Between a Flock and a
Hard Place

ALSO BY DONNA ANDREWS

*Let It Crow! Let It Crow!
Let It Crow!*

Birder, She Wrote

Dashing Through the Snowbirds

Round Up the Usual Peacocks

The Twelve Jays of Christmas

Murder Most Fowl

The Gift of the Magpie

The Falcon Always Wings Twice

Terns of Endearment

Owl Be Home for Christmas

Lark! The Herald Angels Sing

Toucan Keep a Secret

How the Finch Stole Christmas!

Gone Gull

Die Like an Eagle

Lord of the Wings

The Nightingale Before Christmas

The Good, the Bad, and the Emus

Duck the Halls

The Hen of the Baskervilles

Some Like It Hawk

The Real Macaw

Stork Raving Mad

Swan for the Money

Six Geese A-Slaying

Cockatiels at Seven

*The Penguin Who Knew
Too Much*

No Nest for the Wicket

Owls Well That Ends Well

We'll Always Have Parrots

*Crouching Buzzard,
Leaping Loon*

*Revenge of the Wrought-Iron
Flamingos*

Murder with Puffins

Murder with Peacocks

Between a Flock and a Hard Place

A Meg Langslow Mystery

Donna Andrews

MINOTAUR BOOKS

NEW YORK

First published in the United States by Minotaur Books, an imprint of St. Martin's Publishing Group.

BETWEEN A FLOCK AND A HARD PLACE. Copyright © 2024 by Donna Andrews. All rights reserved. Printed in the United States of America. For information, address St. Martin's Publishing Group, 120 Broadway, New York, NY 10271.

www.minotaurbooks.com

Title page illustration by Gabriel Guma

The Library of Congress Cataloging-in-Publication Data is available upon request.

ISBN 978-1-250-89408-3 (hardcover)
ISBN 978-1-250-89409-0 (ebook)

Our books may be purchased in bulk for promotional, educational, or business use. Please contact your local bookseller or the Macmillan Corporate and Premium Sales Department at 1-800-221-7945, extension 5442, or by email at MacmillanSpecialMarkets@macmillan.com.

First Edition: 2024

1 3 5 7 9 10 8 6 4 2

Between a Flock and a Hard Place

Chapter 1

"They're at it again." Gloria Willingham stood on our doorstep, shoulders hunched as if to resist a blow. Her elegant contralto voice throbbed with righteous indignation and a suggestion of barely controlled hysteria. I tried to decide who she was channeling. Lady Macbeth? Hedda Gabler? The Red Queen from *Alice in Wonderland*? Like my husband, Michael—and for that matter, most of their colleagues in Caerphilly College's Drama Department—Gloria tended to reprise her favorite acting roles whenever real life gave her the chance.

"I told you this TV thing was a bad idea," she added, flipping back her mane of shoulder-length braids.

"And I agreed with you." I stepped away from the front door and gestured her inside. "And so did the town council, but unfortunately they couldn't think of a way to stop it."

"At least we tried." Gloria lifted her chin, and her fierce grin suggested that she enjoyed the memory of her dramatic appearance before the council, demanding that they stop her neighbors from having their house redone by one of the many home makeover shows that had spawned to fill whole channels of cable airtime.

"Not even one of the better-known makeover shows," one of the council members had said with a condescending sniff. But the problem wasn't so much that *Marvelous Mansions* was a relatively unknown—and probably low-budget—home makeover show. Any makeover show would have been a disruption to one of the quiet, tree-lined streets of downtown Caerphilly.

And on top of that, it was the Smetkamps' house getting the makeover. The Smetkamps, who seemed to have made a hobby out of annoying their neighbors. A hobby? More like a crusade.

But unfortunately, as long as they and *Marvelous Mansions* filed for the proper building permits and obeyed all the relevant town ordinances, there was nothing the council could do about it.

"Sorry to darken your doorstep at such an ungodly hour," Gloria went on. "But yesterday when I told Michael how horrible it was, he said I could come and use your library the next time things got too noisy next door. And yes, I could work at my office in the Drama Building, but this time of year you can't go five minutes day or night without students showing up to ask for extensions on papers and breaks on exams and—"

"It's absolutely fine." I was suppressing the urge to chuckle at her calling 8:00 A.M. "an ungodly hour." No wonder I got along so well with Michael's theater colleagues. Eight A.M. absolutely was ungodly to a night owl like me. The daily discipline of getting my twin sons off to school on time did not come naturally, but this far along in the school year, I woke early by force of habit, even on days like today when school wasn't in session due to teacher workdays.

Gloria stooped, picked up a battered copier paper box, and handed it to me. It was heavy—full of books and papers, I suspected. Gloria then slung a laptop over one shoulder, heaved a bulky leather satchel over the other, and followed me across the foyer and then down the long hall to our library.

"I'm not normally a fussbudget," she said. "You know me. But

I've got that damned dissertation to finish. If I don't turn it in by the end of the summer, the college might not let me stay."

"I understand," I said. "Sorry I haven't been able to keep them in line. The makeover crew, that is."

"And why is keeping them in line your job, anyway?" Gloria asked.

"Because I'm the mayor's special assistant in charge of nuts and nuisances," I said.

She chuckled at that.

Actually, the official wording was Executive Assistant for Special Projects, but my version was more accurate. I was thinking of asking for a title change to make it official.

And since it was all part of the job, once I got Gloria settled, I'd be heading into town to see what I could do to keep the makeover people from making life unbearable for the rest of the neighborhood.

Perhaps I should offer a refuge to any of them who couldn't tolerate the chaos. Not just the use of the library—we could provide spare bedrooms as well. We were expecting a big crowd of family and friends for Memorial Day, but it would be at least a week before any of them arrived. If the makeover was still going on by then—and still making life unbearable for the Smetkamps and their neighbors—we'd figure something out.

"This is perfect," she said, as we set her stuff down on one of the sturdy Mission-style oak tables in our library. She began unpacking the interesting contents of her box—which I suspected were only a small portion of the books and articles she was using to research her sweeping study of Black women playwrights of the Harlem Renaissance. Maybe I'd peruse some of the plays later. For now—

"So you said they're at it again," I said. "At what? If they started construction before seven—"

"No," she said. "Oh, they were slamming their truck doors and talking at the top of their lungs and doing everything they could to be annoying. They were even making weird animal noises. Gobbling like turkeys, for heaven's sake. But no actual hammering and sawing. In fact, they hadn't even started doing that when I took off. They seemed to be arguing about something."

"Arguing with whom? Each other, or some of the neighbors, or—"

"No idea. I deliberately didn't even look. Just got in my car, backed out of the garage, and fled the scene of the crime. Didn't want to get sucked into any of it."

Nice for her that she could just leave. I didn't want to get sucked into any arguments, either, but it was all part of my job.

"Are you going over there?" she asked, as if reading my mind.

"Unfortunately," I said.

"See if you can talk some sense into Jennifer. That's the student who rents my spare bedroom. She's spent the last few days hanging out in the front yard in a bikini. She seems to think the TV people are going to discover her and put her in the movies."

"Seriously?" I asked.

"Seriously. I live for the day when I can afford my mortgage without renting out the spare room to her and the attic to that weirdo and his forty-seven computers."

"Forty-seven?" I echoed. "He's even got my nephew Kevin beat. And there are worse things than having a tame techie in your basement. Or attic. It's like having a sentient firewall and spam blocker."

"Forty-seven's an exaggeration, but he has at least ten," she said. "And he's not tame. More like feral. Not the least bit helpful like your nephew. The only time he talks to me is when he has a complaint. Remember the twelve-hour power outage we had last week after that huge thunderstorm? He practically had a nervous breakdown by the end of it, and he's threatening to withhold his rent unless I install a generator. Which is rich, considering what he did to my power bill the first month he was here."

"Your power bill?" I echoed.

"First month he was here, the total was up by nearly eight hundred dollars," she said. "And the only thing that was different was him and all his equipment. Did your nephew Kevin's setup do that to you when he moved in?"

"Not that I noticed," I said. "And Kevin's the one who arranged installing a whole bunch of solar panels on the roof of our barn, so these days our electrical bills are next to nothing unless we have a prolonged heat wave or cold spell."

"Wish Chris would do something useful like that," she grumbled. "I told him he either had to pay the difference or find another place to live, and he griped about it for a while, then told me he'd found the problem and my usage should be back to normal. And it was. But I keep my eyes on the power bill, just in case. And if he thinks he can stop paying rent to force me to install a generator, he has another think coming."

"Sounds like a pretty difficult tenant," I said.

"At least I'm not stuck with him much longer," she said. "The student I rented the attic to in the fall had to drop out, and Chris was the only person who answered my ad. I was so desperate to get a new tenant that I probably didn't do as much checking as I should have. But his lease is up at the end of July, and I'm not renewing it."

"Tenant/landlord disputes can be nasty," I said. "If you have any problem getting him to either pay up or move out—"

"Michael already gave me the contact info for your cousin, the lawyer," she said. "And I'm absolutely calling him if I get any more static from the attic. What would I do without you and Michael?"

I got Gloria settled in the library and then dropped by the kitchen to let my cousin Rose Noire know that we had a guest in the library and I'd be heading into town.

The kitchen smelled heavenly. I smiled as I took a deep breath. One of these days, Rose Noire might suddenly decide that she wanted a place of her own and move out of the third-floor bedroom she'd occupied for so many years. But not just yet, thank goodness. I wasn't exactly sure what I was smelling—a mix of coriander, turmeric, cumin, cloves, and several other spices. But I knew what it added up to.

"Curry for dinner?" I asked, in a hopeful tone.

"Oh, no," she said. "This is for Seth's sheep."

She returned to what she'd been doing—vigorously stirring the liquid simmering in our biggest stockpot.

"Do sheep like curry?" I peeked into the pot. Disappointing. It wasn't actually curry—just great handfuls of spices simmering in water. "Curry flavor," I corrected.

"We don't know yet," she said. "We hope so."

"Then why are you cooking it for them?" The only possible reason I could think of was that they were trying to flavor the meat while it was still on the hoof—but Seth's sheep were wool sheep rather than meat sheep. And he didn't even send them to the slaughterhouse when they grew too old to be good wool producers—he moved them to the retirement pasture, where they led a relatively quiet life most of the time. Once a month or so, Seth would give workshops on raising, shearing, or herding sheep—the latter with the assistance of Lad, his champion Border collie—and from what I'd seen the senior sheep rather seemed to enjoy being drafted into service for these events. And they definitely enjoyed spending the summer in their pen in the town square as part of the farm animal petting zoo that had become such a tourist attraction. So no, Seth would have no interest in curry-flavoring his sheep.

"If you have no idea whether the sheep will like it, why are you fixing it?" I asked.

"It's one of your grandfather's projects," Rose Noire said, as if that explained everything. Well, it did and it didn't. Dr. J. Montgomery Blake, the eminent zoologist and environmentalist, almost always had dozens of projects and experiments going. But he was a passionate animal welfare activist, vehemently crusading against any kind of research that caused pain or stress to animal subjects. With both him and Rose Noire involved, the sheep would be fine.

But it would be nice to know what he was up to. And clearly Rose Noire was in no mood to explain.

I'd ask Grandfather later. I pulled out my notebook-that-tells-me-when-to-breathe, as I called my giant combined calendar and to-do list and scribbled in a reminder.

"We might be having a few overnight guests," I said. "I'm going to offer the Smetkamps' neighbors a refuge if they need it. And maybe even the Smetkamps themselves."

"Oh, what a good idea." She abandoned her sheep curry to dash across the room and rummage through the wicker basket she used to haul things to and from her herb drying shed in the pasture behind the house. "And if you're going down to the makeover site, take this with you."

She handed me a small cobalt-blue glass bottle with a black plastic screw top. It was labeled *Breathe!* in elegant calligraphy.

"If anyone gets worked up, try to get them to smell this," she said. "Lavender, orange, rose, ylang-ylang, and myrrh. It's a new blend I've come up with—it's almost magical!"

"Am I supposed to use it on the poor, stressed-out neighbors or the quarrelsome makeover crew?"

"Either," she said. "Both. Just tell whoever needs it to hold the bottle near their nose and inhale slowly and deeply."

"Thanks." I tried, for a moment, to imagine what would happen if I raced up to one of the quarrels that kept breaking out at the makeover site, waving the little blue bottle and ordering everyone to take a drag on it. Well, stranger things had happened there. I tucked the little bottle in my tote bag.

"Will you have time to pick the boys up after school?" she asked.

"No school today, remember?" I said. "Teacher workday. They had a sleepover with Adam Burke last night. Minerva will take them to baseball practice this morning and drop them off later."

"Oh, right," she said. "How silly of me to forget. Maybe I'll make some brownies for the team. And a few extra as a thank you to Minerva and Chief Burke."

I agreed that this was an excellent idea. Then I grabbed a cold soda for the road and headed for town.

I shoved *Marvelous Mansions* and the Smetkamps out of my mind as I drove into town. Although the weather threatened to be unseasonably warm later, for now it was a beautiful May morning. Ordinarily, I'd have been focused on planning Memorial Day activities, both for the town and for the horde of extended family who'd be coming to stay with us for the long weekend. But if there were problems at the makeover site, I needed to take care of that.

Still, I couldn't do anything till I got there. So I rolled the window down and turned on the radio. Someone down at the college radio station couldn't wait for the semester to end—they were playing nothing but summer-themed songs. I hummed along with "In the Summertime," "Hot Fun in the Summertime," and "Walking on Sunshine."

I'd tucked my phone into the little holder hanging on the dashboard where I could see it without picking it up. About halfway through my drive, it dinged to signal the arrival of a text. I glanced over. The text was from Mayor Randall Shiffley. "Big trouble here on Bland Street" it said.

Bland Street was where the home makeover was taking place. How could big trouble possibly have developed this early in the day? Especially trouble big enough that Randall had been called in.

"Nothing I can do about it till I get there," I muttered, and went back to singing along with "Summer in the City."

My pace slowed when I reached town, mainly because the late spring tourist season was in full swing. Especially as I approached the town square, where I could see that the sidewalks were overflowing with pedestrians. Traffic crawled, since most of the cars were either rubbernecking at the various sights or cruising along at a snail's pace, looking for parking. I felt a twinge of impatience, but then I reminded myself that every single one of those slow-moving tourists was here spending money in the shops and restaurants owned by my friends and neighbors. Randall's efforts to promote Caerphilly as a tourist destination were bringing prosperity to the town. So I fought down the urge to honk at the dawdlers, or mutter things under my breath, and focused on smiling at them. Especially the ones who were already laden with shopping bags so early in the day. They must have gone on a buying binge at the farmers market in the town square, since most of the shops weren't even open yet.

Still, I was glad to leave most of the tourist traffic behind when I turned right onto Bland Street. If I'd turned left, the street would have dead-ended at the edge of the Caerphilly College campus after a few blocks. But to the right it led through block after block of peaceful, tree-lined residential neighborhoods. This near the college, the houses were reasonably large, and mostly either Colonial or mock Tudor. After a few blocks, the yards grew smaller, and the sizable Tudor and Colonial houses gave way to Craftsman-style cottages and stucco bungalows from the thirties. And as I knew from the days when Michael and I had been house hunting, the prices dropped from astronomical to merely inflated and unaffordable.

So I'd long ago learned to enjoy this neighborhood as a spectator. And this time of year there was a lot to enjoy. The dogwoods were fading, but the roses, peonies, and rhododendrons were

going strong. I saw at least a dozen residents already at work in
their yards—probably taking advantage of the cool morning
hours before the predicted heat made gardening less enjoyable.
I waved to the ones I knew, mostly Mother's fellow Garden Club
members.

I was in a delightfully mellow mood by the time I reached the
1200 block of Bland Street, where the Smetkamps lived. Whatever they and the *Marvelous Mansions* crew were up to, I could
deal with it. Randall was already here coping, and—

Just then something landed on the hood of my car with a huge
thud.

I slammed on the brakes.

It was a turkey.

A large, full-grown male turkey.

Chapter 2

The turkey staggered to his feet and spread his magnificent brown, black, and white tail feathers. And then he just stood there on my hood, gazing around as if surveying his kingdom. His back was to me, and as luck would have it, he'd landed on the driver's side. All I could see were tail feathers. I'd need to figure out a way to dislodge him before I could keep going.

And why, pray tell, was it raining turkeys here on Bland Street? I tried a few gentle beeps with the horn. He ignored them.

I rapped briskly on the inside of the windshield. No reaction.

I tapped the windshield washer button, with no effect. Not surprising, since the fluid sprayed directly onto the windshield. But turning on the wipers got his attention. Unfortunately. He turned around and gobbled at me, shaking his red wattles vigorously. Then he pecked a few times at the driver's-side wiper, eventually grabbing it with his beak. I turned off the wipers, but he played tug-of-war with the one he'd grabbed until he had twisted the metal arm into a pretzel and stripped off the rubber blade. He shook his trophy from side to side a few times, then took a running start and leaped off my hood, flapping wildly to slow his descent.

"Good riddance," I muttered, as I watched him strut proudly down the street, waving my windshield wiper blade up and down.

Now that the turkey was gone, I could see what was going on around me.

The whole block was overrun with turkeys.

Okay, maybe not the whole block. Apart from a few outliers, like the one that had crash-landed on my hood, most of the birds were near the middle of the block.

The Smetkamps' house appeared to be the epicenter of the infestation. At least ninety or a hundred turkeys were milling about in their front yard. And foraging. Some of them were dining on the contents of Mrs. Smetkamp's flower beds. Others were tearing up the lawn in search of insects. They'd ripped out part of the hedge between their yard and that of their neighbor, and another dozen or so birds were starting to demolish her carefully tended yard. A few of them were perched in the nearby trees, looking menacing and improbable. Every so often, a turkey would begin running furiously across the ground, flapping its wings until it eventually succeeded in taking off and—usually—landing in one of the trees. Occasionally one of the turkeys roosting in a tree would decide it wanted to return to the earth, and would flap down ponderously, often damaging any shrub or garden ornament unlucky enough to be in its landing zone. Another dozen turkeys were strutting about in the middle of the road—mostly male turkeys who were posturing at each other and at the nearby hens, in what looked like the opening rounds of either deadly combat or a mating ritual. Maybe both.

And of course, all of them were busily depositing turkey poop all over the landscape. I made a mental note to ask somebody knowledgeable if turkey poop was unusually nasty and smelly, or if it was just that, given their size, they produced such large quantities of it. Since my dad was an avid birdwatcher, I'd ask him the next time I saw him—which would probably be fairly soon. I couldn't imagine him hearing about the turkey invasion and not showing up to kibitz.

A police car pulled up behind me, lights flashing. I glanced in my rearview mirror and recognized the driver as my friend Aida Butler.

She pulled her cruiser up beside my car and rolled down her passenger window.

"We're closing off this block," she said. "You might want to park your car back there at a safe distance. The birds are pretty territorial."

"And this isn't supposed to be their territory," I said. "Where did they come from? Does one of the local turkey farmers have it in for the Smetkamps?"

"These are feral turkeys," she said. "The ones we've been trying to chase out of town the last couple of years."

"I had no idea there were so many of them," I said.

"Didn't start out that way." She shook her head. "But you might be right about someone having it in for the Smetkamps. Last I heard, we'd managed to encourage this bunch out into the woods on the other side of town, near the high school, and we had hopes of gradually steering them out into Virgil Shiffley's timberland. No way they all suddenly showed up here without human intervention. The chief's hopping mad and determined to find out who's responsible."

"Is there anything he can arrest them for if he catches the culprit?" I asked.

"No idea," she said. "He's got the county attorney working on that. But even if he can't find any law they've broken, you can bet whoever did it's going to get a piece of his mind. I wouldn't want to be in their shoes."

I nodded. The wrath of Chief Burke was legendary. And it was somehow all the more intimidating even though he never used foul language and usually didn't even raise his voice—only told the culprits exactly what they'd done wrong and what he thought about it in no uncertain terms.

"Attention all units," came a voice over Aida's police radio. She nodded to me and rolled up her window, thwarting my curiosity.

Time I got moving anyway. Instead of continuing into the 1200 block of Bland Street I made a left turn and parked beside the house on the corner. I looked around to make sure there were no turkeys nearby, then stepped cautiously out of my car and inched forward so I could get a better view of what was going on.

The Smetkamps' house was in the middle of the block, and next door was the house that belonged to Mrs. Emma Peabody, a widow in her sixties. Yesterday both of their yards had been a bee-hive of construction activity but now they were deserted except for the turkeys. The bits of gear the construction crew had left behind—sawhorses, piles of lumber, a table saw—all either had turkeys perching on them or had been besmirched with turkey poop.

The van and the big truck that the production used to haul its crew and equipment to and from the scene were parked in front of Mrs. Peabody's house, along with the sleek black rental SUV the producer drove around in. The rear door of the truck was open and half a dozen of the camera and sound crew were sitting inside, looking down at the turkey-covered landscape with ex-pressions of incredulity. Or maybe shell shock was the right term. Beyond that, at the far end of the block, another police car was parked sideways to keep traffic from getting any closer. Behind me I could hear Aida moving her cruiser to block off this end.

To my right, I saw Randall Shiffley talking to his cousin Darlene Browning, who lived a few houses down with her husband and four sons—right beside the Smetkamps. Darlene was one of his favorite cousins, and when her husband, a Marine, was overseas,

Randall did his best to make sure her boys never lacked for someone to cheer at their games or toss around a football, basketball,
or baseball. But he and Darlene seemed to be having an uncharacteristically testy exchange. I headed over to see what was up.

"And anyway, who cares who brought the silly things here,"
Darlene was saying when I drew near. "Stupid thing to do, but I
don't see that whoever did it broke any laws."

"We don't know that yet," Randall began.

"And I have no idea who did it," Darlene said. "But if I find
out, I'm going to shake their hand, because that whole thing is
a hoot."

She nodded toward where the turkey flock was milling about
in the street and the Smetkamps' yard.

"And how are you going to feel if they start destroying your
yard?" Randall asked.

"You think they can do anything my monsters haven't done?"
Darlene asked.

She had a point. Apart from a few modest-sized boxwoods
and dwarf Burford hollies around the foundation, her front yard
didn't have much landscaping. What bushes she had were neatly
pruned and the lawn had obviously been cut recently—although
it was more weed than grass. But it was a kid-friendly yard rather
than a picture-perfect one, with a basketball hoop mounted
over the garage door and a small treehouse perched in a black
walnut tree in the right front corner of the lot. Since one of Darlene's sons was around the boys' age, I knew from previous visits
that the backyard held a batting cage, a soccer net, a small above-
ground pool, a playhouse, a semi-permanent camping tent, a couple of hammocks, and a large deck on which stood an enormous
grill. An outdoor paradise for active kids. I wondered if Darlene
would be as mellow about the turkey invasion if she'd realized
how much hosing off and scrubbing would be in her future if the
birds strayed into her yard.

"Like I said, we need to find who did this," Randall said.

"If I hear anything I'll let you know," Darlene said. She strode off down the sidewalk toward the middle of the block—toward the turkeys, which seemed like a pretty silly thing to do. Then, when she reached the border between the corner house and its next-door neighbor, she left the sidewalk and headed for the houses' backyards. As I watched she vaulted handily over the fence between the corner house and the one next door.

The door of her house opened a foot or so, and I saw a face peering out. Then the door opened all the way and three tall, rangy teenage boys dashed out—Evan and Luke Browning, Darlene's older two, and Cal Burke, the oldest of the orphaned grandsons the chief and his wife were raising. They looked around, a little nervously. Were they scoping out how near the turkeys were, or trying to make sure Darlene wasn't nearby? If I lived here, I'd probably have given my twin sons orders to stay inside until the turkeys were gone. Of course, Darlene's boys were a little older than Josh and Jamie. Still—I'd have issued orders to stay clear of the turkeys. Better yet, I'd have taken them somewhere. Somewhere far enough away that they'd be safe, and interesting enough that maybe they wouldn't try to come up with a way to sneak back. Grandfather's zoo. Our friend Ragnar's farm, where they had a standing invitation to ride the Friesian horses whenever they wanted to.

Cal and the Browning boys were loitering across the street from the Smetkamps' house, where they could get a good view of the turkeys.

"You'd think she'd be eager to get rid of those things," I said, stopping by Randall's side. "Granted, she doesn't have any fancy landscaping for them to wreck, but surely she doesn't want her kids playing in all the turkey poop."

"Yeah, and she's kind of defensive, isn't she?" he said. "I think she thinks I think her kids did this. Brought the turkeys, that is.

Or at least helped out with it. And maybe the chief's hopping mad and wants to put the culprits under the jail, but I'm thinking if we figure out who brought them here, maybe get a bunch of them to help us take them away again. So if they did it . . ." His voice trailed off and he shook his head in frustration.

"Any reason for you to suspect Darlene's kids?" I asked.

"Nothing concrete," he said. "Just the way she's acting. And for that matter, the way Evan and Luke are acting."

I nodded absently. I was trying to study the three boys without appearing to stare at them. They seemed eager. Animated. Was this just a normal teen reaction to strange and exciting events happening on their doorstep? Or the glee of pranksters who had pulled off a coup? Maybe I should keep an eye on them.

Just then I spotted Darlene, reappearing from between two neighboring houses. The three teens also saw her and scurried farther down the block. I should definitely keep an eye on them.

"So what's the plan for dealing with this?" I asked. "Or do we actually have a formal plan? Couldn't you maybe chase them out into the countryside? Even chasing them to some other part of town would help. I mean, the town would still have a feral turkey problem, but at least the TV people could get on with their make-over."

"Not a whole lot we can do right now, given how riled up they are," Randall said. "See, a lot of them aren't eating. If we try to shoo them away, the toms and some of the feistier hens will go after us—and some of those things weigh upward of fifty pounds. And the rest will just struggle up into a tree and wait us out. Best thing we could do is to clear everyone out and leave them alone. Once they calm down, we might be able to lure them away with handfuls of corn."

"Is that all?" I asked. "I thought we had a plan for eliminating the town's feral turkey population."

"We do." Randall looked around to make sure no one was

within earshot. "And it's working." He gestured at the flock. "You think that's bad? You should have seen how many of the blasted things we had a couple of years ago."

"So what is the plan?"

"Well, originally we were going to hunt them," he said. "Only during the legal hunting season for wild turkeys, of course," he added hastily. "Which seems okay, seeing as how wild turkeys are pretty much what they are by now. But that means we have to follow all the game laws, which is one reason it's such a slow process."

I assumed the "we" in question was the Shiffley family, many of whom were avid hunters.

"Shouldn't take long with your whole family after them," I said. I felt momentarily sorry for the turkeys.

"Legal limit's three birds per year per hunter," Randall said. "So it's not like we can send a few of our best shots out to wipe out the whole kit and caboodle. In fact, the year we started, we actually lost ground—the damned things bred faster than we could hunt them. Not a lot of natural predators for something that big. Plus we can't hunt them when they're here in town, or for that matter when there are too many people around—a lot of folks are against hunting, or just squeamish. But then we enlisted your grandfather and Clarence to help, and now we're making progress."

"Grandfather and Clarence? What kind of help are they giving?" I could imagine my zoologist grandfather reluctantly helping eradicate the feral turkeys if he thought them an environmental menace, but Clarence Rutledge, our soft-hearted local vet, spent most of his free time rescuing animals from kill shelters and then browbeating the locals into adopting them. And he wasn't a big fan of hunting. Was he planning to rescue the turkeys and find adoptive families for them?

"Er . . . long story." Randall looked uncomfortable. "Behavioral stuff. You should get your grandfather to explain. Anyway, right now we're smack dab in the middle of the spring turkey hunting season, and we were hoping to lure at least some of the blasted things out into the countryside, and then this happens."

"You think there's any chance they just showed up on their own?" I asked. "Could the *Marvelous Mansions* crew be doing anything that would attract them?"

Randall shook his head.

"Pretty sure someone brought them over here," he said. "Almost certainly someone who's been helping out with the project to get them out of town and has learned a bit about how they operate. Yesterday the flock was over by the high school, and I bet when Horace gets cracking on it he'll find some clues. Maybe signs that someone was using handfuls of corn to lure them or something."

"It must have taken more than a few handfuls of corn to tempt all of that lot," I said, eyeing the turkey flock. "And I assume they go to sleep when the sun goes down, like most poultry, so you couldn't lure them then. Wouldn't people have noticed if someone was doing a Pied Piper act with the feral turkeys in broad daylight?"

"True," Randall scowled. "Come to think of it, seems pretty unlikely that someone could have lured them over here while it was still light and managed some kind of camouflage or distraction so that no one even spotted over a hundred turkeys parading across town. Tourists might have thought it was just another entertainment we were putting on to amuse them, but I think a few locals would have noticed. So what probably happened is that someone figured out how to capture them. Maybe used corn to lure them into a truck while it was still light. Or figured out an effective way to shake them down from the trees where they were roosting and then load them into the truck. We've been trying for months to figure out a humane way to capture all of them, but we've only ever managed to get hold of two or three at a time. And here someone finally figures out how to do it, and instead of hauling them out to the woods, they dumped them here."

He sounded exasperated.

"Doesn't sound like something a single person could pull off," I said.

"No." He shook his head. "Definitely a group of people. So call me a suspicious son-of-a-gun, but I'm pretty sure Darlene's two oldest had something to do with it. I mean, take a look at them."

He nodded toward where the three teens stood. I was struck by their facial expressions, which were clearly intended to communicate that they were concerned yet disinterested bystanders. Josh and Jamie, who had inherited some of Michael's acting ability, might have pulled it off. These three weren't even coming close.

And it wasn't just Darlene's two. Cal Burke showed the same suspicious air of innocence. The chief would go ballistic if he found out one of his grandsons was involved.

"I don't think they were the ringleaders," Randall said. "But I'm betting they helped out. If you hear anything, let the chief know. And me."

"Roger," I said. "I should go see if there's anything I need to do. Any idea where Mrs. Smetkamp is?"

"As far as I know, she's still inside making menacing phone calls to everyone she thinks should be doing something about the turkeys," he said. "You planning to talk to her?"

"Not if I can avoid it," I said. "But yeah. Eventually I'll have to, I expect."

"Good luck. I'm off to take care of a few things."

He headed back toward where Aida had blocked off the road.

Darlene strolled over. I hoped she was merely coming to say hello, not making a complaint. But I braced myself anyway.

Chapter 3

"Morning, Meg." Darlene was carrying a large black umbrella. It was open, but she wasn't holding it over her head—probably because it wasn't raining, or even threatening to. It was resting on her shoulder, ready to be deployed if needed.

"Morning," I said. "I notice you left out the 'good' part."

"Yeah." She snorted. "Here." She was holding out another umbrella. It was still furled, but I could tell it was a large one with broad blue and white stripes. Probably a golf umbrella. "You might want to use this if you get too near the trees where Mrs. Smetkamp's yardbirds are roosting. Protection from perils overhead, plus you can use it like a stick, to fend them off, or flap it open and closed to scare them."

"Great idea," I said. "Thanks."

"Just drop it on my doorstep when you leave."

She strode off. I could see that both of her teenage sons and their friend Cal were also outfitted with golf umbrellas, although at the moment they still had them closed and were using them to practice their swordplay in the middle of the blocked-off street.

I glanced back at the turkeys A small number of them were

still strutting up and down the street. A couple were still up in the trees. But most of them were swarming around in the yards in the middle of the right-hand side of the street—in the Smetkamps' yard, Mrs. Peabody's, and now Darlene's. They hadn't yet expanded into the backyards, though that was probably coming. At the moment they didn't seem to be venturing across the street to explore any of the yards to my left. That would probably change when they'd consumed everything edible on the yards they were currently destroying, but for now, the left side seemed reasonably safe. So I crossed the street and began cautiously walking down the left-hand sidewalk in the direction of the Smetkamps' house, with the still furled umbrella at the ready on my shoulder.

Many of the neighbors were out in their yards, watching the turkey invasion. I waved to the people who were sitting on their front steps, which seemed like a sensible idea to me. If the turkeys suddenly headed their way, they could easily run inside. I said good morning to the ones who were standing in small clumps on the sidewalk, eyeing the turkeys nervously. I could tell some of them were dying to interrogate me about what was going on, but since I didn't know anything to tell them, I assumed the sort of busy, distracted look that would give them the impression that I was in the process of doing something useful that would result in the departure of the turkeys, and they merely returned my good morning.

In front of one house, a stucco bungalow painted pale pink with sky-blue trim, Meera Patel, a thirtyish math professor whom I knew from the Garden Club, was watering her front flower beds and frowning at the turkeys. I got the impression that she was planning to turn the hose on them if they threatened her beautiful all-native landscaping. I hoped she had a backup plan for when the thin stream of water her hose could produce did no good.

In front of another house, a beige bungalow, a foursome of

young men—probably college students—were lounging in Adirondack chairs just off the sidewalk, drinking beers and devouring Cheetos and pretzels. They set up a loud, raucous cheer every time the turkeys did anything entertaining, like chasing a pedestrian or flapping up onto someone's roof.

Although they seemed to be paying a lot less attention to the turkeys than to the bikini-clad young blond woman lounging on a beach blanket in the yard next door. I deduced that this house—a quaint, Craftsman-style cottage—must be Gloria's, and presumably the sunbather was Jennifer, the lodger. I nodded and said good morning to her. She frowned, and I realized she probably didn't want me blocking the TV crew's view of her. So I ambled a little farther down the sidewalk. I glanced back at the house. Jennifer was spreading suntan lotion on her skin with great concentration—and the kind of slow, suggestive strokes that suggested she was mentally auditioning for a soft porn film. I looked around to see if anyone was watching. Only the college students, and that half-heartedly.

No, there might be another watcher. The roof of Gloria's house was interrupted by two dormer windows, whose venetian blinds were down and closed. But in the right-hand window several slats had been pushed askew, and I could make out the lenses of a pair of binoculars.

It had to be Gloria's other tenant—Chris, the one she described as a weirdo, with more computers than his landlady could count. But was he bird-watching or girl-watching?

I pretended to be looking up and down the street while keeping tabs on those binocular lenses with my peripheral vision. After several minutes, I didn't see them move, and from this angle it was impossible to tell what their target was.

I made a mental note to keep an eye on the possibly creepy lodger and turned my attention back to the Smetkamps' turkey-besieged house.

It had started out as just another of the block's neat, trim, one-story stucco bungalows, distinguishable only by color from Mrs. Peabody's house next door—it was white while hers was a pale lemon yellow. And it was almost identical in size and shape to both Mrs. Peabody's house and Darlene's Craftsman house on the other side. And, for that matter, most of the other nearby houses. Rumor had it that the builder who'd developed this neighborhood in the nineteen thirties had only bothered to buy a single set of blueprints, which he used for both the many stucco houses and the occasional Craftsman ones, sometimes flipping it so the garage was on the right instead of the left. I'd heard Darlene joke that if it weren't for the furniture she could have found her way blindfolded around any of her neighbors' houses. The houses all originally had a modest living room, galley kitchen, tiny dining room, cramped bathroom, and two small bedrooms. Three of the bungalows on this block—Darlene's Craftsman, Gloria's, and a stucco house on the corner—had been enlarged by building out the attic into a second story, with natural light provided by dormer windows front and back. Finding space for the stairs must have made the downstairs rooms even tinier. The owners of another two had converted their one-car garages into living space. But these modest renovations hadn't changed the essential character of the block. It was old-fashioned but charming. There had been some talk of declaring it a historic district. And it was always a strong contender in the town's annual spring Beautiful Block contest, with two wins and quite a number of honorable mentions.

Although I did wonder sometimes where the residents put their stuff, since the attics weren't that big and none of the houses had been built with basements. I made a mental note to ask Randall if there was a reason for this. Was it impossible? Or merely prohibitively expensive?

Theoretically, I could ask these questions of Randall's cousin

Buck Shiffley, the building inspector, but Dad had just admitted him to Caerphilly General with a bleeding ulcer and would probably disapprove of anyone bothering him. Especially about anything related to the makeover. The *Marvelous Mansions* crew may not have caused the ulcer, but they certainly hadn't helped. And with Buck sidelined, I was a little worried about who would ensure that the makeover crew adhered to the approved plans and the town building codes.

The initial proposal they'd presented to Buck had called for large two-story additions to both the front and back of the house—additions that would have more than doubled its size. But since the existing house was already within a foot or two of the required setback from the property lines on all four sides, Buck had shot down that proposal, and the Smetkamps had insisted on taking the issue over his head, to the town council.

"This whole thing has me worried," Randall had said, after one tempestuous discussion of the makeover plans. "It's as if they don't have anyone connected with the show who knows how to read a floor plan or a surveyor's map."

The plans the town council had finally approved wouldn't change the house's footprint much. They would add another two feet to the back of the house, which meant the kitchen, dining room, back bedroom, and bathroom could be a little larger. Unfortunately, it was the living room and front bedroom where they'd really wanted more space. The council had also granted a variance to allow them to add a roof over the tiny front stoop.

Was that small amount of additional space worth all the hassle of the construction? Not to mention having to pack all of their belongings into a moving pod for the duration. They were reportedly sleeping on cots in the middle of the construction project and living on carryout. And thanks to some testy words I'd overheard between Mrs. Smetkamp and the *Marvelous Mansions* producer, I knew that the show wasn't covering a lot of the extra expenses, like the pod and the cost of repeatedly pulling corrected building permits.

Maybe the cosmetic changes were what they really cared about. No accounting for taste. To me, the design sketches they'd shown the council were depressingly similar to every other house you saw these days on TV shows and magazines. Bland and modern, it would stick out like a sore thumb on the ironically un-bland Bland Street.

A pity we hadn't anticipated the problem and declared the neighborhood a historic district before the Smetkamps had been bitten by the remodeling bug. At least we had vetoed most of the changes they wanted to make to the front façade, on the grounds of preserving the architectural integrity of the neighborhood.

Just then I spotted my grandfather standing a little way down the sidewalk. He was observing the turkeys through binoculars. Definitely the turkeys, not eager Jennifer.

I went over and wished him a good morning.

"Ah, there you are," he said, giving the impression—as usual—that he'd been looking high and low for me and that I'd been willfully dodging him. "We need to talk to whoever brought all these turkeys over here."

"I know," I said. "The chief's trying to identify the culprits."

"No, no!" Grandfather shook his head fiercely. "They won't come forward if he keeps threatening to arrest them. We don't want to scare them away. We want to talk to them. Find out how they did this."

He waved his arm in the general direction of the turkey flock.

"Why?" I asked. "So you can capture them and turn them loose in the woods where the hunters can go after them without upsetting the townspeople?"

"No, not at all." He scowled at me. "Hunting's not the answer. I've got a habitat all set up for them out at the zoo. They can live their lives there quite happily without bothering the towns-people, and I have a useful research project I can do with them. But so far Randall and his crew have only managed to catch half a dozen of them for me. I need more than that, or I can't do any of the research I want to do."

"So what do you want to do to them if you catch them all?" I asked. "Feed them curry?"

"What? No, that's for the sheep. Although, come to think of it, that could be an interesting idea." He fell into thought.

"Interesting why?" I asked. "What does eating curry do for sheep?"

"Reduces the amount of methane they produce when they belch or fart," Grandfather said. "We've been experimenting with adding coriander, turmeric, and cumin to their feed. They act as a sort of natural antibiotic, killing off methanogens—the methane-producing bacteria in the sheep's stomachs—without harming other, beneficial bacteria. Reduces their methane emissions by up to forty percent."

"So it's like probiotics for sheep," I said. "Will it help with the smell?"

"Of course not," he said. "Methane gas is odorless. The smell comes from the other gases they emit—hydrogen sulfide, meth-anethiol, dimethyl sulfide, ammonia. But methane's a big contrib-utor to climate change. Eighty times more potent than carbon dioxide. If we can cut down on the amount of methane the sheep produce, we can reduce the negative impact they have on the environment. But you might have something there. Turkeys pro-duce methane, too. Turkeys and other domestic poultry. Once we've got all the feral turkeys rounded up, I could try the curry on them."

"So if you weren't planning on feeding curry to them, what did you have in mind?" I asked.

"Coming up with a humane way to whittle down the size of the flock, and eventually eliminate it," he said. "A trap, neuter, and release program."

"For turkeys?" I asked. "You're spaying and neutering turkeys?"

"No, that's not very practical," he said. "Labor intensive, and pretty invasive. We just do vasectomies on the males. Easier, and not as hard on the birds. And remarkably effective, especially if we can get the big, dominant toms. But those are exactly the birds Randall's crew finds hardest to catch. All I have so far is five hens and one scrawny half-grown tom. But whoever did this caught the whole damned flock! In one night! It's amazing! We need to learn their methods."

"If you say so." I studied his expression for a moment. "Are you really planning to keep the turkeys out at the zoo after you've finished neutering them?"

"Sterilizing, not neutering," Grandfather corrected. "And yes, of course. I need to keep them around to make sure the vasectomies are effective. And permanent—they are in humans, but what if turkeys can regrow the vas deferens? Birds aren't mammals, you know—in a lot of ways they're a lot more like their dinosaur ancestors. We can't assume what works for mammals works the same with them. Plus we need to make sure there's no long-term effect on their health. If all goes well it could lead to a whole new humane method of controlling unwanted feral bird populations. But quite apart from that, the turkeys might fit in nicely with our current methane-reduction studies. We want to work on cows, eventually. Your average cow produces ten times the methane as a sheep—partly because it's so much larger, of course. Sheep, being smaller, are easier to work with. But we might be able to modify the fart-box to fit a turkey. We'll need a much bigger one when we start working with cows."

"The fart-box?" I echoed.

"In the research papers we call it the ovine methane emissions measurement chamber, of course," he said. "But that's quite a mouthful. Around the lab, the researchers and I just call it the fart-box."

Clearly Grandfather relished the term. I wondered how any of his researchers who happened to be female felt about it. Or any who were older than twenty-five.

"How does it work?" I asked instead. Actually, I could easily imagine it, but I got the impression Grandfather was eager to explain.

"We put a sheep in there for a few hours—with food and water available, of course—and measure how much methane it emits. Doesn't hurt the animals. In fact, now that they've learned that they get their favorite treats in the box, they all try to shove their way in when we bring it around. Gets challenging to keep the alpha sheep from taking more than their share of turns in it. I'm sure the turkeys will love it once they try it."

He seemed rather pleased with himself for having invented a way to brighten the sheep's lives.

"So if I get a clue to who dumped the turkeys here, you want me to tell you so you can get them to catch the turkeys for you," I said.

"That would be helpful," he said. "And it might help if you could talk to the chief. Tell him to take it easy on whoever did this."

"Why don't you try that?" I said. "Because maybe the chief won't give you a hard time for trying to tell him to go easy on a mischief-maker. I'm not sure I want to try."

"Hmm." He frowned slightly. "I'll mention it to him. Getting back to the methane-reduction project—I'm in touch with some researchers in New Zealand who are breeding sheep that have naturally lower methane emissions—up to fifteen percent lower, without any negative effects on wool quality or general health. I'm negotiating with them to get some breeding stock and see what we can do over here. And we're testing all of Seth Early's sheep to see if he has any that are already natural low methane emitters.

Ah—there's Randall. He might know if the chief's found our turkey rustlers."

He dashed off toward the other end of the block, where Randall and Aida were leaning against her police cruiser as they
watched what the turkeys were up to.

I thought of joining them, but then another nearby snatch of
conversation caught my attention.

"You've got to do something."

Chapter 4

I flinched slightly. I'd been hearing "you've got to do something!" all too often. Then I relaxed as I realized that for a change those all-too-familiar words weren't aimed at me.

Mr. Smetkamp was standing across the street talking to another man whose back was to me. The other man was tall, stoop-shouldered, and cadaver-thin, which made him an odd contrast with the short, plump, balding Mr. Smetkamp. I decided it would be a good idea to see how they were taking the turkey invasion, so I headed that way. When I drew closer, the taller man turned and I recognized him: Charles Jasper, the man from whom the Smetkamps had bought their house a decade or so ago. I'd run into him repeatedly while here on Bland Street over the last few days, so I assumed he'd moved to another house nearby—though I didn't know precisely where.

"You can't just stand by and watch," Mr. Jasper was saying. "Those horrible birds are ruining the privet hedge."

"Not much I can do about it." Mr. Smetkamp held up his left hand, which was adorned with a wad of gauze and first-aid tape. "One of those things came over and attacked me this morning when I was trying to get out of the house. I had to sneak out the back door. I'm not going anywhere near them."

"But look what they're doing to the landscaping," Mr. Jasper moaned.

Curious that he seemed far more upset about the turkeys' depredations than Mr. Smetkamp. And maybe it was my imagination, but he seemed to come very close to saying "*my* privet hedge" and "*my* landscaping."

"Well, I think the makeover people were planning to do something with the yard anyway," Mr. Smetkamp said. "I'm sure they'll make it all look nice again."

"Do something with the yard?" Mr. Jasper echoed. "What are they thinking of? Do they have any understanding of how much time and work it took to get the yard in such good shape? You can't just let them—"

He suddenly seemed to realize how odd it was for him to be making such a fuss over what was planned for someone else's yard.

"It really isn't going to be that big of a deal, this makeover," Mr. Smetkamp said. "Mostly cosmetic. A pity, really. I'd like a nice space for my woodworking. My shop's in the shed in the backyard, which isn't really big enough, and besides, it's only really comfortable in the spring and fall."

"Not enough space to add a workshop," Mr. Jasper said—a little smugly, as if he disapproved of woodworking.

"No, there isn't." Mr. Smetkamp looked gloomy. "I did ask if they'd consider adding a basement, but—"

"A basement!" Mr. Jasper gasped. "No—that would be a terrible thing. It would ruin the whole look of the house."

He looked so distraught that my first impulse was to whip out Rose Noire's little cobalt aromatherapy bottle. But I quickly decided that he probably wouldn't respond well, even to the most beguiling lavender. And the way things were going, I might want it for myself later.

"Don't worry," Mr. Smetkamp said in a soothing tone—although from his expression, I suspected he was wondering the same thing I was: how could a basement possibly ruin the look of a house? "I'm pretty sure the county regulations wouldn't let us have a basement even if we wanted one."

"Why not?" I asked. I hoped they wouldn't consider me rude, barging into their conversation uninvited—but I happened to know quite a few houses in nearby neighborhoods that had basements.

"There's an underground spring in this part of the neighborhood," Mr. Smetkamp explained. "Very localized problem—only affects this block and a few others nearby. I've been told the technology does exist to dig a basement here and make it watertight, but it'd be very expensive, and there'd be no guarantee how well it would work, and our insurance would go through the roof, and there might even be some kind of environmental issue, which is why the county forbids it in the affected area. So given all that, no basement, ever, as far as I'm concerned."

"Good," Mr. Jasper said. "Sensible. Isn't someone going to do something about those horrible pests?" he asked, turning to me. His expression showed that he assumed I should be the someone.

"We've got people working on it," I said.

"Hmph!" He glared at me and then began striding down the street to where Randall and the chief were now talking to Grandfather. In doing so, Mr. Jasper passed too close to one of the larger tom turkeys, who resented the intrusion and gave chase. The last we saw of Mr. Jasper, he was sprinting down the street, just barely managing to outrun his pursuer.

"Spry for his age, isn't he?" Mr. Smetkamp remarked, with a sigh. He was looking his own age this morning. Maybe more than his age. He'd only recently retired, and was somewhere in his sixties, but at the moment he looked far older, and worryingly worn and frail. Especially compared with Charles Jasper, who was

about the same age but was still vigorous and energetic enough
to outrun the turkeys.

"Feel free to tell me it's none of my business," I said. "But has
he always been that . . . possessive about your yard?"

"Oh, yes." He sighed again. I'd already noticed he did that a
lot. "At first I thought it was rather nice that he cared so much
about the place. Seemed to be a sign that he'd taken good care of
it, you know. Which he definitely had. And of course it was understandable that he'd have a sentimental attachment to it. He and
his wife moved in there as newlyweds, and they spent their whole
married life there."

I was opening my mouth to ask if Mrs. Jasper had died there,
but realized in time that if she had, it might not be something he
wanted to be reminded of.

"How long ago did she die?" I asked instead.

"She didn't." Mr. Smetkamp glanced around as if to make sure
Mr. Jasper was out of earshot. "At least not that we know of. Not
here, anyway. She ran away with another man."

"How did I miss hearing about this?" I said.

"Well, the college kept it pretty quiet."

"She worked at the college?" That made it even more surprising that I hadn't heard the gossip.

"Yes, but under her maiden name," he said. "Barker or Barber
or something like that."

"That sort of rings a bell," I said. "I don't think I ever met her,
though."

"She wasn't faculty," Mr. Smetkamp said. "She was in finance."

Okay, that explained why I'd never met her. I shared Michael's
jaundiced view toward the college bean counters, and they certainly didn't socialize much with the Drama Department.

"How long ago was this?" I asked.

"I don't know precisely," he said. "A few years before he sold the
house to us, so maybe twelve or thirteen years. Apparently she was

the main breadwinner in the family—assistant to the chief financial officer, and in line for the top job when her boss retired, or so
they say. I expect that's why they kept it so quiet. Jasper works at
the college, too—he does some kind of admin job in the Building
and Grounds Department—not nearly as well paid, so after she
left, he couldn't keep up with the mortgage. After struggling for
a few years, he sold his house to us." He shook his head. "Moved
into a studio apartment in the College Arms, poor soul."

"Quite a comedown," I said. The College Arms, locally known
as The Armpits—or just the Pits—was a run-down garden apartment complex that constituted the closest thing Caerphilly had
to a bad neighborhood. Mr. Jasper had indeed come down in the
world if he'd moved from this neighborhood to the Pits. And why
the Pits? There were other places in town—or better yet out in the
county—that, while not quite as cheap as the Pits, were consid-
erably more affordable than Bland Street. I could probably have
steered him to some. Back when Michael and I had been house
hunting, we'd quickly realized that any house we could afford in
this neighborhood would be a tight squeeze for us as a couple and
completely impractical for the family we were hoping to start. Before stumbling on our farmhouse in the country, we'd spent a lot
of time hunting in neighborhoods less quaint and charming but
much more reasonably priced.

Mr. Jasper must have circled around through the nearby streets
to shake loose the turkey that had been chasing him. Or possibly
the nearby backyards. He was down at the other end of the block
now, complaining to Randall and the chief about something.

"I think he misses the neighborhood," Mr. Smetkamp said. "He
still comes over here for his daily walks. Morning and evening.
And hangs around a lot in between. Knows more about what's
going on in the neighborhood than most of the people who still
live here."

I nodded and made a mental note to be sure the chief knew

this. If Mr. Jasper spent that much time lurking around the neighborhood, he might have seen something that would help the chief figure out who had lured the turkeys here.

Or what if Jasper had done it himself? The arrival of the turkeys had certainly brought the makeover to a sudden halt. And the fuss he was making about what the turkeys were doing to his beloved hedge could be his attempt to divert suspicion from himself.

Then again, even if he'd lured the turkeys here, his reaction could be an honest one. He might have thought the birds would merely interfere with the *Marvelous Mansions* crew, not realizing that they might also do real damage to the house and yard he still loved.

"Maybe Mr. Jasper still thinks of this as his neighborhood," I suggested. "Hard to imagine anyone feeling at home anywhere near the Pits. Maybe he's hoping his financial situation improves and he can buy the house back from you someday."

"I rather doubt it," Mr. Smetkamp said. "He must be close to retirement—he's only a few years younger than I am. Doesn't seem likely that he'll be able to buy a house on just social security and whatever pension the college will be giving him."

"Especially not here on Bland Street," I said.

"Exactly. So if he wants a house—any house—he probably needs to buy it now, while he's still getting paychecks, and Imogen doesn't want to sell ours. Even if she did, I can't imagine her agreeing to sell it to him. She can't stand him."

Imogen—that must be Mrs. Smetkamp. I'd never even tried to get on first-name terms with her. Interesting that he seemed to assume the decision on whether or not to sell would be his wife's, not a shared one.

"He could have savings," I suggested.

"He could," he agreed. "But I rather doubt it. After all, why would anyone stay on at the Pits if they could afford anything else?"

Actually, I could think of a reason—what if Mr. Jasper was living there so he could save every penny he could to make it possible to buy back what he obviously still thought of as his house? I glanced over to see where he'd gone. He'd given up haranguing Randall and the chief and was standing on the sidewalk near Gloria's driveway, shoulders hunched, hands in pockets, staring at the turkeys. He was a sad, shabby figure. I couldn't think which was the sadder—the idea that he was living at the Pits because he couldn't afford any better, or the possibility that he was deliberately living there to save up enough money to move back to Bland Street. I had a depressing vision of him in his well-worn clothes, living on ramen or cans of pork and beans. I could even imagine him sitting at a secondhand table tiny enough to fit into the cramped space of his breakfast nook, gazing up wistfully at a picture of his former house, and maybe one of his fugitive wife.

And what if he did manage to save enough money to buy back the house, or one like it here on Bland Street? It wouldn't bring back the wife who'd run away, or the life he'd had when he'd lived here.

"Snap out of it," I told myself. I was depressing myself with the sad picture I was painting of Mr. Jasper's life. Maybe he was indifferent to his surroundings, and perfectly happy at the Pits. Or as happy as he'd be anywhere that wasn't Bland Street.

"I wonder if this will discourage them." Even Mr. Smetkamp's speaking voice sounded like a sigh. "The TV people, I mean. They're already rather annoyed about some of the extra things they weren't expecting to have to do."

"Like filing plans that comply with the town building code?" I asked.

"I suppose." He turned to look over at the *Marvelous Mansion* vehicles. Some of the crew members had climbed on top of the big truck, and they were busily filming the turkeys. "I overheard that producer fellow grumbling that maybe they should go find a

town that would be properly grateful for what they were doing."
A wisp of a smile crossed his face, so slight that I almost thought I
imagined it. "And a less assertive client."

"Did he really say assertive?" I asked. It didn't sound like something the producer would say.

"Actually, he said bitchy," Mr. Smetkamp said. "But he was
rather upset at the time."

"I expect your wife is keeping them up to the mark," I said.
"He's probably used to having his own way."

He nodded, and I thought I spotted that ever-so-faint smile
again, just for a second. And then he stiffened slightly. I turned
to see that Randall was approaching. He was wearing a hard hat
and carrying another.

"Morning," Randall called out. "You doing okay?"

"As well as can be expected, considering." Mr. Smetkamp gestured vaguely toward the turkeys.

"We're working on that," Randall said. "I suppose the chief
already asked you—"

"If I saw who dumped the turkeys there," Mr. Smetkamp said.
"And no, I didn't. I had such a hard time getting to sleep the first
few nights of sleeping on that miserable cot that last night I finally
broke down and took a sleeping pill. Can't say I feel very rested,
but at least I didn't spend the whole night tossing and turning."

"I can imagine how difficult that was," I said. "Look, we've
got several spare bedrooms out at our house. You and your wife
would be welcome to one if you'd like a more comfortable place to
sleep—a place where there's no danger of getting pecked to pieces
coming and going."

"Thanks." He looked pleased, and a little wistful. "I'm not sure
if Imogen would want to leave the house just now—she's very focused on the makeover. But I'd definitely be glad to get away." He
glanced back at his house. "Assuming I can get inside to pack a
few things."

"If you can't, just show up and we'll try to come up with what you need." I pulled out my notebook-that-tells-me-when-to-breathe, tore out a blank page, and scribbled down directions. "If I'm not there, just tell my cousin Rose Noire I sent you."

"Thanks." He folded the slip of paper and tucked it into his shirt pocket. Then he flinched. "It looks as if Charles Jasper is heading this way again. I'm going to make myself scarce, before I have to listen to another lecture about what barbarians we are for even thinking about remodeling the house."

He scurried away, past where Horace's cruiser blocked off the street and out into the wide world beyond Bland Street.

"I'd just as soon avoid Mr. Jasper myself," Randall said. "If he comes this way—"

But Mr. Jasper stopped several houses away and stood staring at his former home.

"We expecting rain?" Randall gestured at the golf umbrella I was still carrying.

"Not that I know of," I said. "Protection in case I have to go any-where near where the turkeys are roosting." I demonstrated the flapping motion Darlene had recommended to repel any turkeys that tried to interfere with me.

"Smart," he said. "I'll grab one myself next time I get a chance. Meanwhile, want to come with me? I'm going to go in and talk to Mrs. Smetkamp and that television producer fellow. What's his name—Bloom something, right?"

"Blomqvist," I said. "Jared Blomqvist. Spelled with a 'qv' that sounds like a 'k.'"

"Blomqvist. Blomqvist." Randall frowned. "Am I saying it right?"

"You're doing fine," I said. "But I think it makes him a little ner-vous when you call him Mr. Blomqvist. Not sure if it's a California thing or just that he's so ridiculously young to be running a tele-vision show. He won't mind if you call him Jared. In fact, I think he'd prefer it."

"Then I'll call him Mr. Blomqvist," Randall said. "I want the bastard off balance. I'm tired of him trying to bulldoze everyone around him. And I want a look inside that house. Remember how much trouble Buck had with him back when they were planning this fiasco?"

"Vividly," I said. "If it weren't for *Marvelous Mansions,* Buck probably wouldn't be in the hospital. Although it's probably a good thing he wasn't at that last horrible meeting. I think that was what really got to him, when Blomqvist pitched that fit and insisted on going over his head to the town council. At least it was just before that meeting that Dad ordered him into the hospital."

"True," he said. "But I think the outcome of the meeting might be helping Buck's recovery."

"Knowing the town council has his back?"

"Yeah, he was pretty happy about how that turned out." Randall smiled at the memory. Not only had the town council backed up every "no" Buck had issued, it had reversed several of the concessions he'd made. "And now he can rest easy, knowing I've appointed a fierce, picky, and highly qualified acting building inspector who won't let them get away with anything."

"That's good news," I said. "So who did you appoint to fill in for Buck?"

"Myself," Randall said. "No way I'm delegating this thing."

"That should be fun," I said.

"Not really," he said. "I've been studying my copy of the plans the town council finally approved. And keeping an eye on what's been coming out of the house. That first day of work especially, there was way more stuff going into the dumpster than seems reasonable if they're following the plans they filed with the town. And they made sure to haul the trash out to the dump twice that first day. Hoping we wouldn't notice just how much they were ripping out."

"What is it you think they're up to?" I wasn't sure why he cared that the makeover was generating more trash than he expected.

"Could mean they're gutting the interior," he said. "Which was not in the approved plans—mainly because those clowns don't seem to understand the concept of load-bearing walls. Or building codes. Or environmental regulations. Or—you get the idea. We need to find out what they're up to. Let's get it over with."

Chapter 5

Yesterday, after deciding to get his confrontation with Blomqvist over with, Randall would have stormed across the street and marched up to the Smetkamps' front door. Now, he glanced left and right, as if assessing something.

"Let's try this way." He nodded to the left. "Slightly longer, but I think we'll run into fewer fences. And here—assuming we get inside the house, it'll be a construction area. Wear this." He handed me his spare hard hat, bright blue with the words SHIF-FLEY CONSTRUCTION COMPANY printed on the front, flanked by tiny icons of hammers.

"Good idea," I said. "Could also come in handy if we run into any turkeys flying overhead." I donned the hat with satisfaction. Between the hard hat and the umbrella, my anti-turkey arsenal was growing.

We turned left and went to the end of the block. The residents of the four houses between Mrs. Peabody's house and the corner waved from their yards and looked as if they'd like to have stopped us to ask what was going on, but Randall and I waved back and did our best to look like people who were on their way to an important meeting.

We kept up this brisk pace until we reached the corner house. Then Randall stopped and said good morning to the man who appeared to be weeding his already immaculate front flower borders.

"Got to talk to the Smetkamps and their TV people," Randall said. "But with all those turkeys running around, it would be a lot safer to go through your backyard to get there, if that's okay with you."

"Feel free," the man said, gesturing graciously with his weeding fork. "You working on something that will get rid of those blasted turkeys?"

"Hope so," Randall said. "Get rid of them, and maybe find out who's responsible for them being here in the first place."

Then he raised his hand to his forehead in a mock salute and headed down the sidewalk toward the man's backyard. It was unfenced, and several graceful, rustic oyster-shell paths wound through it. Unfortunately, the paths would only take us so far, since the neighbor next door had an eight-foot privacy fence.

So Randall and I wound our way along one of the paths till we reached the corner yard's back border. There we stopped to explain ourselves to a lady who was scooping leaves out of her koi pond. After a few minutes of chatting, the koi lady shouted to get the attention of her next-door neighbor, who was at the far side of her own backyard sitting atop a stepladder so she could see over the privacy fence and take pictures and video of what the turkeys were up to a few houses down.

It was slow going, making sure before entering a yard that its owner knew we were there, and why, but given that the neighbors were probably already on edge from the turkeys, we didn't want to barge in anywhere uninvited. Once we had to wait until the homeowner could leash a small but very vigilant watchdog, and once we had to climb over a low fence to get from one yard to the next. But at last we found ourselves in the yard behind the Smetkamps. Only one more fence stood between us and our goal. One more fence and a couple of middle-school kids who reacted to our arrival by running inside the house yelling, "Mom! Mom! More people going to the Smellybads!"

Randall and I glanced at each other, then quickly looked away and worked on not cracking up.

"Shouldn't those two be in school this time of day?" Randall asked.

"Teacher workday," I explained.

"That's a relief," he said. "I didn't want to bring it up with Darlene, but I was worried her boys were playing hooky."

I nodded. I was studying the yard we were in. It was fenced in—a split-rail fence reinforced, almost invisibly, with green wire mesh—the sort of fence that suggested it was designed to keep a dog confined. We'd been able to use a gate to enter from the yard next door, but we'd have to go all the way out to the street if we wanted to continue in the same direction. And there was no gate leading to the Smetkamps' yard. No gate, and along the entire back stretch the fence was not only taller but reinforced every few feet by vertical stakes with vines growing up them, as if to block out even the sight of their unloved neighbors.

A harried-looking woman dashed out of the house and frowned at Randall. Then she spotted me and her face relaxed. I recognized her as Myra Lord, one of Mother's favorite fellow Garden Club members, passionate about eradicating invasive species and eschewing pesticides. She was also a frequent volunteer at Grandfather's environmental protests and cleanup efforts.

"Nice to see you, Meg," she said. "And you, too, Mr. Mayor. What's up?"

"Randall and I need to talk to Imogen Smetkamp," I said.

"Preferably without having to fend off any turkeys. Is there any way we can get through your fence into her backyard?"

"Of course." She turned to the kids, who were trying to look as if they weren't eavesdropping but merely roughhousing with their dog, a large and shaggy Heinz fifty-seven variety pooch. "Jason, Eli—go get the stepladders."

The two boys—and their dog—scurried away.

"I don't suppose you're here to shut down that so-called make-over," Myra said. "Honestly—if she wants to live in a cookie-cutter McMansion, why doesn't she just move over to Westlake?"

I had to resist the impulse to chuckle at this. The residents of Westlake considered their pricy little enclave to be the most desirable—and possibly the only civilized—neighborhood in Caerphilly. The rest of us had a less rosy view of the place, considering its residents snooty, standoffish, and demanding. They accounted for a large percentage of the nuisance calls I had to deal with in my job as Randall's assistant. And Randall still had a hard time forgiving his great-uncle Thaddeus Shiffley for selling off his small farm to Westlake's developer.

"If I'd known then how Westlake would turn out, I'd have tied him up and made him listen to Wagner until he agreed to sell it to me," Randall had once said.

"I gather Great-Uncle Thaddeus wasn't an opera fan," I'd said. I'd been about to ask what music his elderly great uncle had liked—country? Bluegrass? Big band?

"Oh, he was a big opera fan, all right," Randall had retorted. "Puccini, Verdi, Mozart, Rossini, Donizetti, Tchaikovsky. Bizet—just not Wagner."

Okay, maybe Great-Uncle Thaddeus didn't have such bad taste in music. But I still hadn't forgiven him for making Westlake possible. And Myra had pegged it. The Smetkamps—Mrs. Smetkamp, at least—would fit in perfectly if they moved to Westlake.

It occurred to me, just for a moment, to wonder if Myra had

had anything to do with the arrival of the turkeys. But no—I could tell from her anxious expression when she glanced over the fence that she was dreading what the turkeys would do if they eventually moved in her direction.

"I wish we could shut down the makeover, ma'am," Randall said. "But as long as they stick to the plans they filed with the county and follow all the building codes—"

"Don't hold your breath on that one," Myra said. "She's been setting off mosquito foggers again."

"She's not allowed to do that," Randall said. "Remember we passed that new town ordinance that you can't use any kind of pesticide unless you can keep it on your own property."

"And a fat lot of good it's doing so far," she said. "She does it in the middle of the night. If she thinks we don't notice, she's deranged. You confront her with it, and she just claims she can't smell a thing, when the whole neighborhood reeks from the fumes. And before you ask, yes, we call the police, and they can smell it, too, but they can't prove it's her doing it. I'm pretty sure sometimes she sets them off right across the property line in her neighbors' yards, in the hope that they'll get blamed."

Just then her two kids returned, each carrying a stepladder. I could tell Randall was conflicted. However impatient he was to tackle Mrs. Smetkamp and the producer, he didn't want to appear insensitive to the very valid concerns of a citizen.

An idea came to me.

"Would you be willing to let us use your yard for a stakeout?" I asked Myra.

"Sure," she said. "But it could be a long wait for whoever's doing the stakeout. She doesn't do it every night. Doesn't seem to have any kind of a schedule. I think if she sees a bug—any old bug, not just a mosquito—she goes out, buys another industrial-sized fogger, and sets it off that night."

Randall was frowning, as if equally dubious about my suggestion.

"I was thinking more of an electronic stakeout," I said. "We get my nephew Kevin to set up a couple of motion-sensitive low-light video cameras in your yard, aimed at hers, and not only will we catch her in the act, we'll have hard evidence."

"Oooh," she said. "I like that idea. Mi casa es su casa—or would that be mi yard es su yard?"

"Why didn't I think of that?" Randall said.

"You don't have a mad computer scientist living in your basement." I pulled out my notebook and added calling Kevin to today's tasks. "I'll see what we can arrange. We probably won't be able to do it until the turkeys are gone, though," I said, turning back to Myra.

"Yeah, getting rid of them's the important thing for now." She turned to her sons, who were standing nearby, each holding a battered metal stepladder.

"Which side?" one of them asked.

"The back," Myra said.

The boys goggled at that.

"Ms. Meg and Mr. Randall need to visit the Smetkamps," Myra explained. "So set up the ladders for them. And then hold Squeaky so he doesn't trip them or try to steal their shoes while they're on the ladders."

Squeaky? That struck me as a rather incongruous name for such a big, shaggy dog. I wondered if the kids had chosen it.

The kids—Jason and Eli, I reminded myself—set up the two ladders so they were side by side and straddled the fence. One had the steps on our side of the fence, so you could climb up on it. Then you could slide over onto the other ladder and descend, since its steps were on the other side. The two boys then stood back and watched as Randall and I headed for the ladders.

You'd think we were going into combat from the anxious looks on their faces.

Then again, maybe they were right to be anxious.

"You've helped someone else into the Smelly—er, Smetkamps' yard?" I asked.

"That snotty TV producer," Myra said. "I think he's still over there."

Randall took the lead and climbed the first ladder, stopping at the top to scout out our destination.

"Any turkeys in the backyard?" I asked.

"Not that I can see," he said. "But I figure it's only a matter of time. Someone's rigged up some chain-link fence to try to keep the birds in the front yard, but that won't stop them for long. There's a couple roosting in their backyard trees."

"Did I remember to thank you for this hard hat?" I asked.

He chuckled, then slid over onto the second ladder and began climbing down. I followed him. I checked to make sure I could unfurl my umbrella in a hurry if the need arose, and we stood for a moment, surveying our surroundings.

The back of the house was surrounded by a ten-foot-high plywood construction fence a foot or so out from the walls, with blue polyethylene tarps covering the small gap between it and the roof. The only break in the fence gave access to the back door.

For a construction site, the yard was remarkably tidy. No random bits of the drywall and lumber they must have removed from the house. No empty water bottles or fast-food trash. No construction tools or supplies—they'd put all that on poor Mrs. Peabody's front lawn. Nothing marred the pristine perfection of Mrs. Smetkamp's lawn and flower beds.

"This yard must drive Myra crazy," I said.

"Why?" Randall asked. "It's a little . . . prim and manicured. Not that bad."

"Myra's passionate about planting only native species," I said.

"And this yard is like a museum of every invasive species Myra probably doesn't want spreading into her yard." I pointed at some of the nearby culprits. "Bradford pears. Chinese wisteria. Burning bush. English ivy. Japanese barberry. Wintercreeper. Royal Paulownia. Nandina. A privet hedge."

"That sounds a lot like the list of plants your grandfather and the Garden Club have been trying to get us to outlaw selling here in the county," Randall said. "You think that's a coincidence, or do you suppose they planted some of them just to spite Ms. Lord?"

"Your guess is as good as mine."

"Any of them on the Federal Noxious Weed List?" he asked. "Because those would be illegal, right?"

"I suspect a couple of them ought to be, but you'll need to ask Dad about that. Let's get this over with."

I squared my shoulders and braced myself. Randall appeared to be doing the same. And then, since sneaking up on someone as volatile as Mrs. Smetkamp seemed like a bad idea, I made sure I was fully visible from the back door and gave a shout.

"Mrs. Smetkamp!" I called. "Are you there?"

"Where else would she be?" Randall murmured. But he, too, stood waiting.

Chapter 6

A frowning face appeared inside the screen door.

"About time," Mrs. Smetkamp snarled. Then she disappeared back into the house.

"I'm going to take that as an invitation to come in," Randall said.

"I think I'll wait a minute or so before I jump to that conclusion," I replied. "If she walks out and throws a giant-size mosquito fogger at us, I get first dibs on the ladder."

But she didn't reappear, so after a minute or so, we headed for the back door.

"Uh-oh," Randall said under his breath.

Words that always get my attention.

"What's wrong?" I stopped halfway across the lawn.

"See how the roof is kind of sagging there, a little to the left of the back door?" He glanced around to see if anyone was around before pointing quickly. "Left as we're looking at it."

I peered in the direction he'd indicated.

"I think so," I said. "Are you sure it's just not an irregularity on how they've spread out the blue tarps?"

"Maybe," he said. "And maybe I'm just super suspicious, but it sure looks to me like what you'd get if some boneheaded wannabe contractor went and knocked out a load-bearing wall."

"Don't they kind of have to knock out that back wall if they're going to add two feet to the house?" I asked. "And I seem to recall that the new plans called for a lot of glass along the back."

"Yeah," he said. "But if you think back, those plans we approved also called for a couple of big old heavy, well-supported beams to carry the weight of the roof. One on either side of the back door. And any competent contractor would know that you can't just knock out a load-bearing wall and ask the load to support itself in mid-air till you get around to putting in a replacement. You put in temporary supports, and plenty of them. Not doing that is just the sort of bone-stupid, dangerous shortcut I can see those clowns doing. And if they have, I might need to declare the whole place unsafe for human habitation."

"Should we even go in there?"

"To tell you the truth, I'm not keen. But I kind of think we have to." He spent another minute or so studying the exterior of the house. "If I suddenly yell 'get out,' don't stop to ask questions. Just head for the nearest door."

"Even if the nearest door leads out into the middle of the turkeys?"

"Fighting off a few turkeys sounds a lot more survivable than having the whole roof of a house cave in on you. Well, let's do it."

He strode toward the back door.

As I followed him, I realized that at the moment I was feeling very mellow toward the turkeys. The turkeys and whoever had brought them to Bland Street. Thanks to them I'd gotten through half of the morning without having to talk to Mrs. Smetkamp or any of the *Marvelous Mansions* team.

Of course, I might be seeing a lot more of Mrs. Smetkamp than I liked if she accepted my invitation to stay with us while the turkey infestation made staying in her house difficult. Even more difficult than it already was. Why hadn't she and her husband arranged someplace else to stay during the makeover? Maybe they didn't want to spend the money on a hotel or B&B—or hadn't thought far enough ahead to get reservations before the tourists filled up every available room—but didn't they have friends who could put them up?

He probably did, I decided. The idea of having him out at the house didn't bother me at all. He was so mild-mannered and retiring that we'd probably have a hard time noticing he was around. But Mrs. Smetkamp? As Michael would say, "Aye, there's the rub." Having her around would be . . . unpleasant.

But asking her was probably the right thing to do. And who knew? Maybe showing her a little kindness would help us get along better.

I deliberately put on as calm and friendly an expression as I could manage while Randall knocked on the back door.

Mrs. Smetkamp appeared at once, frowning with impatience. Then again, I'd never seen her without a frown—maybe that was her normal expression. Resting frown face. At a casual glance she looked noticeably younger than her husband, but a closer look revealed that she wasn't really younger—just more determined to keep up a youthful appearance. Her hair appeared to have what Angel and Ruth at the Caerphilly Beauty Salon called "dramatic blond highlights"—their euphemism for a complete dye job. I'd never seen her when her face wasn't perfectly made up, and I was pretty sure she always wore what we now referred to as "shapewear"—even Mother had given up using the word "girdle."

Some days I felt a certain amount of sympathy for someone who was so clearly unhappy about what the inevitable passage of time does to us all. And maybe even a little admiration for someone so determinedly fighting the good fight, even if it wasn't one I thought worth the effort. But she generally managed to banish both sympathy and admiration the second she opened her mouth.

"What are you doing about those horrible turkeys?" she demanded.

"Everything we can," Randall said. "And we could use your help on that. Mind if we come in?"

"Construction zone!" came a high, nasal male voice from inside. "No admittance!"

"That's why we wore our hard hats," Randall said—to Imogen, as if she were the one who had spoken. "If we may?"

He took half a step closer, and she stepped back to allow us inside.

I heard Randall stifle a gasp as he glanced around. I had to repress the urge to turn and run back outside.

The kitchen wasn't just a construction zone. It was more like a war zone.

No wonder the roof drooped in at least one place. It was almost a miracle the whole thing hadn't all fallen in. The entire back wall of the house had been removed, and the roof was held up with jerry-rigged pillars made of unfinished four-by-fours set on enough scraps of plywood to bring them up to the needed height.

They'd also removed most of the interior walls, so apart from the bathroom the entire house was one big unfinished area. If Mrs. Smetkamp was hoping to achieve the kind of open, airy space you saw in so many articles in decorating magazines, she probably had a reason for being in a cranky mood. At the moment, the house looked more like a half-demolished warehouse than a contender for a feature in an upscale decorating magazine. You could still tell where the walls had been, not just by the interruptions in the flooring, but also by the line of makeshift four-by-four pillars holding up the ceiling. Evidently some of those interior walls had also been load bearing. I spotted half a dozen places where the weight of the roof had brought down parts of the ceiling, revealing the beams and joists above and depositing little foothills of plaster and insulation on the floor below. In one place, a joist—or maybe even a beam—had broken in the middle and was held up by a small forest of four-by-fours.

It looked ghastly to me, and I had the distinct feeling that Randall, with his greater expertise on what was happening above and around us, was even more alarmed than I was.

After studying the interior of the house for a minute or so with an expression of horror and disbelief, Randall shook himself slightly, rather like a dog coming in after a walk in a rain shower and turned to Mrs. Smetkamp.

"I'm hereby declaring this dwelling unsafe for human occupancy," Randall said.

"You can't do that!" Jared, the producer, hurried forward.

"Watch me," Randall said. "Meg, can you take some pictures of this disaster?"

I pulled out my phone and began doing so.

Jared sighed dramatically and rolled his eyes. I wondered if he'd started out as an actor—he always gave the impression that he was preening in front of a camera. He was about my height, five ten, but looked taller, partly because he was so thin and partly because his clothes seemed cut to subtly emphasize the vertical.

"Don't worry," Mrs. Smetkamp said. "They'll be fixing it."

"Damn right they will," Randall said. "Although if I were you, I'd kick them out and find someone competent to do the fixing. But we can talk about that later. Right now, everyone needs to evacuate this deathtrap."

"Absolutely not," she said. "I can't possibly—"

"You can leave under your own steam," Randall said. "Or I can call the police and have you forcibly removed. Your call. But no one's staying here, and no one's coming back in until we've inspected this place and seen what needs to be done to make it safe."

"Nonsense!" But her voice sounded less assured.

"If you force us to leave now, we might not be able to continue with the project," Jared said. "We can't possibly hang around this one-horse town until—"

"If you try to leave town before we resolve this, we'll arrest you for destruction of property and see what we can do to assist the owners with their lawsuit," Randall said. "Breach of contract—you do have some kind of contract with these clowns, I assume?" he added, turning to Mrs. Smetkamp, who frowned anxiously. "Or maybe even fraud, if we find anything fishy about your contractor's credentials," he went on, turning back to Jared. "For now, I want you to vacate the premises. Now," he added more forcefully, when Jared began to protest.

Jared clenched his jaw as if not arguing was difficult for him to manage. But to give him credit, he realized it wasn't wise. He turned to Mrs. Smetkamp, nodded, and strode out. I drifted over to the back door and watched. At first I thought he was heading for the shed in the back corner of the yard, looking around nervously all the while. But then I realized that there was a break in the hedge right beside the shed. He slipped through it into the neighboring yard.

"He gone?" Randall asked.

"Yes," I said.

Randall closed his eyes, took a breath, then opened them again and turned to Mrs. Smetkamp.

"You need to leave, too," he said. "I know you don't believe me, but those people have created a very dangerous situation here. You need to stay out until we assess what needs to be done to make sure this whole house doesn't fall down around our ears."

"That's ridiculous," she said. "I'm not going anywhere. You're just taking revenge because *Marvelous Mansions* didn't hire you as the local contractor. If—"

Just then we heard a loud thud on the roof, and part of the

living room ceiling collapsed, raining down plaster and debris on
the floor. We all froze until the dust had settled.

"Turkey on the roof, I think," I said. "Maybe a couple of them."

Randall nodded. Then he took a deep breath and turned back
to Mrs. Smetkamp.

"This house is unsafe," he said. "You can leave under your own
steam, or I can have Chief Burke send in some officers to forcibly
remove you. Your call."

"I already told your husband that if you need a place to stay,
we have several spare bedrooms," I said. "You'd be very welcome."

She glanced briefly at me, then returned to scowling at Randall.

"I'll need to pack a few things," she said.

"Make it quick." He folded his arms and frowned at her.

She walked over to the area that would once have been the
front bedroom. I could see two cots with sleeping bags on them.
Two small old-fashioned hard-sided suitcases stood nearby. As we
watched, she threw a few things into one of the suitcases. She
made a quick trip into the bathroom for a few more things. Then,
without saying a word to either of us, she walked past us and out
the back door.

"Let's go while the going's good," Randall said.

"What about her husband?" I pointed to the bedroom area,
where the second suitcase was still standing. "She doesn't seem to
have given him any thought."

"Blast," he said. "Let's pack his stuff up, quick. There can't be
that much of it. I'll check the bathroom."

I made my way carefully over to the bedroom area, using my
umbrella to test the floor ahead of me for soundness before putting my weight on it. I threw any personal items remaining in the
bedroom area into the other suitcase. A pair of shoes, a canvas
laundry bag, a bedside alarm clock. Randall returned from the
bathroom with a few toiletries and tossed them in.

"Okay, we're out of here." He slammed the suitcase closed and picked it up. "After you."

I didn't wait for a second invitation. An immense feeling of relief washed over me when I stepped out into the air. Even looking up and seeing two turkey hens perched on the roof, peering down into the backyard, didn't spoil my joy.

As we headed for the back of the yard, where Myra's ladders awaited us, I could hear Mrs. Smetkamp's voice coming from Mrs. Peabody's yard. She was ranting at someone about something. But not at me, so I did my best to ignore her.

"I'll be heading down to Buck's office to get the signs and caution tape we need to block off this building," Randall said. "And we'll probably have to get the chief to assign a deputy to make sure none of them try to sneak back in."

"How long is it likely to take to make the place safe for them to move back in?" I asked. "I'd like to have at least a rough idea how long we'll have her underfoot if she takes me up on the invitation."

"I hate to say it, but I have no idea," he said. "I'm not sure that mess actually can be fixed, or that it's worth doing even if it can be. And who knows how long it could drag on if she decides to try to take that *Marvelous Mansions* outfit to court over what they'd done."

"Oh, great," I said. "Did I just saddle us with a pair of semi-permanent house guests?"

"Don't worry," he said. "My cousin Ernie's got a mobile home he's been thinking of selling. I'll tell him to hang on to it, and if it looks like you're going to be stuck with the Smetkamps for the long haul, we can set it up here and tell them it's at their disposal for the duration."

"You think they'd go for it?" I asked. "I can't imagine her agreeing to live in a trailer."

"She strikes me as the kind of person who doesn't like being beholden to anyone," Randall said. "And if she balks, we'll find a way to convince her."

"Like reminding her about the obscure county law that might let squatters claim their land if they're not living on it," I suggested.

"Like that." Randall was climbing up the first of Myra's stepladders. "I had no idea we had such a law."

"I doubt if we do," I said. "But you think she'll know that?"

Randall laughed so hard he almost fell off the ladder.

"I've already ordered my workers to set up barricades at all the surrounding intersections," Randall said, as he climbed. "To create a one-block buffer zone on all sides. And I'm having someone standing by at every intersection, to fend off pedestrians and cars that might try to bypass the barricades."

"Sensible," I said. "The last thing we need is a bunch of tourists wandering in here. They'd get themselves killed trying to take selfies with the turkeys."

"That was my thought." He stepped off the ladder and reached over to steady it for me. "And so far we haven't seen too many tourists wandering this far from the center of town, but it's early yet. Most of them are down at the farmers market right now, but when that closes they'll start wandering everywhere. And sooner or later some of them are going to start asking why they can't drive through this part of town. And if they find out what's going on, they'll all swarm over here. How can we possibly fend them off?"

"Pretend we've detected a possible gas leak," I suggested. "Have your workers tell them the rest of the town's perfectly safe, but the utility company's ordered everyone out of these few blocks until they've traced the problem and fixed it."

"Good idea," he said.

"And better yet, don't have your intersection guards just come out and tell them it's a gas leak," I said. "Have them look around to make sure no one's listening, then whisper the news about the gas leak and make them promise not to tell anyone. That will make it much more believable."

"And ensure that the rumor spreads like wildfire," he said with a chuckle. "I like the way you think. I'll make a few phone calls and get that going."

We were both in a better mood now that we were safely back in Myra's yard.

Chapter 7

Myra seemed relieved at our safe return.

"Mission accomplished, I hope," she said. "Jason, Eli—you can get the ladders now."

The two boys raced over and each of them grabbed a step-ladder. But instead of putting them away, they moved them to a corner of the yard, climbed up, and began doing something. Practicing their mime act, perhaps? It looked as if they were pretending to tie strings between the trees along the back fence.

"Fishing line," Myra said, seeing my puzzled look. "Works for the deer—they bump into something well-nigh invisible and it spooks them and they turn back. We're hoping it works the same for turkeys, once they get into the Smetkamps' backyard. Something your dad suggested," she added to me.

"I swear," Randall said. "If I ever catch whoever brought those blasted turkeys over here . . ."

He let his words trail off, but he frowned as if plotting a dire fate for the malefactors.

"But didn't you bring them?" asked a high voice.

We looked down to see a small child sitting on the ground

beside Squeaky the dog. Presumably, from the family resemblance, a younger brother of Jason and Eli.

"I didn't bring them," Randall explained. "And I don't know who did, either. If I—"

"Yes, you did," the child insisted.

"Tyler Lord!" his mother exclaimed. "Don't be rude and stop making things up."

"Not making up." Tyler buried his head in Squeaky's plentiful fur, but then peeked out again. "He brought them," he insisted, pointing his finger defiantly at Randall.

At Randall . . . or at his hard hat? Tyler's small, grubby forefinger was aimed straight at the bright blue hat with SHIFFLEY CONSTRUCTION COMPANY printed across the front.

"Tyler Fenton Lord," Myra began.

Understanding that the use of his middle name was a dire portent, Tyler hunched his shoulders and looked as if he was fighting not to cry.

"No, wait," I said to Myra. I turned to Randall. "Let me have your hard hat for a second."

Looking puzzled, he took off the hat and handed it to me.

As I halfway expected, Tyler's pointing finger followed the hard hat. I held it up to my matching hat.

"You saw a truck that looked like this, right?" I asked Tyler, pointing at the hats. "This color, with words like this?"

He nodded.

Myra gasped.

"Holy Toledo," Randall muttered. "One of my trucks?"

"Can you tell us what happened?" I asked.

"I woke up and had to p—had to go to the baffroom," Tyler said, with great dignity. "And I looked out the window while I was—while I was there, and I saw one of his trucks." He pointed at Randall. "A big one. He has a lot of big trucks," he added, sounding impressed.

"What happened then?" I asked.

"The men got out of the trucks and carried the turkeys into the Smellybads' yard," Tyler said. "With webelos."

"Webelos?" Myra echoed. "There were Cub Scouts helping them?"

"No," Tyler said, sounding impatient. "Just big men pushing webelos."

"Pushing webelos," I echoed. Inspiration struck. "You mean like wagons with only one wheel at the front?"

"Yes," Tyler said. "Webelos."

"Wheelbarrows," I said.

Tyler nodded, as if graciously acknowledging that my pronunciation was also acceptable.

"They were carrying the turkeys in wheelbarrows," I said. "So what happened then?"

"They dumped all the turkeys on the ground and cut their feet with a knife."

"Cut their feet?" Myra sounded alarmed.

"I expect they put some kind of restraint on the turkeys' legs," I said. "Because even if the culprits managed to catch the turkeys while they were asleep, they'd have awakened and gotten a little feisty during their trip in the truck. Does that sound like what happened, Tyler? They tied up the turkeys' feet and then cut off the ties?"

"Yeah." He nodded. "They cut something so the turkeys' legs were free. And then the turkeys started chasing them, and they ran away, and the turkeys started flying up into the trees. They're pretty bad at it," he added. "Because they're so fat."

"And then the truck left?" I asked.

Tyler nodded.

"There you are." I turned to Randall. "I bet if Horace checked all your company's trucks, he just might find one containing evidence the turkeys left behind. Feathers or poop or something."

"Dang," Randall said. "I bet I could have found that evidence myself if I'd known to look for it. Might be able to find it now. And if I check the security cameras down at the construction office parking lot, I just might find proof that someone was making unauthorized use of that truck." He squatted down so he was closer to Tyler's height and held out his right hand. "Tyler, my man— good work!"

"You have the makings of a detective," I said, while Randall was shaking Tyler's hand.

Tyler grinned, revealing several spots where he'd recently lost baby teeth. And then, overcome with embarrassment at our praise, he buried his face in Squeaky's fur.

"Good grief," Myra said. "I had no idea I had the star witness in the turkey caper under my roof. Tyler, remember, it's SMETkamp, not Smellybad."

"I like Smellybad," came Tyler's muffled response. "They're always making our yard smell nasty. And killing the good bugs."

"He's got a point," Randall said. "I'm going to have a hard time not calling them the Smellybads after this." He was pulling out his phone as he spoke.

"You did good, Tyler," Myra said. "We should celebrate—pizza for dinner?"

"Yes! Pizza!" came a muffled voice from beneath Squeaky's fur.

From their position atop the ladders, Jason and Eli also expressed their approval of the plan.

"Chief," Randall was saying into his phone. "We may have a clue to who dumped the turkeys here." He waved at Myra and strode off, presumably to retrace our circuitous route through the neighbors' backyards.

"Thanks for everything," I told Myra.

"Drop by anytime you need to," she said.

"I'll be in touch about those surveillance cameras," I said. "And meanwhile, give us a call if you see that they're up to anything."

"Who?" she asked. "The turkeys or the Smetkamps?"

"Either."

I waved again at the observant Tyler and turned to follow Randall. I realized that he was heading out in the opposite direction from the one we'd come in by—picking his way carefully through some flower beds over the fence into the yard that backed up to Darlene's yard, all the while talking on his cell phone to someone.

"Can you hold down the fort here for a while?" he asked, as we strolled across Darlene's backyard. "I'm going to head down to the construction office. See what the security cameras show."

"No problem," I said.

He strode off along the side of Darlene's house—the side farther from the Smetkamps' house. I followed more slowly. When he came to the corner of the house, he stopped and peered around. Then he ventured out into the front yard, walking briskly. I deduced that if the turkeys had found their way into Darlene's yard, they weren't yet dangerously close.

I followed suit, pausing to reconnoiter. Two turkeys were foraging in Darlene's front yard, but at the far side, near the hedge that separated it from the Smetkamps' yard. Another one was sitting on the roof—and from the look of it, had initially tried to perch on the basketball hoop, which was now bent until it was perpendicular to the ground.

I walked as quickly as I could to the relative safety of the street. Down at the other end of the block, I spotted Randall, talking to Chief Burke and gesticulating wildly.

"I don't know why we ever decided to come to this hick town." I recognized the annoying Jared's voice and turned to see him talking to Darlene at the closer end of the block. No, make that venting to Darlene. "And does that stupid mayor really think he can push us around and interfere with our filming?"

Just then he saw me and blanched.

"Yeah, he probably does think that," Darlene said. "And odds are he's right. Meg, honey—what have you and my cousin Randall been doing to upset this poor boy?"

"Your cousin?" Jared frowned at Darlene, as if she'd somehow tricked him into badmouthing Randall in front of her. "Damn."

"That's small towns for you," I said. "Always safe to assume everybody's related to everybody else."

Darlene was smiling at him, and maybe he thought it was a kindly smile. To me it looked like the kind of smile that went along with the words, "Bless your heart," and signaled that the recipient was on very thin ice.

"I should get back to the Inn," he muttered. "It's not like we'll be able to get anything done if they can't keep the livestock under control."

"You have a nice rest of your day," Darlene said.

Jared didn't respond. He was staring up at the nearby street signs.

"Bland Street," he said, with a deprecating sniff. "What a name. Who actually names a street that, anyway?"

He looked more cheerful, as if finding something to mock made him feel better.

"A lot of places in Virginia, I suspect," I said. "It's named after a real person—James A. Bland, the African American musician who wrote 'Carry Me Back to Old Virginny,' which used to be our state song."

"'Used to be,'" he repeated. "What happened to it?"

"It didn't wear well," I said. "The lyrics were all nostalgic about pre–Civil War plantation life, not to mention full of politically incorrect language, so in the nineties the legislature officially declared it our state song emeritus and started trying to figure out a new state song."

"Bet that took a while," he said, with a chuckle.

"Almost twenty years," I agreed. "And now we have two state songs—'Sweet Virginia Breeze' is officially the state popular song, and 'Our Great Virginia' is the state traditional song."

"Never heard of either."

"You'd recognize 'Our Great Virginia' if you heard it," I said. "Someone wrote new words to the tune of 'Shenandoah.'"

"We don't have that problem in California," he said. "We've got 'California, Here I Come.' Good song. Everyone knows it."

"But it doesn't happen to be your state song," I said. "That honor belongs to 'I Love You, California.' Written by a guy named Frankenstein."

"No way," Jared said.

"Way," I said. "Look it up. Abraham F. Frankenstein."

Jared didn't seem to find this nearly as entertaining as I had when Josh and Jamie had told me.

"I should be going," he said.

"I'm envious, though," I said. "You've even got a state lichen—we don't. The lace lichen. Very attractive, as lichens go."

But Jared was off, walking as if the feral turkeys were breathing down his neck.

"Good job," Darlene said. "I thought I was going to have to be rude and tell him to get lost. Maybe I should look up the words to our state songs and sing them to him the next time he shows up. What's got Randall so fired up?"

"The *Marvelous Mansions* workmen tore out so many load-bearing walls that he's declared the Smetkamps' house unsafe for occupation,"

"Yikes," she said.

"And on top of that—"

"Uh-oh," Darlene muttered.

Never words I wanted to hear. Or did *uh-oh* count as words? I turned around to see what she was concerned about.

"*Uh-oh* is right," I said.

A panel truck had turned in to the block. I recognized the distinctive gray body and bright blue curved arrow that identified it as an Amazon delivery truck.

"How'd he get here?" I asked.

"Ran over the curb to get around Aida's cruiser," Darlene said. "I'm surprised she's not coming after him."

"Maybe she figures the turkeys will take care of that for her," I suggested.

The Amazon driver had apparently spotted a trio of the male turkeys who were gobbling and displaying at each other in the middle of the road. He slowed down to scope out the situation. Slowed and then stopped. I wished, just for a moment, that I could be a fly on the ceiling of his truck cab. He stayed there, about two houses into the block, for a minute or so. Then he continued slowly down the street, navigating around the turkeys. Was he heading for the Smetkamps' house?

Chapter 8

Darlene and I stood anxiously watching the Amazon driver's slow progress.

"Normally, I give delivery drivers what-for if they just toss my packages by the mailbox," Darlene said. "But this guy definitely gets a pass if he wants to do that."

Unfortunately, this driver seemed to have a highly developed sense of duty. And no common sense. He parked his truck in front of the Smetkamps. We could see him turn to pick up something behind him.

Bystanders began shouting at him.

"Look out!"

"Don't do it!"

"Stay away!"

"Go back!"

"For the love of God, man, stay in your truck!"

But he ignored them—or possibly didn't realize they were talking to him. He got out of his truck and plodded around the front of it, startling a small and exceptionally timid turkey hen, who ran away shrieking. He halted, as if trying to figure out how to navigate around the several turkeys who were sunning themselves on the front walk.

Several of the larger turkeys began converging on him.

"We've got to do something," I said. "Come on! And bring your umbrella."

I opened my umbrella partway as I raced down the street toward the Amazon driver. As I drew near the turkeys, I began vigorously flapping my umbrella open and closed. And twirling it, which seemed to enhance the effect. Darlene was right behind me, flapping and twirling her umbrella. Up and down the street, other bystanders sprang into action. Several also had umbrellas. Two of the college kids who'd been swilling beer on their front lawn dashed toward us, holding their lawn chairs in front of them like lion tamers. Meera Patel tossed her hose aside and ran into the street carrying a pitchfork.

Unfortunately, the turkeys were also converging on some of the would-be rescuers, so the college kids and one of the umbrella twirlers ended up having to defend themselves while retreating from aggressive toms. But Meera and several other umbrella twirlers reached the side of the luckless Amazon driver. We formed a circle around him, flapping our umbrellas while Meera gently fended off any birds who tried to slip past the umbrellas, using the back of the tines rather than the points.

"Get back into your truck," I shouted at the driver.

He stood, frozen.

More birds were converging on us.

The driver was wearing a blue-and-gray vest with the Amazon logo on the right side of his chest. On the left he had added a blue-and-gray pin that said HI! I'M BENNY!"

"Benny!" I shouted. "Into the truck!"

"But I have to deliver this." He held up a cardboard box, slightly larger than a shoebox, with CAUTION: CONTENTS MAY CAUSE HAPPINESS printed on the side.

I took one hand off my umbrella, grabbed the box, and heaved it over the umbrellas and the heads of the surrounding turkeys. It landed on the front walk, right beside the mailbox.

"Delivery complete," I said as I shoved him toward the passenger side door of his truck. "Time to make our escape. Everyone, into the truck with Benny. We'll drive to safety."

I began flapping my umbrella again to clear my way around the front of the truck to the driver's-side door. As I climbed into the driver's seat, Darlene scrambled in through the passenger side door, dragging Benny behind her. One of the umbrella wielders was helping Benny up with a strong shove to his rear end, while the two others and Meera covered them with umbrellas and pitchfork.

Darlene propelled Benny through the doorway between the driver's section and the cargo area, then scrambled after him. The other umbrella twirlers swarmed in after her. As I eased off the parking brake, Meera hopped up into the doorway.

"Grab me!" she shouted.

One of the umbrella crew did, and I eased the truck slowly out into the road, with her still standing in the half-open truck door, holding on to the doorframe with one hand while she wielded the pitchfork with the other.

I brought the truck to a stop at the end of the block, where my cousin Horace's police cruiser was parked sideways to block access to the street. I suppose I could have driven around him, as Benny must have done to get himself into this mess in the first place, but I wasn't sure I could do it without damaging either the truck or the corner house's flower beds.

Horace was standing on the far side of his cruiser, with a stunned look on his face. His hand was hovering near his service weapon.

I rolled down the driver's-side window a few inches.

"They're following us!" I shouted. "Take cover!"

Horace began scrambling into his cruiser.

Just then a tremendous blast of water surged past us, knocking the closest turkeys off their feet. I peered in the direction it was coming from and saw that Michael and several of his fellow volunteer firefighters had arrived in the pumper truck. They were using short blasts of water from their hose to fend off the birds.

Michael waved at me and gave me a thumbs-up.

Horace backed up his cruiser until he'd made enough room for me to drive the Amazon truck past without going up on the sidewalk. I pulled across the intersection and parked it—across the street, I noticed, from a Shiffley Construction Company truck.

"I think we're safe now." I set the truck's parking brake and turned off the engine.

"We did good," Meera said with a grin, as she climbed down.

"We did awesome," one of the umbrella twirlers replied, as he climbed down.

The other umbrella warriors followed him, and the four of them began exchanging high fives.

"My packages," Benny was moaning as he peered from behind the seats. "I'm sure some of them are crushed."

"Just be glad you made it out of there alive," Darlene said, as she emerged from the cargo area. "You should apply to the post office. Neither snow nor rain nor heat nor gloom of night nor feral turkeys stayed you from the swift completion of your appointed rounds."

"She'll report me," Benny moaned. "The lady in the turkey house. She always does. She reported me once for leaving a package too close to her house, so her screen door hit it when she went out. She'll go ballistic over this."

I thought of explaining that she wasn't even in the house, and probably had a few other things to worry about today, like whether she'd be returning to a house or a pile of rubble. But he was probably right. She'd make a stink when she found the package. Especially since it was already looking a little battered, having been thrown onto the sidewalk and then pecked at by several of the turkeys, either to see if it was edible or maybe to demonstrate their dominance over it.

"Here." I reached into my pocket and pulled out a business card. One of the ones from my job as Randall's special assistant— I'd had a hunch they'd come in useful today. "If she reports you, and you need witnesses to what really happened, call me."

"Absolutely," Darlene said. "We can get you plenty of witnesses."

"And video," I added. I'd already seen several people with cell phones or video cameras, filming the turkeys. I had no doubt that a few of them had documented Benny's brush with death by feral turkey. For that matter, the *Marvelous Mansions* crew had set up their cameras and other equipment on the top of their big truck, so I'd be astonished if they hadn't gotten high quality video of the whole thing.

"Witnesses, yeah," Benny said. "I may need to take you up on that."

"Just call," I said. "Have a safe rest of your day."

"Thanks," he said, as he eased the truck into motion.

"Stop!" Horace shouted. He began running after the Amazon truck.

"What's wrong?" I called after him. Then I noticed that there was a turkey perched atop the truck. One of the smaller toms.

Benny braked and Horace ran up to the driver's side of the truck to explain. Benny looked panic stricken, jumped out of his truck, and ran up onto the sidewalk.

"Michael," I called.

When he turned, I pointed at the truck. Michael shouted to the other firefighters. They'd turned off the hose after herding the turkeys back into the Smetkamps' yard. But now they turned the hose around, and one firefighter raced back to the truck.

"Wait! Wait!" Grandfather came running up.

"Don't worry," Michael said. "We're not using that much water pressure. Just a little spurt to nudge him off the truck."

"That's fine," Grandfather said. "But as long as we're nudging him, let's catch him while we're at it. Clarence, hurry up!"

Clarence Rutledge, Caerphilly's local vet, came running, which set all the bits of chain dangling from his biker clothes to jingling—and since Clarence was well over six feet and built like a tank, he had room for a lot of chains. He was carrying a bundle of something. He ran over to the Amazon truck and took up a position on the side away from Michael and the pumper. He unfurled the bundle to reveal a large blue tarp, which he spread out on the ground beside the truck.

"Okay, nudge away." Grandfather strode toward Clarence.

The firefighters began releasing brief spurts of water at the turkey. The first one merely annoyed him. The second moved him partway across the top of the truck. The third convinced him to abandon his post, and he fluttered down from the truck . . . right onto the tarp. Clarence and Grandfather quickly bundled him up until only his head was free. A larger-than-life-sized turkey burrito. And not a happy burrito—he was gobbling furiously, and pecking at anything that came near him. But he was caught.

"We'll haul this one out to the zoo," Grandfather said. "Can someone give Clarence a hand? His truck's right over there."

Several firefighters hurried over to help Clarence pick up the wriggling bundle and carry it to the Caerphilly Veterinary Hospital van, which was parked nearby.

Meanwhile Benny returned to his truck. He checked the roof and the cargo area before settling in his seat again.

"I hate this route," he muttered, softly enough that I wasn't sure if he was talking to me or to himself. "Something weird always happens here."

With that, he released the parking brake and drove off again.

I noticed that he was going appreciably faster than the speed limit. Horace noticed, too, but I could tell he was deciding to give Benny a break, given everything he'd just gone through.

"Well, that's one down," Horace said. "No idea how many to go."

"Two hundred and eleven," said Grandfather, who happened to be striding past us on his way to Clarence's truck.

"Good grief," Horace exclaimed as we watched the truck depart with its lone captive. "We can't possibly do that two hundred and eleven more times."

"No," I said. "Even if we could somehow lure them up on top of two hundred and eleven trucks. But it looks as if Grandfather and Clarence have some idea how to wrangle them. There's hope."

"Good." Horace had turned to look at the Shiffley Construction truck, from which a small posse of Randall's employees were unloading a supply of orange-and-white barricades and sawhorses.

"Good idea," I said, nodding toward the truck. "Maybe you can go back on patrol when they get those in place."

"Actually, once they unload them all, I get to process the truck to see if someone used it to bring the turkeys here," he said.

"That's great," I replied.

"It'd be greater if the chief could figure out any kind of law they broke by bringing the turkeys over here," he said. "Not sure how useful it is to gather evidence for something that may not even be a crime."

"Doesn't unauthorized use of one of Randall's trucks count?" I asked. "Plus maybe trespassing in the parking lot at his construction company."

"You're right." Horace looked more cheerful at the thought. "Thanks."

Watching the Amazon driver's adventure must have convinced the *Marvelous Mansions* producer that carrying out whatever plans he had for the day was a lost cause. While Randall's crew were still putting the barricades in place, the film crew's trucks and the producer's rental SUV exited the block—although to my surprise and disappointment, they didn't leave altogether—they just parked in the next block. In the SUV, the producer and some of his senior people were having what looked like a heated discussion.

An ancient though still sporty-looking black MGB convertible with Gloria Willingham in the driver's seat pulled up to the construction barriers.

Chapter 9

"What's going on?" Gloria asked. "Has that miserable TV show done something to—what the hell?"

I turned to see what had so alarmed her and saw that a large turkey had ventured across the street and was being herded back to the Smetkamps' yard by a trio of umbrella twirlers.

"Did the TV people bring those things?" Gloria asked. "Part of their plan to make us look like a bunch of clueless hicks?"

"We don't know yet," I said. "But it's more likely someone brought them as part of a plan to make things difficult for the TV crew."

"Good cause, bad execution," she said. "The TV crew can just leave—we residents can't. Is it safe to go in there? I'd like to park my car in the garage."

"You should be fine if you put your top up," Horace said. "And the fire department's standing by in case anyone needs rescuing."

He pointed to where Michael and his fellow volunteer firefighters had parked the pumper—on the cross street, just outside the barricaded area. They'd also brought out lawn chairs and were sitting in the shade of a large oak tree, drinking sodas or lemonades.

A peaceful scene. In fact, when I glanced up and down the street, it was mostly peaceful. The turkeys had all descended from the trees and were busily destroying the surrounding landscape, but since no one was trying to bother them, they were doing it with quiet intensity. People were still sitting on stoops or in lawn chairs in front of a good half of the houses, but given how sedate the turkey flock had become, most of them were also entertaining themselves with books, phones, or iPads. Waiting for the next flurry of excitement, I supposed.

I helped Gloria wrestle her MG's top into place, and Horace and I moved two of the sawhorses aside far enough for her to drive in.

She paused beside me and rolled her window down.

"Given all this, I'm definitely going to head back to your house for the afternoon," she said. "As long as that's okay. I only really came home to pick up a couple of books I needed and fix a quick lunch."

"Fine with us," I said. "And if for any reason you want to flee the neighborhood until the turkeys are gone, take a suitcase with you when you go back. We'd be glad to put you up."

"Thanks," she said. "I'll think about it. Although I'm not sure I want to leave my house undefended."

"I doubt if the turkeys can break in," I said.

"Actually, I was thinking about my creepy tenant," she said. "I think he snoops around when I'm not home."

"That's not good," I said. "I'd worry about my financial information—my social security number, my passwords, my bank account information—"

"All locked up," she said. "And not here. I'm a little paranoid about security, so when I started renting out rooms, I got a top-quality locking file cabinet for my office down at the Drama Building and made sure anything I didn't want a nosy tenant to see was locked up there. Plus a lock on my bedroom closet so my purse and things are safe. Bothers me that he might be snooping, but he's not likely to find anything he could exploit. Still, it will keep me safe when he's careless. A couple of times I came home to find my front door unlocked. Closed, mind you, but unlocked. If he's going out and doesn't expect to be gone long, he doesn't even bother locking the outside door—he just makes sure the attic is locked so his stuff is safe. I've read him the riot act, but I doubt if he pays any attention, so I just make sure everything valuable's locked up."

"Smart," I said. "So Chris, your weird techie tenant—is that short for Christopher? And what's his full name?"

"Chris Smith," she said. "And that's what he put on the lease. No idea what it's short for—could be Christian. Or Chrysanthemum, for all I know. I was so glad to get a signature from a paying tenant that I didn't ask—why?"

She looked . . . concerned? Uneasy?

"Well, I was going to lie," I said. "And say that since he's a techie, maybe I should see if he and my nephew Kevin knew each other. Actually, I was thinking maybe I could get Kevin to check him out. Because if he really strikes you as creepy . . ."

"I'd like that," she said. "Because I'm not kidding—he's seriously creepy. So creepy I'm thinking of pretending I have a friend who needs the room so I can get rid of him early. He never leaves the house—hardly ever even comes down from the attic. If I try to start a conversation, just to get to know him, or maybe to find out a little more about him, he weasels out of it. He says he works remotely on computer stuff that's too technical to explain to a civilian like me. Maybe he's just a loner with no social skills, but it would be nice to make sure he wasn't an international terrorist or an escaped ax murderer or anything."

"How old is he?"

"Young," she said. "Maybe twenty-five?"

"Okay," I said. "I'll see what Kevin can find out."

"Thanks."

She set the car in motion and headed down the street at a snail's pace, obviously keeping an eye out for any stray turkeys. I watched as she drove up her driveway, waited for the garage door to open all the way, and then disappeared inside. I kept watch myself, to make sure no stray turkeys barged in before the garage door was all the way closed.

When I was sure Gloria was safe at home, I pulled out my notebook and scribbled down "Chris Smith," just in case. It struck me as a very forgettable name. Could it even be a fake one? Maybe not. After all, if I were choosing a fake name, I'd probably avoid anything as generic and fake-sounding as Smith—but when you came down to it, why did it sound so fake? The last time I'd checked it was still the most common last name in the U.S. There must be at least a million real Smiths in the country. Probably more. Christopher regularly appeared in the lists of top ten boys' names, with Christian not far behind. There would probably be a lot of genuine Chris Smiths out there. It wasn't necessarily suspicious. But having such a popular first and last name would make it harder for Kevin to check out Gloria's renter.

I was pulling out my phone to call Kevin when the noise of a door slamming interrupted the fragile peace that had descended over the neighborhood.

"Stupid birds!"

Evidently Mrs. Smetkamp had taken refuge next door. Now she stood on Mrs. Peabody's front stoop with her hands on her hips, scowling at the nearby turkeys.

"Uh-oh," I muttered. That really was the word of the day.

Mrs. Smetkamp stomped down the front steps and marched through the surrounding turkeys toward the sidewalk. She must have caught them by surprise. None of them attacked her, and a few even moved out of her way. When she reached the sidewalk she turned and kept going until she reached her own front walk and stooped to pick up the package.

I didn't hear what she said as she examined the slightly battered and definitely poo-stained package, but I could tell from her expression that she wasn't uttering glad cries of joy. She looked up and down the street, scowling. Was she looking for me? Maybe she knew I was the one who'd tossed the package there and wanted to give her a piece of her mind about its condition. I rather hoped she didn't know. In retrospect, it would have made more sense to carry the package with me, out of the turkey zone, and give it to her later. But hindsight is always twenty-twenty, and I had been focused on rescuing the Amazon driver.

She turned, and it looked as if she was about to head back to Mrs. Peabody's house. Not a good idea. She'd taken the turkeys by surprise when she left the house, but now they were stirred up and milling about. And she wasn't even looking at them. She'd started opening her package, carefully prying the tape that sealed one end—and began slowly walking along the sidewalk as she worked.

The turkeys spotted her. The toms began gobbling, displaying in her direction, and inching closer. She was focused on her package and didn't even seem to notice what the turkeys were up to.

Fortunately, the volunteer firefighters did. Small spurts of water began pelting the turkeys in her path, distracting them and nudging them away, first from the sidewalk and then from the walkway that led up to the house, clearing a safe path for the preoccupied Mrs. Smetkamp.

She didn't seem to notice any of it—not even when one of the largest turkeys headed right for her with murder and mayhem in his eye. A little of the water the firefighters used to fend him off dampened her left sleeve. Only when she got to the front door did she look up from her package. And then she only brushed at her sleeve and glanced up to frown at the sky, as if chastising it for daring to rain on her. Then she disappeared inside the house, apparently unaware of the close calls she'd just been through. Or maybe just predictably ungrateful for the help she'd been given.

"Good job!" I shouted to the firefighters. Michael and several others gave me a thumbs-up.

After that, things grew quiet on Bland Street. The pumper remained parked in front of the corner house, whose owner soon set up a picnic canopy for the firefighters in his front yard. Since it was getting on for lunchtime, the firefighters brought over the huge grill they used at the firehouse and began cooking hamburgers, brats, and portobello mushrooms. One of them took off in his pickup truck and came back with the bed full of folding tables and chairs—borrowed, according to the stencils on the chair backs, from the nearby New Life Baptist Church. Neighbors from up and down the block began showing up with salads, side dishes, breads, and desserts, and the whole thing turned into a giant impromptu neighborhood potluck picnic.

I noticed a couple of the *Marvelous Mansions* crew members gazing longingly at the picnic, but before long one of the guys in the SUV emerged and issued curt orders to the drivers of the trucks. Then he hurried back to the SUV, and the whole bunch of them drove off. Back to their rooms at the Caerphilly Inn, I supposed.

From time to time, the firefighters would spring into action to discourage the turkeys from leaving the Smetkamps' yard or move the barriers aside for a resident to drive into the block. But mostly they sat, keeping watch. Individual firefighters would come and go, as their job or family responsibilities called. And as the day wore on, the impromptu festival grew bigger and bigger.

I snagged a burger and some Caesar salad. Then I found a quiet spot and called Kevin.

Instead of saying "hello" or "what now?" he began whistling into the phone. Or had I misdialed and reached a wrong number? No, my phone screen showed his name and number.

It occurred to me that maybe this was some obscure reference to one of his podcasts. Kevin and a friend hosted *Virginia Crime Time,* which covered crimes and cold cases in the state of Virginia. I didn't always listen to their episodes the night they dropped—in fact, I liked to save them until it was broad daylight, in case they were covering a particularly grisly or creepy case. So had I missed knowing that they were covering a serial killer who'd been nick-named "The Whistler"? No, that was from one of P. D. James's books.

"Cut it out, Kevin," I said. "Or explain why you're whistling at me."

"Don't you get it?" he said. "The tune?"

He whistled a few more bars. I recognized it now. "Turkey in the Straw."

"Hilarious," I said, in a tone that hinted at what I really felt. "May I recruit your help for a project?"

"Something to do with the turkeys?" he asked.

"Alas, no," I said. "Although I think Randall Shiffley is making plans for a great turkey roundup tonight or tomorrow. You could volunteer for that if you like."

"Awesome," he said. "So what tedious non-turkey-related task do you have for me?"

"I have two," I said. "One involves doing a camera setup so we can catch a neighborhood miscreant in the act."

"Miscreant," he said. "I like it. You're good for my vocab. This miscreant of yours—what's he up to?"

"Actually, the malefactor's probably a she."

"Ooh, another good one," Kevin said.

I explained about Mrs. Smetkamp's clandestine use of insecticides, working in "offender," "reprobate," "wrongdoer," and as many other synonyms as I could think of.

"Cool beans," he said. "An environmental transgressor. Got to protect our pollinators. So yeah, we can get the goods on her. Should earn me points with Great when I tell him about it."

"Yes, your great-grandfather will be pleased," I said. "But you can't tell anyone about it until we catch her in the act."

"Roger. When do you want me to set them up?"

I wanted to say, "Now! As soon as possible! Yesterday!" But realistically, did Mrs. Smetkamp have any bandwidth right now for poisoning mosquitoes and neighbors? As long as we got the cameras in place before she did, that would be fine. Plus there were the turkeys to think of. Kevin, like so many of my family—the men, at least—had the ability to focus on what he was doing to the exclusion of everything going on around him. Great if you were trying to concentrate in a busy room. Not so great if you were so focused that you didn't notice any nearby dangers—like homicidal turkeys.

Still, it would be a good thing to have Kevin set up the cameras while Mrs. Smetkamp was focused on other things. And what if whoever pulled the turkey prank had more tricks up his sleeve? The sooner we got the cameras in place, the sooner we could detect any wrongdoing on Bland Street.

"Can you plan on doing it tomorrow?" I asked. "Probably in the afternoon. That's assuming whatever Randall's planning works and the turkeys are gone. I can let you know if we run into any problems and need to postpone. And we have no idea where she sets off her insecticide bombs—it's probably not in her own yard—"

"So my setup needs to cover more than just her yard," he said. "Check. A pity we didn't do this a few days ago. Might have given us a clue to who dumped the turkeys."

"I was thinking the same thing," I said. "Though I think the chief's got some clues. But with luck, the only furtive activity going on in the dark over here tonight will be the turkey roundup. At least I assume the roundup will be in the dark—safer if they're asleep, at least when we start. And I think Mrs. Smetkamp has a few things other than mosquitoes to worry about right now."

"I'll start working on it. Maybe I should bring over a few web-enabled cameras. If I set them up so they have a good view of the turkeys, I can post the feeds online. A live turkey cam could be a hoot."

I winced. Yes, a live turkey cam would be a hoot. But would it make Caerphilly look ridiculous?

Probably no more than some of the town's other past adventures. And with luck, by this time tomorrow, the turkeys would be out at Grandfather's zoo. If Kevin moved his turkey cam out there, it wouldn't matter if the turkeys became celebrities or tourist attractions.

"Whatever floats your boat," I said. "Just be careful. We don't want you pecked and clawed to death by rampaging feral turkeys."

"It'd get me into the Darwin Awards," he said. "Didn't you say you had two chores for me?"

Chapter 10

"Yes, I do have a second chore for you," I said. Kevin was surprisingly—make that suspiciously—cooperative today. "Chore two is a background check on one Chris Smith. Male. No idea if that's his full name or if it's short for something like Christopher or Christian. Mid-twenties. Rents the attic of a house across the street from the turk—from the Smetkamps."

"Not exactly a unique name," he said. "What do you suspect him of doing?"

"No idea. His landlady thinks he's creepy. Hardly ever leaves the attic. Dodges questions about himself. Works from home, using what seems to her like an excessive number of computers, but then she's a drama professor, not a techie. I know it sounds as if she's being paranoid—"

"Actually, it sounds like the opening of a true crime story," he said. "She's smart to trust her instincts. Sometimes our subconscious senses danger long before our conscious mind recognizes it. According to—"

"Let's make sure it's an opening that goes nowhere," I said, interrupting what I was sure would be another impassioned recommendation that every person—and especially every woman—should read Gavin de Becker's *The Gift of Fear*. One of these days I'd get him to remember that not only had I read *The Gift of Fear*, I was the one who'd given him his copy.

"I'll start looking," he said. "But see if she's got any other information. References, previous addresses, maybe even a social security number . . . anything."

"Will do."

I texted Gloria to ask for any other information she had on her tenant. She replied, almost immediately, that she'd drop by her office and see if she had anything else in her files.

"Mainly what I remember is that he paid in advance for three months," she added.

Which sounded suspicious to me. Probably a good thing we were checking out this Chris Smith dude.

I went back to the picnic. Two more picnic pavilions had arrived, which was a relief—they'd protect us from both sunstroke and flying turkeys. Mr. Jasper was lurking nearby—not partaking of the buffet but frowning at it as if trying to recall some obscure town ordinance he could invoke to shut it down. I'd like to see him try.

I began to recognize familiar foods. Darlene's Atomic Buffalo Wings, for example. I knew better than to eat the things—just looking at them almost gave me heartburn—but eating them was a point of pride for teenage and pre-teen boys—Josh and Jamie adored them. So I snagged a dozen before they all disappeared and had Michael put them aside to give to the boys when they showed up—as they were bound to do, sooner or later. I wasn't sure who made the hot German potato salad with bacon bits, but I made a mental note to find out, so I could beg for the recipe. Someone was dishing out cups of a wonderfully savory potato-leek soup and were those homemade potato chips? I spotted half a dozen different enticing salads. And since the county's strawberry farms were going strong at the moment, perhaps it wasn't surprising that we had strawberry shortcake, strawberry tarts, strawberry crumble, strawberry cheesecake, strawberry cobbler, chocolate-covered strawberries, and just plain fresh strawberries so ripe it would have been a waste—in fact, a sin—not to finish them off immediately, lest they go bad.

And I was impressed with Mrs. Peabody, who showed up with two desserts—chocolate meringue cookies with a chewy fudge-like base and tops so flaky and light that they melted in your mouth like cotton candy and high-test chocolate bourbon balls. I had Michael put aside a few of those, too, so I could pig out on them when I got home and didn't have to worry about driving under their influence.

I spotted her sitting at the far end of the yard, holding a plate that contained a dab of nearly every dish on the buffet and nibbling as she listened to the conversation of several of the more outgoing picnickers. She was a small, neat, pleasant-looking woman. Her salt-and-pepper hair was braided and then arranged around her head like a crown—an old-fashioned style, but one that flattered her. She was wearing faded jeans and a T-shirt printed with flowers and the motto GARDENING—BECAUSE MURDER IS WRONG. If you'd put her in a flowered dress and apron instead, she wouldn't have looked out of place fifty or a hundred years ago. Maybe that was why I had such a hard time thinking of her as anything but Mrs. Peabody. She might actually prefer being called Emma.

And although she was trying to smile bravely, she looked a little forlorn.

I went over and took the folding chair next to her.

"How are you holding up?" I asked.

"Oh, don't worry about me." She looked flustered, as if she'd really rather be left in peace.

"I can't help it," I said. "I worry about everyone in the neighborhood, but especially you. First the makeover from hell takes over your front yard and now the turkeys. This whole thing is making your life difficult."

"I don't mind, really," she said. "It's quite interesting, watching everything that's happening."

"I'm not sure I could be that philosophical if the turkeys were digging up our yard," I said. "And our landscaping's not nearly as nice as yours is." Maybe I shouldn't have mentioned her yard. She glanced involuntarily in that direction, and her face fell slightly.

"Well, that is a little discouraging." Her voice and her brave smile tickled my memory. Where had I seen that before? "But of course, the garden's always a work in progress. Reg says he can talk the TV people into fixing it up, as long as they're here."

I nodded, wondering all the while who Reg was.

"Frankly, I doubt if they will," she said. "And I'm not really sure my old-fashioned kind of garden's really something they know much about. But I'll get it back in shape. I'm still pretty handy with a trowel, and of course Reg is always so helpful. You couldn't ask for a better neighbor than Reg."

Aha. Reg must be Mr. Smetkamp.

Interesting that she only mentioned him. I couldn't imagine that Mrs. Smetkamp was anything but a nightmare of a neighbor. She got points for honesty.

"Look, things are pretty crazy around here right now," I said. "And they could be even crazier early tomorrow morning. Randall Shiffley's trying to organize rounding up the turkeys, and that will need to start well before dawn."

"Oh!" She looked anxious. "What's going to happen to them? The turkeys, I mean."

"Don't worry," I said, "My grandfather's got a habitat ready for them out at his zoo. The plan is to let them live out their lives there, and he can use them for his research. Comparing their behavior to those of wild turkeys and things like that," I added, in case she thought Grandfather's research might be fatal to the birds.

"That's so kind of him," she murmured.

"Anyway," I went on. "If you'd rather get away from the chaos, we've got plenty of guest rooms, and you'd be welcome to join us. Heck, for the duration of the makeover, if you like—it can't be a lot of fun, living next door to a construction site."

"Living in the middle of a construction site, actually," she said. "Of course, I'm absolutely fine with them using my yard for the overflow. It's always nice when you can be a help to your neighbors, isn't it? But it has been a lot more . . . lively than I expected."

I suddenly realized who she reminded me of. Greer Garson in *Mrs. Miniver*, valiantly maintaining a stiff upper lip in the face of yet another blow from fate.

"Just pack a suitcase and come on out." It suddenly occurred to me that I hadn't seen a car in her driveway, and the TV show had appropriated her garage for workspace. "Or let me know if you need a ride. I've already told Mr. Smetkamp that they'd be welcome, so they may be coming out, and I can always swing by to collect you."

"Thank you." She looked relieved. "I'll take you up on that. And I'll ask Reg if it would be convenient to give me a ride. I'm sure he won't mind."

"There you are." Randall Shiffley strode up. "We're going to have a planning meeting in a few minutes. Make sure we're all on the same page about tomorrow's roundup. Getting started as soon as your grandfather and Doc Clarence get here."

"Last I saw of them, they were delivering a turkey to the zoo," I said. "That can't take too long."

"No." Randall frowned slightly and looked at his phone. "But when I texted him just now to tell him about the meeting, he said he'd come back soon but at the moment he was communing with his favorite warthog. What do you suppose he means by that?"

"I have no idea," I replied. "It's going to take me a while to get my mind around the idea that someone could even have a favorite warthog."

"If anyone does, it would be your grandfather," Randall said. "Ah. He says the danger is past and he'll be here soon."

"What danger?"

"We can ask him when he gets here," Randall said. "We're meeting in the smallest pavilion." He pointed to the pavilion in question, which was in the side yard, a little removed from the heart of the picnic. "See you there."

He tipped an imaginary hat to us before dashing off. I could see him striding through the crowd, occasionally collaring someone and shooing them toward the smallest pavilion.

"Such a nice man," Mrs. Peabody said. "I think it's a shame, how those TV people treat him."

And then she dug into one of the dabs of food on her plate—the temptingly rich-looking potatoes au gratin. She smiled with delight as she tasted it, and I decided this might be a subtle hint that she wanted to eat in peace.

"Enjoy," I said.

I headed for the smallest pavilion—veering past the buffet table on my way, for another few ham biscuits and just a few more strawberries. The smallest pavilion contained a table at one end, with a few stray paper plates and cups on it, and a lot of New Life Baptist folding chairs arranged to face it in auditorium style.

Randall strode in, followed by Horace and Chief Burke.

"That's no problem," Randall was saying. "I've got pretty good sources with the *Marvelous Mansions* worker bees. Not the camera and light people, but the carpenters and plumbers and such."

"Good." The chief nodded his approval as he took a seat behind the table.

"I guess you did a little carpenter-to-carpenter bonding," I said to Randall.

"I did," he said. "But what really won them over was the fact that I rescued them from the Clay County Motor Lodge."

"The Clay County Motor Lodge?" I echoed. Most of us here

in Caerphilly referred to it as either the Roach Motel or Bedbug City. "What were they doing there? I thought the show was putting up its people at the Caerphilly Inn."

"Only Mr. Blomqvist, originally," Randall said. "He got his reservation in early enough to snag one of the Inn's nicer rooms, but it didn't occur to him to take care of his people."

Randall's scowl suggested that he considered this a mortal sin. I agreed.

"And he tried to sent them over to Clay County?" I asked.

"The tech crews—sound, lighting, camera, and such—took one look at the Roach Motel and threatened to quit. They were damned lucky that the Inn had some last-minute cancellations. Only a couple, of course, so I hear they're five or six to a room, but it's still an improvement over Clay County. But when the skilled building trade workers protested about the Roach Motel, they were told 'Fine—we can replace you.' So they checked in, but they weren't happy."

"And then you rescued them?" I asked "How?"

"Set up a little village of tents and travel trailers," he said. "Out at the fairgrounds, where we let the exhibitors camp when we have an event. It's not the Inn, but there are decent bathrooms and shower sheds, electrical hookups, and a lack of bedbugs. Plus I had their stuff fumigated so the bedbugs would stay in Clay County."

"Fabulous," I said. "I wish we'd been able to hint to them that they should stay around for the picnic."

"I already did." Randall chuckled. "Told them to drive around for a few minutes, then come back and grab a plate. There's three of them now."

He pointed to three young men in jeans or overalls who were hovering by the grills and the buffet tables. The firefighters seemed eager to load them down with burgers or brats, and the several neighbor ladies who had appointed themselves hostesses were coaxing them to help themselves and not be shy.

"A couple of them have volunteered to help with the turkey roundup," he said. "Not sure if they really think it will be fun, or if they're worried that their jobs with the show will disappear if the turkeys aren't dealt with. Either way, they're in."

I noticed that Horace and the chief had been having a quiet conversation. Neither of them looked happy. I edged closer and tried to think of a subtle way to ask what they were discussing with such glum faces.

Nothing came to mind. I decided subtlety was overrated.

"What's wrong?" I asked.

Chapter 11

"Horace has found pretty solid evidence to prove that one of Randall's trucks was used to transport the turkeys," the chief said. "Unfortunately, he didn't find anything to indicate who was using it."

"That's unfortunate," Randall said. "Because I looked at the security video before I sent it over to you, and identifying the culprits from that may not be possible. They wore ski masks when they borrowed the truck out of my lot."

"Did you authorize them to use the truck?" the chief asked.

"Of course not." Randall scowled at the idea.

"Then they stole the truck," the chief said. "Stole, not borrowed. The fact that they returned it later doesn't wipe out the fact that they took it without permission. And if we study the security video long enough—"

"I know," Randall said. "Sooner or later we'll find them. If nothing else, the rumor mill will out them eventually. But we could use their expertise now. I have a sneaking suspicion about who might be involved."

"Darlene's two oldest boys?" the chief asked.

"Exactly," he said.

"Do you have any evidence?" the chief asked.

"No," Randall said. "It's the way they're behaving. I know those kids. When their dad's away, I try to check in with them pretty often. Make sure they've got someone to play a game of catch with."

I was tempted to point out that Darlene, the star pitcher of her team in the town's coed softball league, was probably capable of playing catch with Evan and Luke. But that was beside the point. Randall knew the boys. They weren't themselves.

"I doubt if they were the ringleaders," Randall went on. "I think they were involved, though. But there's not much we can do without any proof."

"Call them in here," I said. "And let's see if we can get them to come clean."

"They're minors," the chief said. "I can't interrogate them without a parent present."

"And Darlene isn't likely to let you," Randall added.

"You're not going to interrogate them," I said. "In fact, maybe it would be better if you left. Stay where we can see you, though. Over there, just outside the tent. And continue that intense, worried-looking conversation. Randall, call them over here on some pretext or other. You want to ask them for some scoop on a couple of the neighbors."

Randall nodded. He pulled out his phone and began texting.

"We don't want to do anything that would—" the chief began.

"I'm only going to urge them to tell you anything they happen to know about the turkeys," I said.

"I think Randall's already done that."

"Randall's not a mother," I said, "of boys only a bit younger than those two. Let me give it a try."

The chief chuckled. Then he and Horace moved to two Adirondack chairs just outside the tent.

A few minutes later Evan and Luke strolled into the pavilion.

They stopped when they saw Horace and the chief and exchanged a worried glance. Their faces cleared when Randall gestured for them to come over to where he and I were sitting. They seemed suspiciously happy to put more distance between them and the chief.

"My nephews," Randall said. "Luke and Evan. Boys, you know Ms. Meg."

The boys smiled the sort of polite smiles my boys would have used if Michael or I called their attention to a random and not particularly interesting adult.

"She has something she wants to ask you," Randall said.

Luke and Evan tensed slightly.

I decided on my strategy.

"More like something I want to tell you." I glanced over at where Horace and the chief were talking—making sure my glance was the hurried, surreptitious glance of someone who wants to make sure she isn't overheard.

"You know my cousin Horace," I said.

"Deputy Hollingsworth," Randall added.

Nods from the two teens.

"He's been collecting forensic data from one of your Uncle Randall's trucks," I said.

Luke and Evan were definitely listening now.

"How'd Horace even know to do that?" Randall asked, playing along.

"Apparently the chief has an eyewitness who saw the turkeys being unloaded from a Shiffley Construction truck sometime last night."

That hit them. Evan flinched visibly. Luke's face just grew stonier.

I glanced over my shoulder again at Horace and the chief. Randall did the same, and then nodded at me, as if reassuring me that it was okay to talk. Were we overdoing it?

No. Luke and Evan were hooked.

"One of my trucks!" Randall's tone of surprise was completely believable. "So that's why the chief asked me for last night's security video."

"Yes," I said. "And that video showed the truck being driven out of your construction yard, but the perps wore masks, of course—they weren't stupid."

"Perps?" Luke echoed, his voice breaking into a soprano squeak in mid-word.

Horace had reliably informed me that cops didn't actually say "perp" outside of the movies—at least not here in Caerphilly—but I figured the boys wouldn't know that.

"So the chief doesn't know who did it . . . yet," I said. "But with Horace around, he has ways of finding out. Forensic ways."

Evan swallowed hard.

"Like DNA?" he whispered.

"Um . . . is there a reason you're telling *us*?" Luke managed to keep his voice down in its newfound tenor/baritone range, but it seemed to be an effort.

"We figure you know people," I said. "People who might have the mindset to do this. And the skill set."

They both just frowned slightly and remained silent.

"So if you have any idea who did this—or even a suspicion—tell them now's the time to speak," I said. "The chief's hopping mad, but right now he's also focused on getting those turkeys out of the neighborhood and safely housed in the zoo."

"And we figure he'd probably be inclined to go easy on anyone who can help him with the problem." Randall had picked up on what I was doing.

"But you know how it goes," I said. "The first one to bring the cops the information always gets the sweetheart deal."

Randall nodded vigorously.

"So if you know anything—" he began.

"Or if you think you know anyone who knows anything," I continued. "Tell them to spill to the chief."

"Get there first," Randall said.

"Before Horace starts sending evidence bags down to the crime lab in Richmond," I said. "And before Dad talks the chief into letting him try hypnosis on that witness."

"Oh, yeah." Randall sounded enthusiastic. "It'll all come out when Dr. Langslow gets going with his forensic hypnosis."

Evan and Luke exchanged a look.

"We might know some useful stuff," Evan said.

"Chief's over there," I said. "Now's probably a good time to talk to him, while he's waiting for the meeting to start."

"Should we interrupt him?" Evan asked. "He looks kind of busy."

"Don't worry about that," I said. "If you like, I can interrupt him, and then if he's annoyed, he'll be annoyed with me."

So I led the boys over to where the chief was sitting.

"Chief," I said. "Sorry to interrupt, but Evan and Luke may have some useful information for you."

And then I cleared out, so the boys could make their confession without the embarrassment of multiple witnesses. I went back to where Randall and I had been sitting. He'd been joined by three unfamiliar faces—young men in work clothes and hard hats or baseball caps. I realized they were the ones he'd pointed out earlier as the construction workers from the *Marvelous Mansions* crew. One of them, a tall young redheaded man, was saying something, rather vehemently. I drifted closer so I could eavesdrop.

"Hey, Meg," Randall said. "Come over and meet some of our volunteers. Guys, this is Meg Langslow, my special assistant."

So much for eavesdropping. All three young men stood up and shook hands with me. Randall introduced them as Loren, Kaden, and Todd, the redhead. I said a few words of welcome and then took one of the nearby chairs.

"Okay," Randall said when the introductions were complete. "Let me get this straight—you haven't yet started work on the house?"

"No, sir." Todd seemed to be their spokesperson. The other two nodded vigorously. "We only got here yesterday, and they told us we'd be starting work today. The turkeys ruined that. So we had nothing to do with the way the TV people butchered that house."

"Then who did?" Randall said.

"They brought in a bunch of day laborers from someplace," Todd said. "No idea where, and they kind of made sure to send them away before we could get a chance to talk to them. They probably just hired some guys with no construction experience at minimum wage."

"No way any of us would mess up a place like that," one of the others said. "I mean, they must have built that house eighty or a hundred years ago. That's good, solid construction—you can see that the minute you drive up to it. And they go and mess it up like that."

"It's criminal," the third man muttered.

"And then they expect us to clean up after them." Todd sounded disgruntled.

"We should just go home," the third one said.

"Where is home?" I asked.

"Pulaski," Todd said. "A ways from here."

I nodded. I thought I'd detected a faint hint of a familiar southwest Virginia accent—Pulaski was in the middle of the Blue Ridge Mountains.

"Four- or five-hours' drive, isn't it?" Randall asked.

"Yes, sir," Todd said. "Took us nearly five."

"And if you're wondering why they hired a bunch of construction workers from the other side of the state, your guess is as good as mine," one of the others said.

"Californians," the third said. "They probably don't have a clue how far apart Pulaski and Caerphilly are."

"They told us there weren't any skilled construction workers in town," Todd said.

"And they were either mistaken or lying," I said, before Randall could explode at the idea.

"Yeah." Todd said. "I figured it was more like there was no one in town who'd do the work for peanuts. Things have been a bit slow down our way lately, so it was kind of worth our while to take the job, even with what they were paying, since they said they'd be providing room and board."

"We almost turned around and went straight back home when we saw that dive they wanted to put us up in," another said.

"We appreciate the tents, sir," Todd said to Randall. "And the good food." He nodded in the direction of the buffet tables.

"Take as much as you want back to your campsite at the fair-grounds," I said. "And let Randall or me know if whatever meals *Marvelous Mansions* is providing aren't appealing—"

"Or aren't showing up at all," Randall added. "We'll manage something. No need for any guest in Caerphilly to go hungry."

"Or eat bad food," I added.

"Thanks," Todd said. "Look, sir, is it true you're going to do something tonight to get rid of the turkeys?"

"Yes," Randall said. "Early tomorrow morning, actually."

"If there's anything we can do to help out, just say the word," Todd said. "'Cause the TV people told us to take today off, and I'm pretty sure they mean without pay. I don't think they plan on paying us until we can get into the house and do some construction work."

"That's not fair," I said.

The three workers all nodded.

Randall studied them for a minute.

"If you want to help us round up the turkeys, show up right

here tomorrow morning at four A.M.," he said. "Even after that, it could be a day or two before we figure out if the house is safe to work in, so if you'd rather earn a few bucks than sit around—"

"Absolutely," Todd said, and the other nodded.

"See that guy in the blue plaid shirt?" He pointed toward the buffet line. "He's my project supervisor. Go talk to him. Tell him what your skills are—and say I sent you. This isn't the only construction job in town, and I'll pay a fair wage for whatever you can do."

"Thank you, sir," they all chorused. And considering how quickly they all got up, nodded to both of us, and strode over to where Randall's supervisor was eating, I suspected that they not only wanted but needed to get some paid work sooner than *Marvelous Mansions* was likely to provide it.

"Do you really need workers?" I asked.

"Actually, yes," he said. "We're already having a busy spring, and all the work my guys are having to do to deal with the turkeys is putting us even further behind than we already were. If they have any kind of skill, we can find a use for them." He glanced at his watch. "Meeting should start soon."

The two of us were pretending not to be looking over where the chief was talking with Luke and Evan. Eventually the chief stood up, said a few last words—stern ones, from the expression on his face—and pointed at something. Both boys hurried off in the direction he was pointing. The chief came over to sit behind the head table. Randall and I joined him.

Evidently Randall was also giving up on subtlety.

"Any luck with the kids?" he asked.

Chapter 12

"With Evan and Luke?" the chief asked. "Some. They helped with bringing the turkeys here, all right. I sent them over to tell Dr. Blake how they did it, to make sure nothing about what they did would be dangerous to the birds. They refused to tell me who else was involved—they say they want a chance to warn the other guilty parties to give them a chance to come forward on their own. I expect it will turn out to be mostly kids from high school. But not the ringleader. They think he was older, and they can't identify him."

"Can't or won't?" I asked.

"Can't, I think." The chief frowned slightly. "They were all wearing ski masks, you know."

"If they don't know him, how did he recruit them?" Randall asked.

"He or she," I corrected.

"Probably a he," the chief said. "By email. And unfortunately they can't give much of a description. The ringleader was tall, around five ten—"

"My height," I said.

"But definitely male," the chief said, with a smile. "He recruited them through email. At least that's how Luke and Evan heard about it, and I'm going to check with any others I identify. They got an email saying if they wanted to help with a cool exploit involving the feral turkeys, they should show up behind the high school at midnight, dressed in black and wearing ski masks. Whoever it is knew that Luke and Evan were Randall's nephews and could probably figure out how to borrow a Shiffley Construction truck."

"Steal, not borrow," Randall said. "At least that's what you told me."

"I was quoting what the ringleader told them," the chief said.

"Apart from his height, could they give any description of him?" I asked.

"Not much of one." The chief grimaced. "The ringleader was wearing night-vision goggles on top of the ski mask, so they couldn't tell the color of his eyes. They think he's Caucasian, because they did occasionally see a little bit of pale skin on the back of his neck, where the bottom of his black ski mask didn't quite meet the top of his black turtleneck. And recognizing his voice is out, because he only spoke through one of those kids' voice changers—you know the things you hand out at parties. Looks like a plastic megaphone and makes your voice sound like a robot or a monster or something."

"Great," I said. "Around five ten, probably male and Caucasian. There must be a thousand people in town who fit that description, and that's assuming the ringleader is from here."

"The kids think he is," the chief said. "He seemed to know his way around town like a local. And he knew them. Knew their names and emails. Knew bits of information about them."

"I assume you're going to ask Kevin to trace the ringleader's email," I asked.

"Already have. And Aida's going over to Darlene's in a few to work with Luke and Evan on figuring out how someone could have gotten hold of their emails—she's going to see what lists they're on, or what organizations they might have given their emails to. And when I talk to any other culprits, I'll be telling them that if they help with the roundup and cooperate with our attempts to find the ringleader, we won't be charging them with anything dire. In fact, I pretty much told Luke and Evan to say as much to anyone they know was involved."

And then we stopped talking about the subject, because people started arriving for Randall's meeting. Several of the chief's deputies, along with three unfamiliar uniformed officers—two men and a woman—presumably deputies borrowed from nearby counties. Michael and nearly all of the volunteer firefighters. Many of the people who lived on the affected block—Darlene, Mrs. Peabody, Gloria, Jennifer the renter, and Mr. Smetkamp among them. Mr. Jasper was there, looking anxious, as if he suspected our roundup efforts might do damage to the house or yard he still loved from afar. Todd the redhead arrived with half a dozen of his fellow out-of-town workers. Evan and Luke with a small pack of their fellow high school students. A scattering of Randall's employees, most of them displaying at least a vague resemblance to Randall, which meant they were probably also his cousins. Dad, Grandfather, and Clarence, seated with two zoo employees and several people whose faces looked vaguely familiar—probably either local birdwatchers or members of Blake's Brigade, the group of enthusiastic volunteers who showed up whenever Grandfather put out the call for help with an environmental protest or an animal rescue.

At some point Randall must have decided that everyone he needed had arrived.

"Welcome," he said, in the loud, resonant voice he used for speechifying, as he called it. "I think most everybody's here."

He glanced around with visible satisfaction. "So let's get started. Here's the plan."

He looked down at the table. Then, with a sweeping back-handed gesture, he knocked its contents off onto the floor. Okay, the only contents were a greasy paper plate and a couple of empty paper cups. Still, a dramatic gesture.

"I always wanted to do that," he said, with a satisfied smile.

But instead of unrolling a map, as I expected him to do, he reached down, pulled up something, and set it on the table—one of those tri-fold cardboard presentation boards so familiar to every parent whose child has ever had to prepare a science fair project. He hadn't made use of the side panels, but taped to the main center part was a large map of the 1200 block of Bland Street. All the houses were drawn in and labeled with the own-ers' names, along with all the trees, sidewalks, fences, and other features of the landscape. The Smetkamps' house, Darlene's, and Mrs. Peabody's were enclosed by a red line. Actually, a whole series of short red lines joined end-to-end.

"Ten-foot-high chain-link construction fence," he said, indicat-ing the red line. "We go in to set it up after dark tonight—once all the turkeys have roosted. Then we let them settle down for the night and we come back before dawn and surround the en-closure. We start making noise, startle the turkeys, and they'll start bailing out of the trees. We'll have volunteers standing by with tarps to wrap them up and whisk them into the trucks. And it should be easy to work with them, since they'll be half asleep."

"So will we if it isn't even dawn yet," shouted one of the fire-fighters, to general laughter.

"But we won't be sharing our coffee," Randall said, to more laughter. "Dr. Blake's going to bring a crew of aviary staff from his zoo, and he put out the word to Blake's Brigade, so a lot of them will be coming as well."

The zoo staff and the random collection of people clustered

around Grandfather all raised both fists over their head in a Rocky-style salute.

"Blake's Brigade?" one of the borrowed deputies asked. "Are you bringing in the military?"

"That's what Dr. Blake calls the volunteers who help him out with stuff like this," Randall said. "Seasoned bird wranglers."

Which was true—the Brigade members did a lot of bird banding and rescuing, although I wasn't sure any of them had ever dealt with anything as large as the feral turkeys.

Randall was pointing to a spot along the red line—a spot that appeared to be in the middle of Bland Street.

"The gate will be here," he said. "And we'll line up the trucks nearby. We'll create a narrow path leading up to the opening, like a cattle chute. We back each truck in turn up to the gate and set down the ramp. Easy for the volunteers to carry the birds up into the truck. And if any of them are too fast for us and run off when they hit the ground, before we can wrap them up, we'll herd them in small batches onto the trucks. And then we whisk them out to the habitat Dr. Blake has prepared for them out at his zoo."

He turned back to his audience and frowned.

"We will be very careful not to harm any of the turkeys," he said. "Dr. Blake and Dr. Rutledge will be on hand to make sure of that. And before you ask, no—no one will be eating these turkeys. They will live out their lives in comfort and safety at the zoo, where Dr. Blake can study their behavior."

Most of his listeners nodded approvingly.

"For what it's worth, even if we did try to cook them, a lot of you might not like them," he added. "The meat would probably taste much more gamy than domestic turkey. At least that's generally the case with wild turkeys, which these critters greatly resemble," he added, probably to make it clear that he hadn't been dining on any of the feral flock. "So a word to the wise, if you were thinking of absconding with one and celebrating Thanksgiving early,

you're forewarned. These are not your pre-plucked tender But-
terballs."

Muted laughter greeted this remark, and if any of the volunteers had been anticipating free turkey dinners, they were savvy
enough not to show their disappointment in front of such a large
crowd of bird lovers.

"Sunrise tomorrow is at five fifty-five A.M.," Randall said. "So
everyone: be here at four A.M. sharp."

The crowd greeted this with a few groans and a small ripple of
laughter.

"And wear some kind of protective gear," Randall said. "No
shorts. No short sleeves. No open-toed shoes. Find yourself a hard
hat or a bicycle helmet or something like that. And some safety
goggles. Bring gloves. Those things are big, and they're feisty, and
they can do a lot of damage if you don't protect yourself. And if
you've got a garden rake, bring it. And I mean a garden rake, the
kind with sturdy metal tines—those birds can do a number on a
leaf rake." He held up the ruins of a leaf rake, its flexible bam-
boo tines either crumpled or broken off entirely. "No pitchforks,
either. I know some of you have been using them successfully to
fend off a few of the birds, but in all the chaos of the roundup it'd
be much too easy to injure one of the birds—or yourself."

"Don't forget to tell them about the first aid tent!" Dad piped up.

"That's right," Randall said. "Dr. Langslow and Dr. Rutledge
will be staffing the first aid tent—for humans and birds. It'll be
right here on the corner, where we are now. So if you get injured
or if you spot a rescuer or a turkey that's injured, bring them here.
Any questions?"

There were a few questions, but Randall seemed to have covered most of the information people wanted to know. People were
already shifting in their seats when Mr. Jasper announced that
he had a question and launched into a long, rambling diatribe
about how unacceptable it was that the town had allowed *Marvel-*

ous Mansions to undertake a project that would ruin not only the Smetkamps' house but the entire character of the neighborhood.

People began drifting away. I stayed, listening to Mr. Jasper's rant, and becoming more and more uncomfortable by the minute. I actually agreed with most of what he was saying. Why did he make it sound so selfish, unhinged, and laughable?

At least Randall was answering him, sounding a lot more patient and courteous than he probably felt. Better him than me.

After a while, the only other people in the pavilion apart from Randall, Mr. Jasper, and the chief were half a dozen avid local gossips, who were taking in every word. The whole town would probably know all about the confrontation by noon.

No, actually the whole town probably already knew. These were modern gossips, busily texting as fast as their fingers would allow. I was pretty sure one of them was even taking a video with her phone.

Mr. Jasper finally lost his temper and stormed away. The gossips quickly scuttled out, probably to find a quiet corner where they could dissect the whole thing. I strolled up to where Randall and the chief were sitting.

"Bad enough I have to placate the people who actually live here," Randall was muttering. "Where does he get off, claiming to know what's good for the neighborhood when he doesn't even live here anymore?"

"He doesn't?" The chief looked surprised. "Then where does he live?"

"The Pits," I said.

"Good to know." The chief pulled out his notebook. "I think I'll have my deputies keep an eye on Mr. Jasper. Given the strength of his dissatisfaction with the makeover project."

"You think he might try to interfere with the roundup?" Randall asked.

The chief shrugged. Randall looked at me. I shrugged.

"I have a hard time thinking he'd have anything against the roundup," the chief said. "He's quite frantic about the amount of damage those wretched birds are doing to the yard that he's so obsessed with."

"Maybe he thinks the TV people will do even more damage," I suggested.

"He might be right about that part," Randall muttered. "And maybe that's just the kind of thinking that got the birds over here."

"Are you suggesting that he might be responsible for the turkeys?" the chief asked. "That he could be the unidentified ringleader?"

"Well, I wasn't actually suggesting that," Randall said.

"But it's an interesting idea," I said.

"He's weird enough," Randall said. "And given how much he hangs around the neighborhood, he knows everything about everybody. He'd know Luke and Evan were my nephews and probably had access to my trucks."

"But how would he get their emails?" the chief asked.

"From the town message website," I said. "Luke and Evan posted a couple of weeks ago that they were available to do odd jobs this summer. I remember it because I steered Mother to them—she's been having Josh and Jamie weed her vegetable garden, and I knew she wanted to find someone who could fill in for them in July when we all go on that turtle rescue thing Grandfather is organizing. Mr. Jasper could have recruited all of the others the same way—I bet a lot of the high school kids have posted on the website, either looking for work or selling stuff."

"True," the chief said. "For that matter, even if Mr. Jasper's not the ringleader, whoever is could have used the town website for emails."

"Does Jasper fit the description of the ringleader?" Randall asked.

"Since the only description we have is Caucasian and around five foot ten, he does," the chief said. "So do half the people who were in this tent a few minutes ago."

"True," Randall agreed.

"I'll keep him in mind as I interview the others I'm hearing from," the chief said. "Evan and Luke have been doing a good job of spreading the word that it's better to turn yourself in than get caught."

"And I should leave you to it," Randall said. "Got plenty of other things to worry about. What time does it get dark, anyway?"

"Not till about eight," the chief said.

"That's going to be a pain," Randall said. "It'll take a few hours to get the perimeter fence set up, and then some of the same people who'll be doing that will need to be back by four A.M. to prep for the roundup. Not much time for sleeping. Of course, maybe we could get a different crew for the setup, or—"

"Is there a reason we have to wait till after dark to set up the fence?" I asked. "I understand starting the roundup while the birds are still asleep, but setting up the fence is another thing. You can ask Grandfather to be sure, but I bet as long as we're not putting the fence so close that the turkeys feel threatened by it, it will be fine. They won't guess what it's for. They might not even notice it's happening. After all, they're bird brains, not rocket scientists."

Randall and the chief exchanged a look.

"She's right," the chief said. "The birds won't have a clue what you're doing."

"It's hard not to think of them as a hostile invading force, actively trying to cause trouble," Randall said.

"I know what you mean," I said. "I've caught myself looking around to see if they're nearby and then lowering my voice if I'm saying anything that might upset them."

"Or give away our plans." Randall shook his head ruefully. "Meg, can you touch base with the neighbors whose backyards we'll be putting the fence in? Make sure they're cool with it. I'll have the guys who are bringing the fencing stay around to set it up."

"Can do."

"Let me know if you need me for anything," the chief said. "I'll be interviewing suspected turkey rustlers."

I pulled out my notebook and began to sketch a quick copy of Randall's map, so I knew which households would be affected.

Chapter 13

I spent the next few hours visiting the neighbors. The front of the fence could go down Bland Street—right in the middle of the road if need be. No permission needed there, or if any was, the chief and Randall could handle it. At the one end, the fence would take a right turn and run through Mrs. Peabody's yard, on the side farthest from the Smetkamps, and then into the yard behind hers. From there it would continue across Myra Lord's lot until it reached the far side of the backyard of the house behind Darlene's. From there, it would return through Darlene's yard—again, running right along the property line on the side away from the Smetkamps—until it joined the fence running down Bland Street.

The family whose backyard adjoined Mrs. Peabody's had a very nice vegetable garden planted right up against the split-rail fence between the two yards and were reluctant to let the workers trample through it to set up the temporary chain-link fence. And we needed to run it through the garden, rather than right up against the property line, because a few of the turkeys had already spread to trees that hung a little way over onto their lot.

"That's okay," I said finally. "We don't have to run the fence through your garden. We can run it through here—right behind the house. With luck, none of the turkeys will run this way when we try to round them up. For that matter, we don't need to put it in your yard at all. We could run it down the street in front of your house."

At that point, the homeowners decided that perhaps they could risk sacrificing a few rows of lima beans and Silver Queen corn to protect the remainder of their crops. I scribbled a reminder in my notebook to tell the workers to do everything they could not to trample the garden. And another to come back after the roundup to see if the crops had suffered any damage. I could always convince Randall to placate them with a few bushels of corn and beans from one of his cousins' truck farms.

Myra Lord raised no objections to the perimeter fence, and offered to bring out the stepladders, in case the roundup volunteers needed to climb over the smaller fence between her yard and the Smetkamps'. We decided that was a good idea—and that we should set them up now, rather than have the rescuers trying to do it in the dark. Jason and Eli scrambled off to fetch the ladders.

The residents of the house behind Darlene's house also had no objection to the fence but warned us that most of the backyard was filled with an incredible amount of poison ivy—a menace that they, as renters, weren't ready to tackle—and one that their landlord continued to ignore. The fence workers and turkey wranglers were welcome to do whatever they liked.

"Just don't blame us if you're covered with blisters afterward," the wife said. "We've given up even going back there."

I managed not to show what I really thought of their feckless attitude.

"Mind if I sic the Garden Club's Weed Warriors on it?" I asked. She liked the idea, so I called Mother to see if she could organize an emergency squad to deal with the unwanted *Toxicodendron radicans* before the turkey wranglers began wading through it in the dark.

"Of course, dear." Mother was almost purring at the idea. "I'll round up a few of the ladies and we'll get right on it."

Mother, of course, wouldn't go anywhere near the nasty vines, since she was known to be incredibly sensitive to them. But she recruited a squad of volunteers and then showed up in her most elegant gardening outfit, complete with a flowered hat and elbow-length gardening gloves, to organize and encourage the actual workers. Half a dozen dedicated Weed Warriors showed up, and then sent for reinforcements when they realized that in addition to the poison ivy—which was a native plant, albeit an unwanted one—the yard in question also contained a bumper crop of garlic mustard, Japanese knotweed, Japanese stilt grass, common chickweed, sour weed, and who knew what other foreign invasive species.

"It's a wonder we haven't found a giant hogweed back here," one of them sniffed.

"The day isn't over," another replied.

They were an impressive sight, all dressed in the disposable Tyvek hazmat suits they kept in stock for just such serious poison ivy infestations. And they kept me busy for quite a while, either fetching more biodegradable yard waste bags from Flugleman's, the local feed and garden store, or driving pickup truck loads full of bags to the town dump. Apparently many of the weeds they were pulling were too invasive even to be composted.

After one of these trips I stopped by the pavilion to get a cold beverage and took a short break as I watched the activity around me. Deputies were fending off the occasional tourist car that ventured near Turkey Central. From the speed with which the tourists departed, I suspect they were, indeed, sharing the gas leak rumor.

Michael and the rest of the firefighters joined forces with

Randall's workers to set up the fence. I spotted Luke, Evan, Cal Burke, and a dozen other high schoolers helping.

Were the other culprits in the turkey prank among them? I thought Luke and Evan had said there were only three or four others. Maybe they were playing down how many people had participated. Maybe they were all culprits, or at least suspects.

Instead of hurrying back to where the Weed Warriors were working, I plopped down in one of the lawn chairs near the pavilion. The bags of weeds would still be waiting if I took a short rest. And while I was sipping my lemonade, I could keep an eye on the kids. See if any of them were behaving suspiciously.

And none of them were that I could see.

With the possible exception of Josh, Jamie, and their buddy Adam, the chief's youngest grandson. They were doing a good job of helping the fence builders, but every so often two of them—or all three—would put their heads together and exchange a few hurried words. If anyone came near or seemed to be looking at them, they'd quickly return to what they'd be doing. Josh and Jamie's air of innocence was quite convincing. Adam looked anxious.

My first instinct was to race over and grab them. Drag them over to my car and drive them home. Interrogate them until I got them to admit what they knew about the turkey prank. Order them to stay in the house—well, okay, in the yard—until the turkeys were safely confined out at the zoo.

But they weren't toddlers anymore. All three appeared to be helping out the firefighters. And Michael was keeping an eye on them. Not just Michael—all the firefighters.

They were perfectly safe. And they'd had a sleepover last night with Adam. They were too smart to sneak out of Chief Burke's house to play a stupid prank, weren't they?

Still, I stood rooted to the sidewalk, watching.

I spotted Minerva Burke, Adam's grandmother, a little way down the block, doing the same thing. I strolled over to join her.

"Did the boys behave themselves while they were over at your house?" I asked.

"Of course," she said. "I just wish I could have talked them into going someplace else today. They turned down offers to spend the day out at Ragnar's, swimming in his pond and riding the horses. If I ever catch whoever brought those blasted turkeys here—"

"You'll have to stand in line for your turn with them," I said. "The firefighters will look after the boys."

"I know," she said. "And it's not as if we can keep them wrapped in cotton wool forever."

"But we can damn well try," I said.

We shared a laugh.

"Don't take this the wrong way," I said. "But is there any way they could have sneaked out of your house last night to help with the turkey prank?"

Minerva turned and frowned at where the boys were working. Josh and Adam had picked up a ten-foot section of chain-link fence and were carrying it over to where a trio of construction workers were waiting for it. Jamie hurried after them with another of the rectangular stands that joined and held up the fencing at each end.

"Pretty sure not," she said. "Since today wasn't a school day, I let the three of them stay up late watching movies and playing video games. They kept me busy fixing snacks right up to midnight. I sent them to bed around one and did a bed check shortly after, and then another around three when the dogs started barking. Anyone comes or goes after dark and they both bark their fool heads off. Everyone was where they were supposed to be then, too. Turns out the dogs were barking at some deer in the backyard. I think they'd have raised Cain if the boys tried to sneak out."

"So they're alibied," I said.

"Pretty much," she said. "But they are acting a little off, aren't they? Maybe they have some idea who did it."

"Maybe," I said. "Or maybe when they first saw the turkeys they thought it was hilarious, and now they feel guilty about laughing."

"Or maybe they feel guilty because I told them to stay far away from the turkeys, and here they are helping corral them," Minerva said. "Who knows with kids their age? If you're worried, I'm going to stay here and keep an eye on them."

"They'll love that," I said. "Mine always complain if they think I'm hovering."

"Mine, too," she said. "So they think I'm here to take pictures of what's going on. To help their granddad's investigation. Henry made sure they overheard him telling me that the person or persons responsible could return to the scene of the crime, or even help with the roundup preparations, so could I hang around and take a lot of photos." She held up her phone and took several pictures of the activity around us. "So if you've got things you need to be doing, don't worry. I'm not going anywhere."

"Thanks," I said. "I'll be hauling dangerous weeds to the dump. Let me know if you need me to spell you."

By five o'clock the Smetkamp, Peabody, and Browning houses were surrounded by the chain-link fence. The jungle of poison ivy and invasive weeds was completely gone. A skeleton crew of volunteers stayed behind to keep an eye on the turkeys until the sun went down and they all roosted. A truck laden with more fencing was parked nearby. If any of the turkeys perched in trees—or on roofs—that were outside the fencing, the volunteers could expand the perimeter.

The boys were still full of energy, so Michael took them out to Grandfather's zoo to inspect the habitat he'd prepared for the turkeys.

I went home and collapsed. Actually, when I first arrived, I volunteered to help Rose Noire fix dinner, but she handed me a glass of freshly made organic limeade and chased me out of the kitchen. I didn't even try to protest.

I had just settled down on one of the comfy couches in our living room when the doorbell rang.

It was Mr. Smetkamp. He looked tired and was carrying the small hard-sided suitcase Randall and I had packed when we chased his wife out of the ruined house.

"Welcome." I opened the door wider and gestured him in.

"Thank you," he said. "This is extraordinarily kind of you. From something I overheard Mayor Shiffley say, I gather fixing whatever's wrong with the house may take a bit of time. I'm going to start looking for another place to stay, in case we can't go back into the house for a while. But you know how that can be in tourist season."

"And these days, tourist season is pretty much year-round," I said. "You're welcome to stay as long as you need to."

I realized we were both standing in the front hall, with the door hanging open. I glanced outside.

"Is your wife with you?" I asked. "Or is she coming later?"

"I have no idea."

Did I detect just a hint of . . . anger? Resentment? His face was the same calm mask. I'd read somewhere that building or remodeling a house was one of those life events that put extraordinary strain on a marriage, often leading to divorce. Was that happening now?

Not something I could ask. None of my business anyway. And I'd find out anyway, sooner or later.

"I'll show you to your room, then," I said.

I led him upstairs and down the hall to one of the nicer guest rooms—one of the ones that had an en suite bathroom. He smiled with pleasure as he walked in.

"Oh, this is very nice," he said. "I don't know what to say."

"Just say that you think you can sleep well here," I said. "It must have been difficult, making do on cots in what had become a construction site."

"More like a demolition site," he said. "I'm beginning to worry about whether those *Marvelous Mansions* people really know what they're doing."

I decided that if he didn't already know Randall's take on that, maybe I shouldn't tell him. It would only worry him, and he looked ready to drop. Why not let him get a good night's sleep?

"We'll be having dinner in about an hour," I said. "Just let me know if you need anything."

And with that I left him to settle in.

Gloria showed up a little later, with Mrs. Peabody in tow. I showed them to two more of the nicer guest rooms, and then went back downstairs.

Dinner was subdued. No, make that peaceful. Even the boys seemed quieter than usual, probably because they'd had a busy and tiring day. I found myself wondering if I could occasionally lend them to Randall to help out with other construction projects. Not all the time, of course. But maybe once or twice a month. It would probably be good for them, too. Character-building.

And they weren't acting suspiciously. Either their acting skills were even more highly developed than I thought, or they didn't have anything to feel guilty about. I filed away their odd behavior earlier to worry about later, when I was less exhausted.

Thank goodness for Rose Noire, who was busily explaining what herbal teas, aromatherapy oils, and breathing exercises we should all be doing to ensure that we could drift off to sleep earlier than usual. Gloria was brooding—was she focused on her dissertation, or worried about leaving her weird tenant behind? Mrs. Peabody seemed quietly resigned, as if trying not to think too hard about what was happening back in her once beautifully landscaped yard. Mr. Smetkamp also seemed preoccupied—worried about his wife, perhaps?

"Just let us know if you want someone to wake you up to join the turkey roundup," Michael said when we'd all finished dessert.

"I'd only be in the way," Mrs. Peabody said, with a small, self-deprecating smile.

"As would I," Mr. Smetkamp said. "I wish I could help, but my night vision is so bad. I'd be more of a hindrance than a help."

"I'm going to set my alarm," Gloria said. "If I can manage to drag myself out of bed that early, I'll see you there."

"And if you can't, that's fine," Michael said. "Save your energy for the dissertation."

"Probably the smart thing to do," Gloria said. "But here—take this." She handed me a ring containing two keys. "My spare house key. Might come in handy if you need an observation post, or a place to hole up. And the master key to the bedroom doors, in case you need to check up on what Jennifer and Chris are doing."

"Good idea." I attached her key ring to my own.

We all straggled off to bed. Michael set his alarm for three thirty. I didn't set mine—it was safer to let him wake me. I'd been known to maim and kill alarm clocks that went off before I was ready to get up, but Michael was very good at waking me gently. And from a safe distance.

"Sleep well," I muttered. I think Michael answered back in kind, but I was already drifting off to sleep.

Chapter 14

"Turkey time!"

I pried one eye open. It was three thirty. In the morning. Make that in the middle of the night.

"Mom?"

"I am rising," I said. "Do not expect me to shine."

I heard giggles. I propelled myself upright. It was dark. Still dark. Well, mostly dark, except for the lamp on Michael's bedside table.

I didn't want to do this.

"Reframe it," I reminded myself. I decided to pretend that I wasn't getting up early—I had taken a nap so that I could stay up even later than usual.

My body wasn't buying it. I closed my eyes again.

"Guys, go get your protective gear," Michael said. "And your mom's and mine. And load it all in the cars."

It sounded as if a herd of buffalo were leaving the room. Good. Anyone who wasn't coming with us to help capture the turkeys would probably be awakened by the racket. Let them suffer a little, too.

I heaved myself out of bed and crawled into the clothes I'd laid out the night before.

"Are you going to be okay to drive?" Michael asked. "Because I know it would be useful to have both cars in town, but if you're not awake enough—"

"Thanks," I said. "I will be by the time I get downstairs."

When we arrived in the front hall, we found Josh and Jamie waiting for us with freshly made smoothies.

Some mornings I couldn't help thinking that we must have done something right, for the boys to have turned out this considerate. Probably something Michael had done right, actually, since this involved early morning thoughtfulness. Not something I had in my DNA.

"It's not that you're a grouch in the morning or anything like that," Michael had said once. "You're just not really there for a while."

Actually, I usually felt pretty grouchy if awakened before I'd had my fill of sleep. I'd just learned, long ago, that no one likes a morning grouch. If I couldn't make a joke about how very much I'd rather go back to sleep, I did my best to keep my mouth shut.

"Thanks," I said. "This is great—"

"We've also got caffeine for you," Jamie said.

"But you should do the healthy stuff first," Josh said.

"Jamie, why don't you ride with your mom," Michael said. "You can make sure she drinks her smoothie." And make sure I found my way to town, instead of crawling back into bed. He could probably even shake me if I looked as if I was dozing off.

Although remembering that one of the boys would be riding with me went a long way toward waking me up.

It was a clear, cool night, and by the time I got behind the wheel I was conscious enough that Jamie didn't need to second-guess my driving. And it was delightful to drive through the streets of town when all the tourists were asleep and there was no traffic.

At least until we drew near the 1200 block of Bland Street, that is, and hit the small but intense traffic jam caused by dozens of volunteers showing up at once. We ended up parking four blocks away, and joined a steady stream of volunteers hiking toward the pavilion that was serving as headquarters for the roundup. The New Life Baptist tables were back, and laden with coffee and doughnuts, with Mabel from the diner handing them out to the volunteers.

Chief Burke was there already, coordinating the efforts of his deputies. And Randall, organizing the volunteers into teams. He assigned Michael and the boys, along with their friend Adam, to a group that would be stationed in Myra's yard, with orders to capture or fend off any turkeys that tried to escape in that direction.

It sounded like a safe assignment. I approved. I didn't want the boys on the front lines. For that matter, I didn't want Michael on the front lines. Not unless he was armed with a fire hose that could bowl the entire flock over.

"Meg, why don't you stay here at the pavilion for the moment," the chief said. "So you'll be handy in case I need your diplomatic skills to fend off curious tourists. Or curious locals."

"Or anyone who's getting in the way instead of helping," I said. "Can do."

So I grabbed an Adirondack chair, sat sipping my diet soda—caffeinated, of course—and tried to pay attention to what was going on so I could pitch in when needed. Periodically Randall would call on me to orient an out-of-town volunteer, fill in a gap in someone's equipment, or perform some other useful task.

By a little past four, the stream of arriving volunteers tapered off, and the last few teams were hiking to whichever part of the fence they were supposed to guard—or lining up near the Shiffley Construction trucks, armed with garden rakes and blue tarps, preparing to pitch in to pounce on the turkeys.

"Things seem to be shaping up nicely," the chief said. "I'm

amazed at how many volunteers turned out at this ungodly hour.
We might even outnumber the turkeys."

"A good thing we managed to keep the news from getting out
to the tourists," I said.

"Good heavens, yes," Randall said. "Although, you know—
once we've got a successful turkey roundup in our rear mirror—"

"Let's not jinx it," the chief murmured.

"We could have a festival," Randall said. "Down in the town
square. It could be a great tourist attraction—the annual com-
memoration of the Great Feral Turkey Roundup. We have a few
turkeys in a pen, we reenact the roundup, sell roast turkey dinners and sandwiches—"

"I realize how much the tourist trade has done to make the
town prosperous," the chief said. "But why don't we finish the actual roundup before we start making plans for the reenactment?"

"Sorry." Randall chuckled. "I get a little carried away sometimes. What else needs doing?"

"Aida and Vern are checking the perimeter to make sure everyone's in place," the chief said. "Before we get started, let's make sure
we know where the occupants of those three houses are. The ones
inside the fence. Optimally, I'd like for them all to evacuate, but
failing that, we should be fine as long as they stay put until things
quiet down."

"Darlene's staying put," Randall said. "But she knows to stay
inside until it's all over. You'll remember that her two oldest are
volunteering their turkey-hauling expertise to the cause, and she
took the younger ones out to Judge Jane Shiffley's farm last night.
They'll be camping out there until we sound the all clear."

"And her husband's still away on active duty?" the chief asked.

"Overseas, yes," Randall said.

"As far as I know, Mr. Smetkamp and Mrs. Peabody are still fast
asleep at our house," I said. "At least their bedroom doors were
closed when I got up, and his car was there when we left. I think

Gloria Willingham decided to sleep in, too—she said something last night about helping with the roundup, but she wasn't awake when I left, and I haven't seen her check in. I left Rose Noire in charge of playing hostess and making sure they're happy—I can ask her to do whatever she can to keep all of them there and warn us if it doesn't work."

"Good idea," the chief said.

I pulled out my phone and began texting Rose Noire.

"We also want to make sure the *Marvelous Mansions* people don't show up here and get in our way," the chief continued. "The staff at the Caerphilly Inn have agreed to let me know if any of them leave the premises, but what about the carpenters and other workers? The ones camping out at the fairgrounds."

"Most of them are helping us out with the roundup," Randall said. "And we recruited a trio of volunteers from Blake's Brigade who are also camping out at the fairgrounds. Ostensibly they're doing a little early morning bird-watching, but they'll let us know if any of the remaining construction workers leave the fairgrounds before the roundup is over."

"That just leaves Mrs. Smetkamp," the chief said. "Meg, you mentioned Mr. Smetkamp. I gather if his wife was out at your place you'd have included her."

"I would have," I said. "But she didn't take me up on the invitation. Her husband did, along with Mrs. Peabody and Gloria. Not her."

"It would be her," the chief muttered.

"Blast." Randall turned toward the Smetkamps' house and scowled. "I already looked and she's not staying next door—Mrs. Peabody was kind enough to give me a spare key, in case we could make use of it during the roundup. I bet Mrs. Smetkamp went back into her own house."

"I thought we were having someone keep watch over her house last night," I said. "To make sure she didn't sneak back in."

"We did," the chief said. "Vern was here all night."

"Of course, he couldn't watch all sides of the house at once," Randall said. "If she really wanted to sneak in, all she had to do was wait until he was at the other side of the house."

"We knew that was a possibility," the chief said. "And Vern was on notice to keep an eye out for signs that someone was in the house. Although frankly, I wasn't expecting her to sneak in. I figured she'd march right up and tell us we had no right to keep her out of her own house. Vern was supposed to call me if she did that, so I could come down and help him deal with her. But he didn't see anything. I already asked."

"If she runs out right in the middle of the roundup, she could spook the turkeys so they run away before we can catch them," Randall said.

"Or she could get hurt," I added.

"Maybe both," Randall said. "And if the turkeys don't get her, the house might. It's already a disaster waiting to happen—what if a couple of the big turkeys flap up onto the roof while trying to escape us and land on a weak spot?"

"So let's go find out if she's in the house," I said. "And roust her out if she is."

The chief grimaced. Then he nodded.

"Yes," he said. "I'd do it myself, but some more deputies on loan from Goochland and Tappahannock just arrived, and I need to brief them. See if she's there. If she is, try to talk her into leaving. And if you can't dislodge her, let me know."

"We'll call you if we need you," Randall said.

"Good." The chief strode off toward where several out-of-town police cruisers had pulled up.

"Time's a-wasting," Randall said.

Chapter 15

He glanced up quickly, as if to assure himself that all the turkeys were still asleep overhead. Then he strode across the street, marched up to the Smetkamps' front door, and tried the knob.

"Locked," he said. "That figures. The whole back side of the house is wide open to any halfway competent burglar, but they lock the front door."

"Plus any halfway competent burglar would know there's not a single thing worth stealing left in the place," I said. "At least the local burglars would know. Try knocking."

"Bet she won't answer," he said. But he rapped firmly on the door and called out. "Mrs. Smetkamp! Are you there?"

He was right—she probably wouldn't answer, even if she was there. I started heading around to the backyard—going through the side yard closest to Darlene's and farthest from the main flock of turkeys.

The backyard was spooky. One of the blue tarps on the roof was flapping slightly in the breeze, and I could see a pair of turkeys roosting on the roof, not that far from the back door. At least

I assumed they were turkeys. The way they were huddled, they looked a lot like crouching vultures.

I tested the back door's knob.

"Any luck?" Randall had given up on knocking and followed me to the backyard.

"Locked," I said.

"Good thing I brought this." He flourished a crowbar. I stood aside and watched as he pried one of the plywood boards off of the barrier that closed off the back of the house. Then he reached around inside and unlocked the door.

"Here." He pulled two flashlights out of his pocket and handed me one. "Don't turn it on till you're inside. We don't want to wake the birds."

He stepped inside. I followed. We turned on our flashlights and scoped out the inside of the house.

Seriously creepy. I hadn't really noticed it in the daytime, but there was a haze of dust hanging in the air throughout the interior.

"What do you think's in that dust?" I asked. "Could it be asbestos?"

"Not necessarily." Randall was slowly playing his flashlight over the house's interior, starting to our right, in the kitchen area. "The houses in this neighborhood were all built in the thirties. That was before the craze for asbestos really took off, at least here in Caerphilly. If we're lucky, they didn't use it. Of course, if any of the previous owners did any remodeling between the forties and the seventies, the odds would have been pretty high that some of the building materials they used contained asbestos. We can't find a record of any building permits in the timeframe, but they might have skipped that formality. Especially if they were doing it themselves. That's why Buck required asbestos testing before issuing the building permits."

"And the tests came back clean," I said. "Which is great, as long as they didn't cheat on the tests."

"Yeah, and after what I've seen now, I wouldn't want to bet on that," he said. "So let's search and vamoose. I'm going to order new asbestos testing—I'll collect the samples myself. And in the meantime, we're not staying any longer than we have to, and this is the last time anyone comes in here without a respirator." His flashlight beam had reached the front bedroom area. I heard him take a sharp breath. The flashlight beam now illuminated— barely—the two cots in the front bedroom area. One of them was clearly empty. The other—

"Is that you, Mrs. Smetkamp?" Randall called.

No answer.

Was it just my imagination, or was there a body on the cot? A sleeping body or—

"Why don't you stay there in the doorway and keep an eye on me while I search," he said. "That way you can run out and get help if the roof caves in on me or anything like that."

"Can do," I said. Nice of him to let me keep my distance from . . . whatever was on the cot.

He walked over to the bedroom area, moving carefully, body tense. He reached down, and I saw him relax as he lifted up a blanket from the cot, revealing that what had looked like a human body lying on the cot was only a tangle of bedclothes.

"Had me worried there for a sec," he muttered. "Just let me check the bathroom and the closets."

It seemed to take forever, although it could only have been a couple of minutes before he headed back to where I was waiting.

"She's not here," he said. "Let's get the hell out of this death-trap."

I didn't wait to be asked twice. We exited, turning off our flash-lights on the way.

"Where do you think she is?" I asked when we were safely back on the lawn, with a good ten feet from us and the house, taking deep breaths of what I hoped was fresh air.

"No idea." He leaned against the fence between the Smet-kamps' yard and Myra Lord's. "Maybe she's staying with friends."

I nodded a little uncertainly.

"I mean she must have friends," he went on, after a pause. "Everyone does."

"Yes, but how are we supposed to go about finding them?" I asked. "I can't think of any way to do that. Well, unless we made a list of all the other really difficult and annoying people in town, on the theory that eventually they'd run into each other and dis-cover they were kindred spirits."

"And even if you made a list like that, would we really want to call them up at this hour?"

"I really wouldn't want to call them up at all."

We pondered for another minute or so. In the distance, we could hear muffled sounds. Occasionally we'd catch a glimpse of the workers who were deploying along the perimeter of the con-struction fence.

"I have an idea," I said. "I'll call Rose Noire and get her to ask Mr. Smetkamp. If anyone knows who his wife's friends are, it would be him. I hate to wake him up this early—"

"But it's worrisome, going ahead with the roundup without knowing where she is," he said. "It's a question of her safety. He wouldn't mind. Or maybe he would mind, but he'd understand. Go for it. I think Darlene's up—I'll ask her if she has any ideas. She can't stand Mrs. Smetkamp, but I bet she knows everything the old bat gets up to, all the same."

"Good idea—the same goes for Mrs. Peabody. I can get Rose Noire to ask her, too." Something else occurred to me. "I can check their shed. Mr. Smetkamp has his woodworking shop there— maybe it's habitable, at least for camping out overnight."

"Good idea."

"Let me borrow the crowbar, just in case the shed door's locked."

He nodded, handed me the crowbar, and strode off toward Darlene's house.

I decided to start with the shed. If I found Mrs. Smetkamp camping in there, I wouldn't have to wake Rose Noire or any of our guests.

As I drew near the shed I found myself marveling at how small it was. Did Mr. Smetkamp actually have a usable workshop out here? Perhaps he did mainly tiny projects. Dollhouse furniture. I had to smile at my mental image of the precise and mild-mannered Mr. Smetkamp with his head bent over a miniature chest of drawers. Maybe with one of those hands-free jewelers' loupes over his eyes as he did almost microscopic carving.

I was letting my imagination run away with me. Lack of sleep will do that, I thought as I yawned.

When I reached the door of the shed, I was startled to find that two turkeys had roosted on the roof. One of them, the biggest hen I'd ever seen, opened her eyes and stared at me.

They really did look like dinosaurs. Most of the time you focused on the feathers and the huge, oversized chest, and maybe the bright-red wattle. But when you were staring eye-to-eye with one it was the head that stood out. The naked, scaly, neck. The sharp curved beak. The glittering black eyes.

I made sure I had a good grip on the crowbar, in case the birds made any threatening moves. To my relief it turned out that I wouldn't need to pry open the shed's door. There was a padlock on the door, still locked on the steel loop, but the hasp had been unscrewed. I hoped it was something the owners had done—perhaps to cope with a lost key. If someone had broken into their shed during the turkey invasion, I was sure we'd hear about it. Mrs. Smetkamp would find a way to blame it on the town.

I pulled open the door, slipped inside, and took a deep breath.

Maybe I should make my phone calls from here in the shed. Give the modern-day dinosaur on the roof time to go back to sleep.

I turned on my flashlight and—

"Mrs. Smetkamp?"

She was lying on the floor of the shed, on a pile of blankets. If I'd taken another step before turning on my flashlight, I'd have tripped over her feet. Her eyes were open, but I didn't think she could see me.

Someone had stuck a knife into her throat.

Chapter 16

I closed my eyes, took a deep breath, and then opened them again. The murder weapon wasn't a knife, I realized, but a knife-like tool called a carpenter's rasp. I had a collection of them in my own workshop.

Then I deliberately looked in a different direction so I wouldn't have to see the rasp, or Mrs. Smetkamp's contorted face, or the bloody floor beneath her. The direction I chose wasn't that much of an improvement. Mr. Smetkamp kept a neat, well-organized workshop. The entire back wall of the shed was covered with pegboard, on which he'd hung all his tools. He'd even painted a precise outline of each tool in its designated spot. Along with the neat rows of hammers, mallets, files, saws, screwdrivers, clamps, vises, pliers, and all the rest, I could see the spot where he kept the rasps. He had a set of five sturdy-looking rasps with wooden handles and sharp points, their blades ranging from four inches to almost a foot. The second largest was missing from the pegboard, and the handle of the rasp that had killed Mrs. Smetkamp matched those of the other four.

I reached into my pocket and pulled out my phone. Time to call the chief. I dialed his cell phone.

"What's up, Meg?" he said, his voice low. "Have you and Randall found Mrs. Smetkamp?"

"Unfortunately, yes," I said. "Someone killed her."

"Someone?" he echoed. "Not the turkeys, I assume."

"Not unless they've developed opposable thumbs and learned to use tools," I said. "She's in her husband's woodworking shed, in their backyard. Someone stabbed her in the throat with a rasp."

"What's a—never mind. Stay there. I'm on my way."

"A rasp's kind of like a coarse file," I said. "This one has a wooden handle and a pointy end, like a knife."

"Are you sure whoever did it is gone?" he said. "If there's any chance they could be hiding in there with you—"

"No chance whatsoever," I said. "I can see every bit of the shed. And it's so small I'm practically stepping on her. Oh, and watch out—there are turkeys on the roof."

"Of course there are," he said. "Yes, I can see them. The noise you hear at the door will be me."

I was glad he'd warned me, but I still jumped when the door opened behind me. There was just barely enough room for me to step aside so he could enter.

He was carrying a garden rake. He was holding it, tines up, in a pose that reminded me of the farmer in the painting *American Gothic*.

"I assume you didn't touch the body," he said, almost absently, as his eyes flickered around the shed's interior.

"I didn't think I needed to. She looked pretty obviously dead."

"Yes." He nodded slightly, reaching into his pocket. "Can you call Horace and get him to come over here? I'm calling your dad. Tell Horace not to let anyone know what's up just yet."

"Okay if I do it from outside?" I asked.

"Of course. Take this, in case that monster on the roof wakes up." He handed me the rake. "And if anyone other than your dad, Horace, or another of my deputies comes into this yard—"

"I'll fend them off," I said.

"Well, don't let them into the shed, but try to keep them here in the backyard until I can talk to them. I just might want to know why they're interested in coming back here."

"Can do," I said.

I took a deep breath, then dashed outside, holding the rake over my head, ready to fend off any attacking turkeys. I managed to reach the back fence without interference, though the larger turkey was definitely getting restless.

Keeping my eye on the turkey, I called Horace.

"What's up?" he asked. "Kinda busy here, you know."

"Can anyone overhear what I'm saying?" I asked. "You don't have your phone's speaker on, do you?"

"No," he said. "Hang on a sec . . . Okay," he said, in a lower tone. "I'm not on speaker, and no one can hear what I'm saying either. What's wrong?"

"Mrs. Smetkamp is dead," I said. "Probably murder, although that's for you and Dad and the chief to figure out. Can you meet the chief in the shed behind the house?"

"Damn. With my forensic gear, I assume."

"Yes," I said. "And the chief doesn't want anyone else to know just yet."

"Won't people be suspicious if they see me getting out my forensic gear? Especially anyone who knows your dad's the medical examiner and sees him heading in the same direction."

"Just tell them the chief found some more evidence to prove who brought the turkeys here," I suggested.

"Smart," he said. "On my way."

We signed off, and I leaned back against the fence. It seemed like a good vantage point for keeping an eye on what was happening in the shed without actually having to share that all-too-tiny space with a dead body.

Horace was the first to arrive, trotting in from Darlene's yard. He nodded to me before knocking on the shed door and disappearing inside.

I glanced up. Was it just my imagination, or was the sky getting lighter? Shouldn't the roundup be starting any minute now?

Or was the chief going to have to cancel the roundup? Would removing the turkeys compromise whatever evidence Horace would be gathering? Surely once the turkeys woke up, they'd do at least as much to contaminate the crime scene as rounding them up would. Maybe more.

I was still pondering that when Dad trotted over from Darlene's yard, with his medical kit in hand.

"In there?" he asked, pointing to the shed.

I gave him a thumbs-up, and he went over to knock on the shed door.

The chief ended up having to exit to make room for Dad to go in. He hovered in the doorway briefly, then decided to put more distance between him and the turkeys on the roof of the shed. He strode over to where I was standing.

"Is it still all systems go on the turkey roundup?" I asked.

"What a mess," he said. "Yes, we're going ahead, with a few small changes. Randall's going to bring his most seasoned team of turkey wranglers over here in a few minutes, so they can start with rounding up the turkeys on the roof of our crime scene."

"We might want them to bag those, too, while they're at it." I pointed to the turkeys roosting on the roof of the house.

"Good point." He pulled out his phone and texted rapidly. "Luckily Horace thinks the murder took place there in the shed. Too much blood for it to have happened anyplace else."

"So at least the roundup won't contaminate your crime scene."

"We don't know that the yard's not part of the crime scene," he said. "There could be footprints out here that would give us a clue to what happened and who did it. Signs of a struggle. Who knows what. But I'm thinking the contamination from the roundup will be more manageable and predictable than just letting the blasted birds continue strutting around my crime scene as if they owned it. Attacking my deputies. Muddying the evidence."

Of course, it wasn't mud the turkeys would be depositing if they stayed, but the chief knew that.

He scowled at the nearest turkeys. Then he pulled out his phone and punched a couple of buttons.

"It's a go," he said into the phone. "But I need to run this crime scene, so you're in charge. Get Vern to liaise with the visiting deputies if they don't like taking orders from you. And is that team on the way to deal with the birds that are here in the backyard? . . . Good."

He hung up.

"Randall?" I asked.

He nodded. Just then Dad popped out of the shed and gestured to the chief.

"I need to see how your dad and Horace are doing. Work with Randall to get rid of those blasted things first." He gestured toward the shed. "If memory serves, you said that Mr. Smetkamp was still at your house."

"Yes, and still fast asleep when I took off," I said.

"I need to break the news to him about his wife." His face fell slightly, as if imagining the husband's reaction. "But there's no need to wake him up to do it. I assume Rose Noire's there taking care of things in your absence."

I nodded.

"Can you enlist her to let you know as soon as he's awake—without letting her know why?"

"Of course." I pulled out my phone.

The chief strode back to the shed door and, after a wary glance at the turkeys, ducked inside with Dad. Dad and Horace. They must be crammed together in there like kids playing Sardines.

I paused with my fingers over the phone, trying to decide what to say. I finally settled for "Let me know when you're awake."

She replied within seconds.

"Already awake," she said. "Baking. What's up?"

"Can you let the chief know as soon as Mr. Smetkamp's up?" I replied. "He needs to ask him something. About the turkeys," I added, which wasn't entirely accurate but would avoid rousing her suspicions.

"Something urgent? I could wake him."

"No, let him rest. It can definitely wait. Or if that changes, I'll let you know."

"Roger. Stay safe!"

I was about to put my phone back in my pocket when an idea hit me. What if Kevin had jumped the gun and started installing cameras in the Lords' backyard. Or a webcam in the Smetkamps' front yard. Either might prove useful to the chief. And given the strange hours he kept, Kevin might still be up. Or the ding of the arriving text might wake him. Though if he was still asleep and missed the ding, the only thing that would suffer would be my curiosity.

"You didn't happen to install those cameras already, did you?" I texted.

Chapter 17

Kevin must have been awake, since he texted back within seconds.

"No. Your reason for waiting sounded good. What's wrong?"

I hesitated. The chief might not want news of the murder to get out quite so soon. But Kevin, in his role as the police department's designated computer forensic expert, would probably get sucked into the investigation sooner rather than later.

"Not for anyone else's ears yet," I began. "Someone murdered Mrs. Smetkamp."

"Whoa!" he texted back.

"So if you have any idea what kind of forensic stuff the chief is going to be asking you to do, you might want to get a head start on it."

"Roger. On it."

I waited to see if he was going to text anything else. The silence was curiously unnerving. I almost wished I'd called instead of texting. The sound of a human voice would be heartening. Or the sight of another human. Even the ding of another text from Kevin. I reminded myself that Michael and the boys were just across the fence. If I listened hard enough, maybe I'd hear them.

And as if on cue, I heard noises from that direction. Not Michael and the boys, though. A crew of half a dozen turkey wranglers began climbing over the stepladders from Myra Lord's yard. Randall was the first on the ground, decked out in a football helmet with the red and gold colors of Caerphilly High School. The other members of his party wore either matching football helmets, Shiffley Construction Company hard hats, or motorcycle helmets. They all wore boots and gloves and carried garden rakes or long poles, except for the last one over the fence, who was lugging a bundle of bright blue tarps.

I was surprisingly glad to see them.

"Two targets on the shed and two more on the roof of the house," I called out, in what I hoped was a sufficiently brisk and military manner. "All hens, I think," I added. I had no idea if that was a useful bit of information—Grandfather had mentioned that the hens, being smaller and less aggressive, would be easier to capture, but easier than what?

"Let's get the ones on the shed first," Randall said to his posse.

That made sense. The shed roof was lower, so the birds there would be easier to reach.

They set up just in front of the shed door. Four of them spread out a blue tarp, and stood ready, one at each corner. The remaining two—Randall and Clarence Rutledge—began gently prodding the larger turkey with their rakes. The turkey tried to ignore them, shifting slightly aside. Then she woke up, uttered a few cranky, outraged squawks, and flapped down to the ground—landing squarely in the middle of the tarp. The waiting crew then pitched in to wrap her up securely. Clarence hovered over the whole operation, calling out a steady stream of advice and warnings to the crew, along with soothing and encouraging words for the irritated turkey hen. Then two of the crew hefted the wriggling bundle and trotted off through the yard on Darlene's side of the house, presumably heading for a waiting truck. The four left behind quickly spread out another tarp and kept watch over the remaining turkey, who didn't appear to have paid much attention to the sudden departure of her companion. In fact, she appeared to be still fast asleep. I wondered how long that would last. In the distance I could hear other shrill squawks, as other posses presumably bagged other low-roosting turkeys.

The two wranglers who'd hauled the turkey away quickly returned, and the squad repeated the nudging and wrapping process with the second turkey—closely observed by Horace and Dad, who cracked open the shed door for that purpose.

Once the shed roof was clear of turkeys, the chief emerged and followed the wranglers as they carried the second turkey around the side of the house.

While that was happening, Randall appropriated one of Myra's ladders and repositioned it so he'd be high enough to nudge the turkeys perched on the roof of the house. They had soon taken care of the remaining two turkeys, and all six of them left with the final bird.

I could hear other sounds in the distance that suggested the rest of the roundup was well underway. Squawks, gobbles, and stray human shouts, along with the occasional rumble of a truck's motor starting up and heading away from Bland Street.

I noticed Dad was still peering out of the shed door. The sky had lightened just a little by now. Was I seeing a wistful expression on his face, or only imagining it? Two of his favorite activities in the whole world—a wildlife rescue mission and the investigation of a murder—were happening simultaneously, and he could do only one. I was torn. For everyone else's sake, I hoped the turkey roundup was taken care of quickly and efficiently, with no injuries to any of the humans or birds. But would it hurt if the tail end of the roundup was still going on when Dad finished his official medical examiner duties? Or if one or two of the wranglers incurred minor injuries so he could patch them up and fuss over them?

Evidently, I wasn't the only one thinking along these lines. Randall appeared, striding briskly along the side of the Smetkamps' house.

"One turkey-free crime scene, as requested," he said. "If any more turkeys show up, call me and I'll bring a crew in to deal with them. And keep this." He handed me a garden rake.

"Thanks," I said. "How's it going?"

"Slow," he said. "But we expected that. Oh, and just between you and me—we found a couple of turkeys that escaped the perimeter and roosted down the block—almost at the corner. Really small ones—probably half grown. I put a little fence around them, and we're saving them for last. I figure we can probably keep them there long enough to let your dad help out with rounding them up—unless his crime scene work takes a lot longer than usual."

"That's very thoughtful," I said. "But let's not tell him we're saving them for him."

"Of course not," Randall said. "Where's the fun in that? Heck, I might even take the fence away and let him be the one to spot them. And I'm keeping a list of people who have minor injuries. Couple of people who tangled with turkeys or hit themselves with their own rakes. Nothing worth interrupting him for now, but we'll have a sick call later on and let him patch everyone up properly. Any idea how soon they'll be bringing out the . . . er, Mrs. Smetkamp?"

"No idea." I shook my head. "Totally depends on how long it takes Dad and Horace to work the scene."

"Yeah." He glanced over at the shed and shook his head. "Well, those turkeys aren't going to round up themselves. See you later."

He turned to go, then stopped long enough to move the ladder back to its original spot, straddling the fence.

"Got to keep our escape routes open!" he exclaimed.

With that he loped back toward the front yard.

I settled in to keep watch.

The shed door opened and the chief reappeared. He glanced around, spotted me, and trudged over.

"If we're lucky, someone will have spotted the killer coming or going." His face suggested that he wasn't really expecting that much luck. "So I'm going to start interviewing any of the neighbors who are awake."

"Which will probably be most of them," I said.

"Most likely," he agreed. "Assuming the coast is clear—or will be soon—I'm going to set up my incident command center in Mrs. Peabody's garage. If anyone's looking for me, steer them that way. And I'd appreciate it if you could keep an eye on things here until I can free up a deputy to handle it. If any humans show up, let me know, and try to detain them."

"And if any turkeys show up, call Randall," I said. "Can do."

He looked around and, spotting the stepladders, used them to exit by way of Myra Lord's yard.

I settled in to keep watch.

The firefighters were now deploying their hoses to encourage turkeys down from the trees, and the amount of squawking, gobbling, and shouting increased.

At one point, a fairly large turkey came around the corner of the house, shrieking like a banshee and heading straight for me. I made sure my route to the stepladders was clear, and then decided that I wasn't going to let a mere bird chase me away. So I leveled my garden rake, and began walking to meet the turkey, while uttering loud, wordless roars—the sort I'd practiced when the boys were tiny in case I had to scare off bears or coyotes or other threats to their safety when we were on camping trips. I'd never tested this technique on live predators, but it seemed to work on the turkey. He veered away, heading for Darlene's yard, but I ran to head him off and steer him back toward the front yard. A posse of wranglers appeared from the front yard, which so demoralized the rogue turkey that he sat down in the middle of a patch of English ivy and uttered the sort of ear-piercing squawks I'd expect to hear if we were torturing him. But the wranglers were surprisingly gentle as they bundled him up in a tarp and hauled him away, shouting their thanks back at me.

The morning wore on, and eventually the squawks, gobbles, and human shouts grew infrequent. At around 6:00 A.M. two EMTs showed up with a stretcher and carried away Mrs. Smet-kamp's body. I wondered if this would give away the fact that a murder had occurred—it was very obviously a body bag on the stretcher, rather than a live patient. Or maybe the rumor had already begun spreading.

Eventually a young deputy—one of the borrowed ones—showed up to take over my post. I made my way cautiously to the front yard. A Shiffley Construction truck was backed up to the gate in the chain-link fence, but it was just parked there. Two volunteers were sitting on the open back of the truck and a third was leaning against it. They glanced up when I rounded the corner, but their faces fell when they realized I wasn't a turkey. All three went back to sipping carryout cups of coffee and looked a little bored.

"Um . . . Meg?"

I turned to see Todd, the redheaded leader of the out-of-town construction workers.

"Morning," I said. "I gather the roundup is slowing down."

"Yeah." He laughed softly. "It was pretty lively for a while. Look, you don't happen to know where the TV people are, do you?"

"I assume they're out at the Caerphilly Inn," I said. "I think Randall succeeded in convincing them that he won't be letting them work on the house until he's had it inspected for safety and tested for asbestos."

"Tested for asbestos?" Todd looked a little anxious at that. "Holy sh—holy cow. You mean they let those workers do the dem-olition without testing?"

"We required asbestos testing," I said. "And the *Marvelous Mansions* people claim they did it—turned in all the relevant paperwork. But now that we've gotten to know them a little better, we're not sure we want to take their word for it. Maybe what they had tested didn't come out of the house. So Randall's going to do his own testing before anyone else goes in there without a respirator."

"As one of the guys who might end up going in there, I approve," Todd said. "Bet that's going to delay things a bit, though."

"Probably," I said. "I know he's going to do the sampling himself, as soon as he ties up any loose ends on this turkey roundup. But he was serious about being able to give you some work while you're waiting. He's got a lot of projects going on, and they all have either deadlines or impatient customers, and this roundup isn't helping."

"Good." Todd looked happier at that thought. "And at least the delay will give me a little time to sort out things with that producer fellow before we start doing any actual work for him. That's who I'm looking for, actually."

"Jared Blomqvist," I said.

Todd nodded.

"I haven't seen him yet today," I said. "Have you seen his assistant? I think she was here a little while ago."

"Talked to her already," he said. "And she's trying to find him herself. She came into town thinking maybe he'd be here, but I gather no one's seen him."

I shook my head. My mind was racing. We should tell the chief about this. Of course, it might not mean anything. Maybe this was normal behavior for Jared. Maybe he often took off without telling his assistant where he was going—especially when unexpected events delayed filming. Maybe hunting him down was an ordinary part of her job.

But maybe the chief would be interested in hearing about someone who suddenly became hard to find right after a murder was discovered.

"It was actually something the assistant said that made me think I should talk to Mr. Blomqvist," Todd went on. "She seemed kind of put out with him, and maybe that made her a little more blunt than usual. She said if we were smart, we'd get our money up front, 'cause otherwise we'd be lucky if we ever saw a penny."

"Yikes," I said. "I don't like the sound of that."

"Neither did I," Todd said. "'Specially since it kind of tied in with something I overheard yesterday."

"And what was that?" I asked.

"I was doing the same thing yesterday," he said. "Trying to find a chance to talk to Blomqvist. I wanted to pin him down on just when our work would actually be starting. And I overheard him having a shouting match with the lady of the house."

"Mrs. Smetkamp?"

"Her, yeah." He paused for a moment. "She's the one they found dead, isn't she?"

I nodded.

"Then maybe I should tell your police about what I overheard," he said. "They were really going at it. There was something she wanted him to do with the house as part of the makeover, and he was saying it wasn't in the plans, they didn't have the budget, the town wouldn't approve it, and so on. They were both getting pretty hot. And then she stopped yelling and her voice got really quiet—but smug and, well, nasty. And she said, 'You'd better do what I want. If you don't make me happy, maybe I'll tell the Rockford people where you are.' And he turned and left without another word. Almost ran out. Looked pale as a sheet."

Chapter 18

A conflict between Mrs. Smetkamp and Jared? I wanted to yell "yes!" and celebrate with a fist pump. But I did my best to hide my satisfaction.

"Interesting," I said.

"Does that ring any kind of bells with you?" he asked.

"No." I shook my head. "I know there's a town named Rockford. In Illinois."

"There's like thirteen or fourteen of them in various states." He held up his phone. "I looked it up. We were wondering, since he's from Hollywood and all, if it could have anything to do with *The Rockford Files*—you know, the TV show James Garner was in."

"Seems far-fetched," I said. "I think that show was on during the seventies."

"Seventy-four to eighty," Todd said. "I looked that up, too."

"Blomqvist wasn't even born then."

"Yeah, but they've tried to do a remake a couple of times in the last few years, according to what I read in Wikipedia. Never got off the ground. He might have had something to do with one of those. Maybe he did something that tanked the thing and lost money for people."

"I think that happens all the time in Hollywood," I said. Although I had to admit that it sounded like the kind of thing Jared could have done. "So I'm not sure her tattling on him would have that much effect. I think it's more likely they're talking about one of those thirteen or fourteen towns named Rockford. But who knows? Why not tell the chief and let him try to figure it out?"

"You think he'd be interested?"

"If someone had a shouting match with someone less than twenty-four hours before she became a murder victim, I can guarantee he'd be interested," I said.

"Yeah." He chuckled softly. "Guess he would be. You know where I can find him?"

"Last I heard, he was setting up his temporary headquarters in Mrs. Peabody's garage," I said. "That's the house to the left of the Smetkamps."

"Then I'll go over and tell him what I know about Mr. Blomqvist," he said. "Thanks."

He strode off.

I went over to the gate and got the volunteers to let me out of the chain-link compound. I stood for a minute or two, taking stock. I didn't see any turkeys. A few residents were still peering out their windows—I waved to Darlene, who was sitting in a rocking chair just inside her living room picture window. I could see Chris's binoculars peering out between the slats of one of his dormer windows, but I didn't think he'd appreciate being noticed.

I headed for the corner, where we'd set up our roundup headquarters.

As I passed Mrs. Peabody's house, I saw that the chief had commandeered one of the borrowed New Life Baptist tables and a few of the folding chairs. Todd was sitting across from him and they were talking intently. Behind them, I saw Horace adding another dozen evidence bags to the already substantial pile on a second table.

A little farther along, I spotted Randall, all dressed up in a fluorescent yellow hazmat suit and carrying what I gathered was a respirator under one arm. Behind him, a junior Shiffley still dressed for the roundup in a red and white football helmet and matching shin guards was lugging a tool chest.

"Venturing into what's left of the house, I gather," I said.

"Going to collect all the samples we need to redo the asbestos testing," he said. "I figure I'll do it myself so I know they're legit. And I'm hoping to get it over with before the day gets any warmer, because this suit is a beast in any weather."

"Be careful," I said.

"I will. Got the firefighters standing by to rescue me if the whole house of cards collapses while I'm in there. Plus some of my guys and equipment."

He gestured down the street, where a construction crane was slowly making its way down the block.

"Excellent," I said. "By the way, have you seen Jared Blomqvist?"

"Not since yesterday. Why?"

I brought him up to speed on what I'd just learned from Todd. A slow smile spread across his face.

"Is it evil of me to hope he turns out to be the culprit?" he asked. "Because that would solve so many problems. I bet we could use it to put a stop to the whole makeover thing *and* force his bosses to fork out some money for whatever we end up having to do to the house. I mean, they're the ones who sent him here."

"Whatever we end up having to do?" I echoed. "You think it's repairable, then?"

"Frankly, I doubt it," he said. "I suspect we're going to end up having to demolish what's left and fight the *Marvelous Mansions* people for enough money for Reg Smetkamp to either rebuild or buy himself a new place to live. And yes, technically it will have to be Reg fighting them, but we'll need to help him. He's not exactly a forceful character. I'm worried that those Hollywood people will run right over him. Talk him into letting them off easy."

"Then let's talk him into hiring a good, forceful attorney," I said. "Before the *Marvelous Mansions* people even know they've got a problem."

"See if you can get your cousin to do it," he said.

I had at least a dozen cousins who practiced law, but I assumed he meant Festus Hollingsworth, who had earned a fearsome reputation for taking on evil corporations and exonerating the unjustly convicted.

"I'll see what I can do."

"Well, the day isn't getting any cooler." He nodded and strode off toward the gate.

I continued on to the corner, where a crowd of volunteers was milling about, eating doughnuts, sipping coffee or sodas, and swapping war stories. I was relieved to see Michael and the boys among them. I knew they'd never been in any real danger, but still.

Michael strode over to greet me.

"Can you take the boys out to the zoo?" he asked. "I need to stay here to help out in case Randall needs rescuing, and then I have classes all afternoon, but your grandfather has invited the boys to help out with getting the turkeys settled in, and they're keen to go."

So after grabbing a doughnut for myself, I found myself chauffeuring Josh, Jamie, Adam Burke, and Eli Lord. They talked nonstop the whole way out to the zoo, telling me what they'd done in the roundup—mostly helping corral the few birds that had tried to escape through the Lords' backyard.

I was happy to listen. I gathered the news of the murder hadn't yet reached them, and the longer the boys remained unaware of it, the better.

Out at the zoo, I used my all-access security card to park in the staff parking lot and let us in through a door marked EMPLOY-EES ONLY. Being what the zoo staff called the designated sane person—the person they called when they needed help talking Grandfather out of something dangerous or impractical—had its benefits. And then, after making sure I knew where Grandfather was keeping the turkeys, I encouraged the boys to run ahead.

I had to badge myself into another secure area before I caught up with them—what Grandfather called the 4Rs area—research, reproduction, rehabilitation, and relaxation. I passed by a pasture in which a bunch of zebras and buffalo were peacefully grazing. They all looked perfectly healthy, so I deduced they fell into the relaxation category—animals Grandfather had judged in need of having some time away from the tourists. The next enclosure seemed to be the maternity ward, containing several heavily pregnant animals—a giraffe, another zebra, and a pair of oryxes. Grandfather also believed in giving expectant animal mothers more peace and quiet than the tourists would allow. Remembering how easily they'd gotten on my nerves when I was pregnant, I approved.

I passed by a large cage containing a solitary and very cranky tiger wearing a tiger-sized Cone of Shame to keep her from licking the half-healed wound on her right front leg, and a cage full of parrots. They looked perfectly healthy, so I went over to get a closer look. A small speaker was just outside the cage, and when I drew closer, I could hear a familiar, resonant voice. Was it—yes. Stephen Fry. I stopped by the speaker to listen.

"Don't forget, Watson," Fry was exclaiming. "You won't fail me. You never did fail me. No doubt there are natural enemies which limit the increase of the creatures. You and I, Watson, we have done our part. Shall the world, then, be overrun by oysters? No, no; horrible! You'll convey all that is in your mind."

I burst out laughing when I realized that Fry was reading a

Sherlock Holmes story. "The Adventure of the Dying Detective," if memory served. Were audiobooks a new form of habitat enrichment for the parrots?

Maybe it was a good idea. The parrots seemed to be listening closely.

I continued down the lane. I could see Grandfather in the distance, leaning on the split-rail fence that surrounded an enclosure. He was talking to a uniformed deputy—Vern Shiffley, from the height—and another man who, from behind, looked vaguely familiar. When I got a little closer, I recognized Grandfather's other companion as Seth Early, owner of the sheep farm across the street from our house. Lad, Seth's Border collie was sitting at Seth's feet, staring intently through the fence. I deduced that Seth had brought some of his sheep in for emissions testing.

But when I drew closer I realized the enclosure didn't contain sheep.

It was full of turkeys.

"There you are," Grandfather said when he spotted me.

"The boys here?" I asked.

"I sent them to help Manoj with something," Grandfather said. "They're pretty focused on the turkeys, though, so they'll probably come back before too long. You're not dragging them away already?"

"No," I said. "They can stay as long as they like. What's with the parrots? Are you trying to turn them into flying detectives? Or just keep them from being bored? Whatever it is, they seem to be enjoying it."

"I'm trying to rehabilitate their blasted unprintable vocabulary." Grandfather turned to scowl in the general direction of the literary parrots. "Some fool let them listen to a lot of George Carlin routines. The 'Seven Words You Can't Say on Television,' and things like that. We started getting complaints that the damned birdbrains were cussing out the tourists. Had to pull them off exhibit."

"You're sure it's George Carlin?" I asked. "You've been known to let fly with some colorful language yourself at times."

"But not in front of the parrots," he said, in an uncharacteristically prim tone. "I'm always careful about that. It's astonishing how fast they pick up words and sounds you don't want them to know."

I had to work to keep a straight face. I could tell Vern was having the same problem. But I made a mental note to tackle my brother, Rob, when he got back from his latest trip. Because I'd bet almost anything he was the one who had corrupted Grandfather's parrots. I'd already had to read Rob the riot act about playing his treasured collection of Carlin's routines within earshot of the boys, whose ability to pick up undesirable words and phrases greatly resembled that of parrots.

"So how's your favorite warthog?" I asked—more to change the subject than anything else.

"Doing fine!" he exclaimed. "She had four healthy little piglets. All doing well."

"Congratulations," I said. "Is this cause for major celebration? Are they endangered or anything like that?"

"No, not endangered," he said. "Parts of their habitat are under pressure, and they're sometimes targeted for their tusks, but on the whole they're pretty resilient. In fact, there have been some reports that feral warthogs are becoming a bit of a nuisance in south Texas."

"Please tell me there's no danger of your warthogs getting loose," I said. "We have enough trouble with the turkeys."

"Don't worry," he said. "Their habitat's secure. They're good burrowers, but we know how to deal with that. And they're all microchipped. Any of them get loose, we can track them down before they get up to anything."

"Like interbreeding with any existing local feral hogs?" I asked.

"Unlikely," he said. "Too many genetic differences. Any inter-breeding's highly unlikely to produce young. And even if it did, the hybrids would almost certainly be sterile."

"Isn't that what they said about the dinosaurs in *Jurassic Park*?" I asked. "'Life finds a way'—isn't that what Jeff Goldblum's char-acter says?"

He frowned.

"Don't worry," he said eventually. "We keep good track of them."

I was about to say, "Famous last words," when he changed the subject.

"What are the boys up to, anyway?" he asked.

Chapter 19

"Up to?" I echoed. "Which boys?"

"Josh and Jamie," he said. "Do you have others you've been hiding from me?"

"No," I said. "But they're not the only boys in town. What makes you think they're up to something?"

"The way they're acting," he said. "Distracted and anxious and maybe even guilty. Their friend Adam, too. When they first got here, the three of them kept slinking off to talk about something. They got a little less distracted after Manoj let them borrow his cell phone to make a call. And then I had Manoj take them over to help with his research—intelligence-testing naked mole rats—and they're acting a lot more normal. But could be he only distracted them. Any idea what they've been up to?"

"Possibly," I said. "Do you think you could ask Manoj what number they called?"

"Already did." Which revealed how worried he was. He patted several of the million pockets in his faded khaki travel vest, pulled out a slip of paper, and handed it to me.

I glanced at the paper. A local number. And one that looked

vaguely familiar. Of course, maybe I only thought that because I recognized the familiar three digits of the local exchange. But I pulled out my phone, checked the contacts app, and bingo! It was Cal Burke's cell phone. No wonder the number looked familiar. Once Cal had gotten his driver's license, he'd been very good about playing chauffeur for his two younger brothers. I must have dialed his number dozens of times to coordinate transportation for Adam and the twins.

"Thanks," I said, handing back the slip of paper. "If it makes you feel any better, I don't think the boys are in any kind of trouble. In fact, I think they're trying to help someone else stay out of trouble."

"And are they going to succeed?" Grandfather asked. "Because it's sure got them worried."

"I think they have a good chance of succeeding," I said. "Since I plan to help them."

"Good," he said. "You'll keep me posted. When's Randall getting here, anyway?"

"Oh, were you expecting Randall?" I asked. "He didn't mention it. What's up?"

"He's supposed to bring some of his turkey wranglers out here," Grandfather said. "And some of that chain-link fence. We need to move the turkeys."

"That's what I'm here for," Vern said. "But we need more bodies."

"I thought you said they could have a happy home here for the rest of their natural lives," I said. "And you already want to get rid of them? Why—"

"No, I don't want to get rid of them." He was frowning furiously. "Of course they have a home here. But not in this enclosure. It's too small, and the fence isn't high enough. They were supposed to go over there."

He pointed to another enclosure. Yes, it was much larger, and had a lot of nice shady trees the turkeys could perch in, and a six-foot chain-link fence instead of the three-foot split-rail one we were all leaning on.

Unfortunately, one of the service roads ran between the two enclosures, leaving a twelve-foot-wide open space the turkeys would have to cross to get to their proper home. And I wasn't optimistic about the odds of the turkeys letting anyone herd them across that open space. I could see why Grandfather was eager to get the wranglers and fencing.

Just then, as if to illustrate what Grandfather was afraid of, one of the younger, leaner turkeys began running frantically across the ground, flapping her wings.

"Blast!" Grandfather pulled out his phone and pressed a couple of buttons. "All hands to the turkey pen! We've got another runner!"

But before Grandfather had even finished saying the words, Lad took off so fast that he was only a black-and-white streak. The turkey very obviously had someplace she wanted to go—or at least a burning desire to put some distance between herself and the enclosure. But Lad headed her off and began gently herding her back toward the nearest gate.

"Let's go help him out," Seth said. So we all three strode around to the gate. Seth opened it and Lad nudged the turkey inside. She was still squawking in protest, but she'd stopped trying to elude Lad.

"I didn't know he could herd turkeys." Grandfather looked thoughtful.

"He can herd anything that moves," Seth said.

Grandfather glanced at me.

"Are you thinking what I'm thinking?" I said.

"If you're thinking Lad could move your turkeys for you, no problem," Seth said. "Probably easier if we take them in small groups. Say a dozen at a time."

By then, three zookeepers had come running up, carrying long padded poles that I deduced were the zoo equivalent of the rakes and umbrellas we'd been using to keep the turkeys at arm's length. So after a few minutes of consultation, Seth, Vern, and the zookeepers began helping Lad relocate the turkeys into their proper home. Actually, all the humans needed to do was open and close gates, and occasionally wave a padded pole at a turkey who was making a more than ordinarily strenuous attempt to escape Lad's control. And Lad was clearly in seventh heaven, with a whole new kind of critter to herd.

"If Lad could open gates, he wouldn't need us at all," I said, as Grandfather and I observed the action.

"He's a very smart dog," Grandfather said. "I bet we could teach him to do it himself."

"Clear it with Seth first, in case he doesn't want Lad to know that." I was still bitter about the time Rob had taught the four-year-old twins how to open childproof caps.

We had drifted across the lane and were now watching the growing flock of turkeys exploring their new habitat.

"What's the deal with that weirdo across the street, anyway?" Grandfather asked.

"What weirdo across what street?" I asked, after glancing around to make sure there were no streets nearby and no one who looked any weirder than we did.

"Across the street from the house where we were doing the roundup," he said. "Guy in the attic kept peering out through the venetian blinds, using a pair of binoculars to watch us work. And laughing like crazy."

"Yeah, I've seen him there myself," I said. "But how can you tell he was laughing? If he was peering out through the blinds—"

"I had my own binoculars," he said. "The ones with twenty x magnification. I knew they'd come in useful for seeing what the turkeys were up to when they were still in the trees. I couldn't just tell he was laughing—I could count his nose hairs and the fillings in his teeth. So do you know who he is?"

"A guy named Chris Smith," I said. "Rents the attic room."

"You might want to tell the chief about him," Grandfather said. "He was enjoying the roundup way too much. At least at first. Started looking a lot less cheerful once we hit our stride and were making real progress clearing out the birds. Looked to me like someone enjoying a mess he'd created, and then getting ticked off that we were cleaning it up."

"A good point," I said. "I'll make sure the chief knows."

"You think he's the kind of creep who might have it in for the birds?" he asked.

"I think it's more likely he had it in for Mrs. Smetkamp," I said.

"Could have had it in for the birds, too," he said. "And thought dumping them in that neighborhood would . . . er, be bad for them, too."

"You were going to say 'kill two birds with one stone,' weren't you?" I said.

"That could have been his aim. Annoy the hell out of the old biddy while putting the turkeys in danger. He might have thought we'd just go in with guns blazing."

"He'd have to be pretty clueless to think anyone would be shooting turkeys in a quiet residential neighborhood."

"They're often pretty clueless, animal haters." Grandfather scowled, then brightened slightly as Lad delivered another dozen turkeys into the habitat. "They're related to velociraptors, you know," he added, apropos of nothing that I could think of.

"Who is?" I asked. "The animal haters?"

"The turkeys." Grandfather was studying several nearby turkeys with a rapt attention that I found ominous, since it so often indicated that he was about to embark on another ambitious project or dangerous undertaking. "They're descended from the theropods—a group of dinosaurs that includes not only velociraptors but also the Tyrannosaurus rex, Allosaurus, Megalosaurus—a lot of really interesting species. Ancestrally carnivorous, although many of the later species evolved to be omnivorous or even herbivorous."

"A good thing the turkeys evolved, then." A vision of Bland Street overrun with aggressive, carnivorous turkeys rose unbidden to my mind, like a nightmare outtake from *Jurassic Park*.

"Theropods are the only dinosaurs with a true wishbone," Grandfather went on. "Which turkeys inherited."

"And chickens?"

"Yes, chickens too. Pretty much all modern-day birds are descended from the theropods."

He continued to study the turkeys. I found myself thinking of our chicken flocks—the calm, friendly Welsummers with their elegant copper and black feathers, and the beautiful but feisty black Sumatras. I had a hard time believing they were related to the feral turkeys, much less the terrifying velociraptors and T. rexes of *Jurassic Park*.

"So, it could be worse," I said. "If the dinosaurs hadn't become extinct, instead of a flock of feral turkeys, we might be battling a flock of velociraptors."

"It really wouldn't have been that much worse," Grandfather said. "*Jurassic Park* exaggerated the size of velociraptors, you know. They were really only about a meter high. Some of these turkeys are bigger than that. And the velociraptors were covered with feathers, too. They've discovered fossilized velociraptor forearms in Mongolia that have quill knobs—little bumps that in modern birds show where the ligaments anchor their flight feathers to the bone."

I studied the turkeys with new respect. No wonder Grandfather was so interested in them. Although he did his best to fight for the welfare of all animals, he freely admitted a sneaking fondness for predators. His enthusiasm for rounding up the turkeys and studying them made sense when you thought of them as modern-day descendants of T. rex and the velociraptors.

"Yes," he said. "If velociraptors were around today, we'd probably think of them as more like big, scary turkeys."

"Or maybe small but worthy descendants of their Mesozoic Era ancestors," I suggested.

"Also true," he said. "And I bet we'd be debating the relative merits of roast turkey and roast velociraptor."

I made a mental note to beg off the next time the boys wanted to rewatch however many movies there now were in the *Jurassic Park/Jurassic World* family.

Something occurred to me.

"Do wishbones have a function?" I asked.

"They help stabilize a bird's skeleton to make it strong enough for flight," Grandfather explained.

"But velociraptors didn't fly, did they? Or T. rexes?"

"Of course not."

"Then what did they use their wishbones for?"

"We don't know." Grandfather frowned as if the question annoyed him. "Not yet anyway. So many questions we have yet to answer. How many of them had feathers, for example, and how many had scaly skin like modern reptiles. And what color were they? And did they vocalize? Oh, for a time machine! Imagine being able to go back to those days—hiking through the humid swamps and jungles, listening to the call of the dinosaurs—would it be trilling? Howling? Shrieking? Trumpeting?"

"Paleontologists don't have any clue what they sounded like?" I asked.

He frowned.

"Not really," he said. "We haven't yet found any evidence that they had vocal cords, which is what they'd need to make the kind of blood-curdling roars you always hear in the movies. We can't prove they didn't, of course."

"The absence of evidence is not evidence of absence," I said, repeating the Carl Sagan quote Kevin was so fond of using in his true crime podcasts.

"True." The idea seemed to cheer Grandfather. "They have found a fossil bird from the Cretaceous period with a syrinx—that's the organ birds use for chirping. Some experts think the theropods might have had a similar organ."

"So T. rexes chirped?" I asked.

"Possibly," he said.

The idea cracked me up. He didn't find it amusing.

"We could be talking about very loud, deep chirps." His voice dripped with disapproval. "Terrifying chirps. And they may also have growled, or hissed, or honked."

"Let's all sing like the dinos sing," I sang. "Chirp, chirp chirp, chirp chirp."

Grandfather snorted in disgust. Should I tell him he needed to work on his sense of humor?

"I should get back to town," I said. "I'll let the chief know about how Chris was enjoying the roundup."

"Good."

"Tell the boys to call when they're ready to be picked up."

He nodded absently, his eyes on the turkeys.

A few feet away, Vern was squatted down beside Lad, scratching him behind the ears while Seth looked on proudly.

"Not in the cards," Vern was saying. "I keep crazy hours, and it's not fair to leave a dog alone that much."

I felt briefly sorry for Vern—he obviously loved dogs. But he was right—a dog would be lonely, left all alone out on his small farm.

On my way, I passed by the cage where the parrots were still intently listening to Stephen Fry reading Sherlock Holmes. I stopped for a moment to listen. I liked Fry's reading. Maybe I should get a copy of the audiobook. It would be fun to listen to while I was driving around on my errands. The boys might even like it.

"Have fun, you guys," I said to the parrots as I turned to go.

"'They were the footprints of a gigantic hound!'" one of the birds exclaimed.

"'Ai! Ai! A Balrog! A Balrog is come!'" shrieked another.

A third rattled off the seven words you can't say on television, in a remarkably accurate imitation of George Carlin's voice.

"No parole yet for you clowns," I muttered as I retraced my steps to the staff parking lot.

Chapter 20

It occurred to me that on the way back to town I'd be passing by the Caerphilly Inn. I decided to stop in and check on the *Marvelous Mansions* crew. See if any of them knew where we could find the elusive Jared.

My spirits rose as I turned in to the Inn's long, tree-lined drive. I could remember when I'd have found driving up to the elegant, expensive, five-star hotel more than a little daunting. But these days it felt familiar and welcoming. The fact that Ekaterina Vorobyaninova, the manager, was one of my best friends helped. So did the fact that on more than one occasion I'd assisted the hotel with problems that could have turned into major PR disasters—including a murder that took place at a conference the hotel was hosting. Most of the staff regarded me as an ally, if not actually a colleague.

So I no longer felt intimidated as I drove the Twinmobile over the spotless white gravel of the parking lot. Rather than parking in the most unobtrusive corner at the far end of the parking lot, I snagged a space close to the entrance, with its overhanging curtain of native wisteria.

Although as I was getting out of the car, I noticed that my former favorite parking area was now occupied by the two trucks the *Marvelous Mansions* crew were using, and a group was clustered around them. No sign of the black rental SUV Jared had been using, though.

Enrique, the bell captain, opened the door for me, and we wished each other *buenos dias.*

"Is Ekaterina here?" I asked.

"Yes," he said. "But . . . she is having a difficult day. There are . . . problems."

"Thanks for the warning," I said. "I'll try not to annoy her."

"I am sure a visit from you will improve her day," he said, with a courtly bow.

I hoped so.

I spotted Ekaterina across the lobby talking to an anxious-looking desk clerk. He spotted me first and nodded in greeting. Ekaterina turned and strode over to greet me, as always, with a smile and kisses on both cheeks.

"I hear you are having a difficult day," I said. "Anything I can do to help?"

"Possibly." Her face grew stern again. "Do you have any idea of the present location of Mr. Jared Blomqvist?" Something about her pronunciation of the surname suggested that Swedish might be another of the dozen or so languages she spoke.

"No," I said. "I haven't seen him since yesterday afternoon. I was rather hoping I'd find him here, or at least be able to ask his staff if they know where to find him."

"*Svolach!*" From her tone and the look on her face, I gathered this was not an expression of great joy.

"What's the problem?"

"He's disappeared," she said. "Vanished. *Complètement disparu.*"

"When?" I asked.

"At six o'clock this morning. I just finished checking all the security tapes. When he walked in—after being out all night, you understand—Enrique asked if he wanted us to park his car, and he said no, he'd parked it himself. He went up to his room and put the 'do not disturb' sign on the door. Then he sneaked out with both of his suitcases—he went out through the loading dock door, which seems to have been where he'd parked his car. And we wouldn't have even guessed he was gone if that assistant of his hadn't begun to worry about him a little while ago and insisted we open the door to make sure he was all right—and he was gone!"

"Let me guess: he didn't pay his bill."

"He didn't pay anyone's bill," she exclaimed. "All of those rooms the television people are occupying are on his corporate card, which has just been declined."

"Let's tell Chief Burke," I said. "Right away."

"Yes." The idea seemed to please her. And calm her slightly. "We will need the assistance of the police to catch him. That nasty thief!"

"He's not just a nasty thief," I said. "He might also be a nasty murderer. If he was out in the middle of the night last night—"

"He drove off shortly before midnight," she said. "I could see that on our security cameras. Whom did he kill?"

"We don't yet know that he did it," I said. "But someone killed Mrs. Smetkamp."

"The lady whose house he was fixing?"

"Yes." I was pulling out my phone and dialing the chief. "Do you have the make, model, and license plate number of his rental car?"

"Of course," she said. "Enrique!" She followed this with a burst of Spanish, so rapid-fire that I could only understand one word in three. Enrique dashed over and handed her a small notebook.

"Hello, Meg," the chief said. "What's up?"

"Jared Blomqvist is on the run," I said. "He was out all night and only stopped by the Inn long enough to collect his luggage and sneak out the back door. Ekaterina has the info on his car."

I handed my phone to her, and she rattled off the license number of the black Cadillac Escalade Jared was driving. Or had been driving when he left the Inn. They exchanged a few more words, and then Ekaterina hung up and handed me my phone.

"What is a bolo?" she asked. "The chief will be out here to investigate as soon as possible, but he says first he must put out a bolo."

"Cop slang for 'be on the lookout,'" I said. "It means he's going to get every other police department in this part of the state to help him catch Jared."

"Good! I will go and prepare the security tapes for his inspection."

"Is Jared's assistant still here?" I asked. "I'm going to see if she has any clue about where he might be heading."

"In the parking lot with the other television people," she said. "What are we supposed to do with them? It's not their fault that their pig of a boss abandoned them without paying for their rooms, but we can't keep them here indefinitely, and there's nowhere else for them to go. All the bed-and-breakfasts will be full, and there is no other hotel for miles."

"Except the Clay County Motor Lodge," I said, a bit mischievously.

"I would not send my worst enemy to that sty!"

"We'll figure out something," I said. "Find some people willing to take them in. Or maybe set up some tents, like the ones Randall got for the carpenters. Let's worry about catching Jared first." I figured there was also at least an even chance that once Ekaterina was convinced they were innocent of their boss's misdeeds she would take pity on them and let them stay a little longer.

She nodded and strode briskly toward her office.

I went out to the parking lot and approached the television people, as Ekaterina called them. They were talking animatedly—possibly arguing. But they all fell silent and looked nervous when they spotted me approaching.

"I hear your boss has deserted you," I said, getting right to the point.

The others all looked at the young woman I recognized as Maddy, Jared's assistant. Evidently they were all silently electing her their spokesperson. She stepped forward.

"We are looking for him ourselves," she said. "We have no idea where he is."

"I gather," I said.

"We don't even know if he's heard about what happened to poor Mrs. Smetkamp," Maddy said.

Which answered one of my questions—they'd heard about the murder. Or at least heard something untoward had happened.

"Maybe you can help us find him," I said. "I'm assuming you flew in to a nearby airport—which one? Richmond?"

"No, Dulles," Maddy said. "Richmond was closer, but Jared didn't like it. Not very many direct flights to L.A."

"You think maybe he's heading there?" I asked. "Back to Dulles, I mean?"

"His return flight isn't for another ten days," she said.

"He might be planning to exchange his ticket," I said.

"He always has me make all his travel arrangements," she said.

"But if he's planning on blowing town and leaving the rest of you holding the bag, maybe he'd do it himself."

"That's true." Her face brightened, and she pulled her phone out of her jeans pocket. "I can log in and see. I have all his account information."

I waited impatiently while Maddy tapped on her phone. For that matter, the rest of the crew were watching her eagerly, as if they hoped the information she found would rescue them from the awkward situation they were in.

"Miami?" She looked up from her phone with a puzzled expression. "He exchanged his ticket back to L.A. for one to Miami. Why would he do that?"

"Maybe he's from Miami?" one of the crew asked.

"No, he's from Anaheim," she said.

"Miami's a good place to head for if you're planning to leave the country," another crew member suggested.

"What time's his new flight?" I asked.

"Three fifteen," Maddy said.

"Then there's still time to catch him," I said. "Hold up your phone and let me take a picture of his flight information for the police."

She obliged, and I texted the picture to the chief.

"Thanks!" he texted back.

I looked up to see that they were all staring at me with anxious faces. It occurred to me that the chief would probably rather interview them without any interference from me. But he'd also probably rather not give them a lot of time to rehearse alibis with each other. Maybe I should try to keep them all busy until he arrived.

"Has he ever done this before?" I asked.

Several of them looked uneasy.

"Don't ask me," one said. "This is my first time crewing for *Marvelous Mansions.*"

"Not surprising," another said. "Since this is only the second makeover they've done."

"He's done it before, though," a tall man in a UCLA Film and Television School T-shirt said. "Remember when the hotel in Chicago wanted to kick us all out because his credit card wouldn't go through?"

"He told us it was a mix-up," Maddy said. "Corporate hadn't paid his Amex bill on time. And it wasn't Chicago, it was Rockford."

"Rockford, Chicago," the UCLA guy said. "I can't keep track of it. I just worry about what airport to show up at."

"Anyway," Maddy said. "He's done it before, and it was a big headache till he showed up and sorted things out. If he doesn't show up soon—"

She stopped herself and resumed chewing on one of her nails. Clearly she, at least, realized that Jared might not be planning to return.

"Were any of you with Jared last night?" I asked.

"No," one of them said.

"He disappeared right after dinner," another added.

"He doesn't like to hang out with us peasants," said a third.

"Look, what's going on?" Maddy asked. "This isn't just about him running out on the hotel bill, is it? Do they think Jared . . . was responsible for Mrs. Smetkamp's death?"

"No idea," I said. "But given his dramatic disappearing act, I bet he's a suspect."

Several of them gasped. But none of them looked particularly surprised. Or particularly upset.

"That jerk," someone muttered. Murmurs of agreement followed.

"Look, Chief Burke will be out here any minute now," I said. "You should stay here, and don't discuss this among yourselves until he has a chance to talk to you."

"But we need to go out and look for someplace else to stay," one of them said. "I don't imagine the Inn's going to let us stay."

"Maybe we don't need to worry about that," another suggested. "We'll probably all end up in jail if Jared doesn't pay the hotel bills. Because I sure can't."

"We shouldn't have to pay them," another said. "It's not our fault—"

"It's not your fault Jared abandoned you," I said. "The chief will know that, and so will the hotel management. Just do what you can to help the police, and meanwhile we'll find someplace for you. If we can't talk the hotel into letting you stay on, we'll find something else."

Just then a police cruiser pulled into the lot, traveling rather faster than the fifteen-miles-per-hour speed limit and sending some of the white gravel flying. I spotted Aida at the wheel. She parked a few feet away from the trucks, got out, and strolled over to us.

"This is Deputy Butler," I said to the television crew.

"I can take over here," she said. "Chief told me to start interviewing these good folks." I deduced that she was giving me, if not marching orders, at least permission to depart.

"Good," I said. "I'm going to start figuring out where they can stay if Ekaterina kicks them out."

I strolled slowly back to my car. Was there anything else I could do here? Probably better to let Ekaterina talk to the chief before I tackled her about whether she'd take pity on the abandoned television people.

I spotted the chief's blue sedan arriving. I pointed toward where Aida and the television people were. He waved and drove over to park beside Aida's cruiser.

I lingered another minute or so, to see if he wanted to talk to me. But he seemed intent on interviewing his new witnesses.

I pulled out my phone and called Randall. If I couldn't stay and kibitz, at least I could have the fun of sharing with someone what the television people had revealed. And I had a legitimate reason to brief Randall.

Chapter 21

"What's up?" Randall asked.

"Jared the producer skipped town around dawn," I said. "And not only does the chief want to interview him about the murder, Ekaterina is gunning for him because the credit card she has on file for him just got declined."

"Good grief," he said. "What do you need me to do?"

"The chief's set things in motion to apprehend Jared and bring him back," I said. "But he's abandoned all his minions, and I'm not sure how long Ekaterina's going to let them stay if *Marvelous Mansions* isn't solvent enough to pay for their rooms. I expect they're all ready to turn tail and go home."

"But I bet the chief doesn't want any of them to leave town just yet."

"Right," I said. "So do you have any more tents? We could send them out to the fairgrounds for the time being."

"I'm sure I can find some," he said. "And maybe something better—leave it to me. I'll let you know what I come up with."

"Or if you need any help," I said.

"Roger. I'll get on it as soon as I finish with these asbestos samples."

"Sorry," I said. "If I'd known you were busy—"

"Not that busy," he said. "Just dropping the samples off. And I appreciate you filling me in on what's happening. Laters."

We hung up. I glanced over at where the chief and Aida were talking to the television people. I was dying to know what they were all telling him, but I knew he wouldn't want me eavesdropping.

Just for a moment, I toyed with the idea of changing jobs. Not giving up my blacksmithing, of course. But what if I quit my job as Randall's assistant and applied the next time the chief had an opening for a deputy?

And I came back to reality and realized that no, I didn't want to be a deputy. The only time I ever envied Aida and Horace was on those rare occasions when they got to help investigate a murder or another interesting crime. I just wanted the inside scoop. And if I did what I could to help the chief and avoided doing anything he'd see as butting in, I'd probably hear as much of the inside scoop as I wanted. More than most people in town, since my status as a part-time town and county employee made the chief regard me as a civilian resource that he could borrow from Randall when the department was overworked and understaffed.

So, in the interest of not looking as if I was spying, or butting in, I got into my car and headed for town.

Back on Bland Street, things were quieter. Not quite back to normal—the chain-link perimeter was still there, the barricades were still up to keep out traffic, and borrowed deputies were on guard in the Smetkamps' front and back yards. A few of the Blake's Brigade volunteers were wandering around, peering up into trees and onto roofs, hoping to spot any rogue turkeys that had escaped the roundup. Neighbors were standing around in twos and threes, discussing the day's doings.

I saw Gloria standing in her front yard, surveying the damage across the street.

"Afternoon," I said. "You missed all the excitement."

"Thank goodness," she said. "But is it true about someone bumping off Mrs. Smetkamp?"

"It is."

"Damn." She shook her head. "Not sure how to take that. 'Any man's death diminishes me' and all, but I can't say I'm going to miss her. I don't mean I'm glad she's dead, or she deserved it, or anything. But I have to admit my life will be a little more peaceful without her on the block."

"I imagine everyone's will," I said.

"Yeah, but mine more than anyone," she said. "Except maybe the Patels."

"Let me guess," I said. "She wasn't a big fan of diversity."

"Got it in one," she said. "Of course, she wasn't an in-your-face, pearl-clutching, how-dare-you-move-into-our-neighborhood bigot. More the condescending kind. First time we met was when my sister was helping me get the place ready before the movers came. Mrs. Smetkamp saw us sweeping and scrubbing and tried to hire us to clean her house."

"Good grief," I muttered.

"If you'd found her dead that week, I'd have been a little worried—my big sister the pediatric surgeon is way touchier than I am about stuff like that. But once I convinced her that no, I wasn't interested in swabbing her toilets, she kind of left me alone. Just told me, every so often, how much she appreciated that I was making an effort to keep up the tone of the neighborhood. And that I was a credit to my people."

"She didn't," I exclaimed.

"Oh, yes she did. And I don't know what she said to Meera Patel, but I've seen Meera go ten blocks out of her way rather than walk past their yard when Mrs. Smetkamp was out there. Of course, that doesn't mean Meera should be a suspect. She wouldn't hurt a fly. Literally. She tries to chase them outside with a paper fan."

I nodded. I didn't see Meera as a very plausible suspect, either. Unless Mrs. Smetkamp had done something to her kids. She'd be a tiger in that case—but even then, I couldn't see her creeping around and stabbing anyone in the middle of the night. Drawing herself up to her full five feet and stepping in front of her children like a human shield, maybe. Sneaking around and stabbing someone with a sharp object? No. Of course, she'd grabbed the pitchfork to defend Benny the Amazon driver from the turkeys, but she hadn't come even close to stabbing any of the birds—she'd mostly just shoved them with the back of the tines.

"Mrs. Smetkamp doesn't like Creepy Chris, either," Gloria said. "Didn't like him, that is. Ever since he moved in last fall, she keeps—kept—asking all kinds of questions about him."

"What kind of questions?"

"Who he is. Where he came from. Why he doesn't ever come out except in the middle of the night. What he does up there all day in the attic. All the same questions I wish I knew the answer to. In fact, maybe that's one reason I haven't managed to find out anything about him. Whenever I think about trying to pin him down to answer questions, I worry that I'll come off as another nosy old neighborhood snoop and I don't do it."

"Then if nothing else, this whole thing will give you a chance to learn more about Creepy Chris," I said. "Because the chief is going to want to question him, and he doesn't take kindly to people trying to avoid giving straight answers."

"Excellent." Gloria smiled as if she enjoyed the prospect of seeing her lodger's discomfort.

Just then I spotted Randall. He'd taken off his glow-in-the-dark yellow hazmat suit, but he was carrying an armload of what I assumed were samples taken from the Smetkamp house. Two of his workers trailed behind him, one carrying his tool chest while the other was toting something wrapped up in a black plastic garbage bag.

"Hey, Meg," he said. "Glad you're here—I was just about to call you. We're taking down the perimeter fence, starting with the parts that run through people's backyards. Can you do an inspection? Make sure we've hauled away everything that doesn't belong there and put things back the way they were?"

"I'm not bringing back all the weeds and poison ivy I hauled away for the Garden Club," I said facetiously.

"Of course not," he said. "Just make sure the residents aren't upset about anything and figure out what we need to placate any that are."

"Can do," I said.

He strode off down the street toward where his truck was parked.

I decided to start my inspection with the Lords' yard. If the ladders over the fence were still there, it would be the closest. So I went through the Smetkamps' yard along the hedge that separated it from Darlene's. I nodded to the deputy who was sitting in a folding chair, watching the shed and the back of the house, and used the ladders to cross to the Lords' backyard.

Myra was there, sitting at a well-weathered picnic table, typing on a laptop. She looked up and waved when she saw me.

"Nice to be able to work outside again without worrying about being pecked or dive-bombed," she said. "What's up?"

"Just checking to make sure we managed to return your yard to the same condition it was in before the turkeys showed up."

"No complaints here," she said. "In fact, I'm pleased with the recent improvements to the neighborhood."

"Improvements?" Did she consider Mrs. Smetkamp's death an improvement?

"The Garden Club's cleanup of that jungle full of invasive species next door," she said. "I'm going to take pictures and show the house's owner how much better it looks and see if I can get them to let the Garden Club re-landscape it with low-maintenance native plants."

"Excellent idea," I said. "And maybe you can talk Reg Smetkamp into doing the same with his yard. After all, his landscaping's going to need a lot of fixing to undo what the turkeys have done to it."

Her face fell.

"That poor man," she said. "He'd probably be fine with the idea, but let's wait awhile before asking him."

"Definitely," I said.

"He's never been anything but perfectly charming," she said. "I have to admit, I won't miss her one bit, but I guess he will, and that's reason enough to be sad about it."

Just then Tyler and Squeaky bounded up to us.

"Squeaky found some evidence," Tyler exclaimed.

Chapter 22

"Evidence?" Myra repeated. "Squeaky?"

When he realized we were looking at him, Squeaky wagged his tail and uttered a bark whose surprisingly high pitch probably explained his name.

Tyler held up a ratty black object. Myra and I both peered at it.

"Looks like a running shoe," she said.

"Or what's left of one," I said. Squeaky hadn't just found the shoe—he'd made a good start at chewing it to bits. It had originally been an all-black leather Nike—I could make out most of the swoop logo in black on black. "Men's size thirteen," I added, as I studied it.

"Not one of ours," Myra said. "Too large even for Jason, and he's the family bigfoot."

"Where did you find it?" I asked Tyler.

"Under the porch steps," Tyler said. "Where Squeaky always hides things. It could be evidence, right?"

"I should never let them watch all those *Murder, She Wrote* reruns," Myra said.

"Depends on when Squeaky found it," I said. "If he always hides things under the steps, it could have been there for quite a while."

"Uh-uh." Tyler shook his head vigorously. "We just had a ten-minute pickup in the yard."

"Today?"

"No, almost yesterday," Tyler replied.

"Almost yesterday is what he calls the day before yesterday," Myra explained. "And he's right. Eli had a baseball game Saturday evening and couldn't find his baseball glove, so I made the boys do a full search of the house and the yard. We found the glove under the steps—so far back I had to get a rake to drag it to where I could reach it. And while we were at it, we completely cleaned out everything else that Squeaky had hidden there. By the time we finished there was nothing but dirt and cobwebs under the steps, and that was two days ago."

"So it probably belongs to whoever brought the turkeys," Tyler said.

"That's very possible," I said.

Of course, it could also belong to whoever had committed the murder, but I wasn't sure how much Myra wanted her kids to know about the real-life crime next door, so I didn't say it aloud. And for all we knew it could be something Squeaky had picked up somewhere else in the neighborhood that had nothing to do with either crime.

"Squeaky probably tried to stop them," Tyler announced. "By biting their feet."

"He doesn't actually bite people's feet," Myra explained. "But he's mischievous. Fond of pulling the shoes off of people when they try to climb the ladders."

"Has anyone other than you touched it?" I asked Tyler.

"Squeaky has," Tyler pointed out.

"I meant other than you two," I said.

"No." Tyler shook his head.

"Put it down on the grass there." I pulled out my phone. "And we'll call the chief to come take a look at it."

Tyler set the remnants of the shoe down and then sat cross-legged on the ground a few feet away. Clearly he intended to stand guard over his find. Squeaky plopped down beside him and rested his head in Tyler's lap—but with his eyes on the shoe.

I'd expected it to take a while for the chief to show up—after all, I'd left him out at the Caerphilly Inn. But he appeared after only a few minutes. I stifled the urge to ask him about it. Horace also appeared hard on his heels.

While Myra and Tyler explained the provenance of the shoe, Horace put on a fresh pair of gloves and deposited it reverently in a brown paper evidence bag.

"It's a well-worn shoe," Horace said, with great satisfaction. "With a fairly distinctive wear pattern, and we can probably get DNA from it."

"Yes." The chief nodded and turned to Myra. "We might need to take Tyler's DNA for exclusionary purposes."

"If it will catch whoever did this, that's fine," Myra said.

"Will that hurt?" Tyler looked dubious.

"Of course not," I said. "Horace, I don't think I touched the shoe, but just in case, why don't you take a DNA sample from me? Show Tyler how it's done," I added, before Horace could protest that if he needed my DNA profile he could always get it from Grandfather, who was doing some kind of massive study of our family genetics.

So Horace swabbed my cheek in the approved fashion, stowed the swab in a test tube, and labeled it neatly. Then, at my suggestion, we swabbed Squeaky. By the time Horace had finished labeling Squeaky's sample, Tyler was impatient for his turn with the swab.

"If you like, we can destroy the sample once we've finished the exclusion," the chief said to Myra.

"Unless you're curious about your family DNA," I said. "In

which case, let me know, and I can ask Grandfather to have his technicians run all kinds of information for you. Where your ancestors came from, whether you have any genetic health risks—all that kind of thing. All the stuff you normally have to pay a service to find out."

"Hmm," Myra said. "Let me think about that."

"I'll take an extra swab of Tyler, just in case you want to do that," Horace said.

Actually, I suspected Horace wanted two swabs so he could send one down to the crime lab in Richmond and take the other over to Grandfather's DNA lab. Courts tended to like the officialness of the crime lab's results, but it could take weeks before we got them. Grandfather had originally started his lab with a focus on animal genetics, but in the last few years he'd greatly expanded their work on human DNA, thanks to Dad's enthusiasm about its importance in solving crimes. Lately Grandfather's staff had been working on expedited DNA testing for law enforcement purposes, so by now his staff could get the chief preliminary results in a matter of hours.

Tyler seemed delighted that we wanted to swab him twice.

"Of course, we don't know if Squeaky grabbed the shoe from Mrs. Smetkamp's killer or from someone involved in the turkey prank," the chief said to me when we had left Myra's yard and Tyler couldn't hear us.

"Couldn't that be the same person?" I asked.

"It absolutely could," the chief said. "So far we have nothing to prove or disprove that it was the same person. Either way, I think it's more likely the shoe was lost the night of the murder rather than the night of the prank. I'll talk to the high school kids who were involved in the prank, but I think they'd have mentioned it if Squeaky had stolen one of their shoes."

"Or if the ringleader had suddenly showed up with one shoe missing," I said.

"Exactly. Do we know what day the trash is picked up in this part of town?"

"Not offhand, but I can find out." I pulled out my phone.

"That's okay," he said. "I can call the trash service."

"You could," I said. "But it will be faster if you just give me a sec to look it up. I have a cheat sheet. That's one of the things people are always complaining about to Randall—that their trash hasn't been picked up, and he usually sends me out to troubleshoot and calm them down, and nine out of ten times they're confused about what day their pickup is. Here you go. Thursdays. So if you're thinking the shoe's owner could have just thrown the matching one in their trash, it might still be there."

"Of course, if he's smart, he'll throw it away someplace else," the chief said. "In a neighborhood that's getting picked up today. Or a public dumpster. But maybe we'll get lucky and he won't think of that. Will you be here for a while?"

"Around the neighborhood, yes," I said. "Making sure the turkey wranglers picked up after themselves and that none of the residents are upset about anything. Speaking of people being upset—what happened with the television people?"

"They're fine." He chuckled. "Evidently Ekaterina had them so cowed that they were afraid to go into the Inn's restaurant to eat and they're all dead broke to boot. So I got Vern to borrow the school bus his brother drives, and he's taking them all out to the Shack for a late barbecue lunch. He'll bring them down to the station afterward for their interviews."

A smart plan, I thought. Anyone who avoided the Shack because of its name was missing out on some of the best barbecue in the state. The television people would probably be in a very genial and cooperative mood by the time they got down to the station.

We'd reached the front yard, where Randall's workers were disassembling the final stretches of the chain-link fence and loading them into a Shiffley Construction Company truck. But the chief wasn't watching that. He was staring across the street, at Gloria's house. He seemed to be studying it.

I reminded myself that I was supposed to be inspecting the yards where the fence had been. And that I wanted to hunt down Cal Burke, to confirm my suspicion that he'd helped with the turkey prank and talk him into confessing to his grandfather. But I didn't want to leave if the chief was about to do something interesting.

"Anything wrong?" I asked.

"If memory serves, you mentioned that Ms. Willingham is staying at your house."

"She is," I said. "Although I saw her back here a few minutes ago."

"She took off again," the chief said. "She has a class to teach. But there's no rush. If she was out at your house all night, there's no chance she saw anything here last night. A pity—she seems like a levelheaded young woman, and her house would be the perfect vantage point for observing anything that was happening across the street."

"You could always check with her tenants," I said. "There's Jennifer—don't know her last name, but she's a Caerphilly College student. You probably saw her sunning herself in the yard all day yesterday. I don't know if Jennifer has the front bedroom or the back one, but the living room windows overlook the street and she'd have had access to those."

"Jennifer Hodges," the chief said. "I've interviewed Ms. Hodges. She didn't see anything during the time period that the turkeys would have arrived. And she had an unsettling encounter with some of the turkeys yesterday and decided to stay with her boyfriend until the neighborhood was safe again, so she couldn't have seen the killer arriving or leaving."

"Well, there's also Chris Smith," I suggested. "The mysterious techie who haunts her attic. He has windows overlooking Gloria's front and back yards, which means he had a ringside seat for anything that was happening at the Smetkamps. And Grandfather thinks you should interrogate him."

"Any particular reason?"

"Because he seemed to find the roundup hilarious—until he realized it was going to succeed." I relayed what Grandfather had reported seeing.

"Interesting," the chief said. "That makes me even more impatient to talk to him. Although so far we've been unable to locate him—he doesn't appear to be home, although a brown van registered to him is parked around the corner."

"What makes you think he's not at home?" I turned to look at Gloria's house. "Grandfather is pretty sure he saw Chris's binoculars peering out from one of his front windows a couple of times this morning. I haven't seen him, but I spent most of the roundup guarding your crime scene. And if his van's still there, he can't have gone far."

"No," the chief said. "But no one's answering the doorbell."

"From what Gloria tells me, Chris might not bother with the doorbell," I said. "According to her, he's never had a visitor, so why would he bother answering the door?"

"Bother." The chief's tone made it sound as if he was saying something a lot worse. "I'm already shorthanded, so it's not as if I can stake out the house until he either returns or reveals that he's hiding inside. I suppose I could get Kevin to set up some of his cameras to watch all the possible exits."

"You could," I said. "Would you like to check inside the house first? Gloria gave me her key, in case we needed it for anything during the roundup. In fact, keys—her front door key, and also what she called a master key, which I bet means it opens up Chris's and Jennifer's rooms."

"I'd need to get a warrant to search the house," the chief said. "Even if Gloria gives her permission, her tenants have an expectation of privacy in their rooms."

"Who's talking about searching the house?" I replied. "We'd only be doing a wellness check on Chris. After all, there's been a murder across the street, and no one's seen so much as one of his eyelashes since sometime yesterday."

"Except your grandfather," the chief pointed out.

"He saw someone in the attic window," I said. "Maybe he assumed it was Chris. What if he's wrong—what if it was the killer, taking a second victim."

"I think that's a little far-fetched," he said. "But I do agree that it would be a good idea to check on his well-being. Let's clear it with Ms. Willingham first."

He waited patiently while I texted Gloria to ask if she'd heard from Chris, and then exchanged a few texts with her, mentioning our worry about him.

"You've absolutely got my permission to search the whole house for him or anything else you're looking for," Gloria said. "Good heavens—I just want to kick him out. I don't want anyone to knock him off."

"Of course, we still can't search his private quarters." The chief was already texting someone. "But you're right—we should do a welfare check on him. And let's bring Horace—useful to have his sharp eyes for this."

So we waited until Horace had responded to the chief's text. Then we marched across the street, climbed Gloria's front steps, and knocked on the door. When several knocks had gone unanswered, the chief nodded to me. I pulled out Gloria's keys and unlocked the front door.

"Let us go in first." The chief stepped inside and glanced around. "Mr. Smith! Ms. Hodges! Ms. Willingham! Are you here?"

No one answered the chief's calls, so Horace followed him in, and I brought up the rear.

Chapter 23

Gloria's living room didn't have a lot of furniture—a sofa, easy chair, and coffee table that seemed deliberately chosen for their clean lines and small size. A wise choice, since it made the room look larger. Or at least not quite so incredibly small. The tiny dining room found in most of the neighboring houses had been sacrificed to make room for the stairs to the attic bedroom and add a few square feet to the kitchen on one side and the bathroom on the other.

Horace and the chief did a quick search of any downstairs spaces where a grown person could hide, calling out "Mr. Smith!" and "Ms. Hodges!" at regular intervals. I followed them, taking pictures of anything that looked interesting. Which was nosy of me, I supposed, but I could always delete them later if nothing in them turned out to be useful.

Gloria's and Jennifer's bedrooms were both unlocked and easy to tell apart—Jennifer's was an untidy mess, with fast-food containers and dirty clothing scattered everywhere and several glamour shots of its occupant hung on the walls. Gloria's was scrupulously tidy and decorated with a few dramatic prints of

African-themed art, like a scene of three lions and an acacia tree
silhouetted against a glorious sunset. At least downstairs, the only
sign of her male lodger was a pair of large, slightly muddy shoes in
the coat closet. Size thirteen. I took a picture of them, just in case.

Then we trooped upstairs to check out Chris's quarters. At the
top of the stairs was a small landing with one door. Chief Burke
knocked on it.

"Mr. Smith?" he called. "Are you here?"

No answer.

After a minute or so he knocked again. When there was still no
answer, he tried the doorknob.

"Locked." He turned to me. "Of course, it's always possible that
Mr. Smith is injured or unwell. We should make sure he's not
inside. Perhaps we could make use of that key Ms. Willingham
entrusted to you?"

I stepped forward, unlocked the door, and knocked again before shoving it open. Then I stood aside to let the chief go first.

"Mr. Smith," the chief called. "If you're in there, I want you
to know that we're coming in. There's already been one violent
death on this block today—we want to make sure all the other
residents are safe."

No response. Horace was frowning, and I noticed that his hand
was hovering over his service weapon. The chief took a breath,
opened the door wider, and stepped inside.

Nothing happened. I wasn't sure what I was expecting—
gunfire? Explosions? Howls of outrage? A bland computer voice
saying, "I'm sorry, Dave, I can't let you do that"? But everything
was quiet. After a minute or so the chief stepped farther inside
and Horace and I followed.

The room was small. I wasn't sure whether to call it cozy or
claustrophobic. A little of both, maybe. The dormer windows—
two overlooking the front yard and two at the back—gave plenty
of light, but the roof sloped so sharply that I could only stand up

completely straight in a three-foot-wide strip along the middle of the room. I had to admit that Chris had made good use of the area under the low, slanted ceilings, installing a row of gray worktables that lined the walls along both sides. At the far end, near the half-open door to the bathroom, one table contained a hot plate, a toaster oven, and a small collection of dishes, glasses, flatware, and food. A half-height refrigerator was tucked under the table. The rest of the tables were filled with computer equipment. Gloria had been exaggerating—there weren't forty-seven of them. But I did count thirteen monitors that appeared to be on and connected to some kind of CPU and keyboard. And dozens of peripherals and other bits of equipment—a rack containing what I deduced were half a dozen servers. Quite a few battery backups and universal power supplies. Rows of external hard drives. Speakers. Printers. Mice. CDs. Cables snaking everywhere. Dozens of other items that Kevin would probably have recognized in an instant, but that I just had to lump into the category of random computer gear.

"Wow," Horace said. "I hope Gloria was savvy enough to get a separate utility meter installed up here. Because otherwise all this stuff is totally jacking up her electric bill."

"It did," I said. "And she already read him the riot act about it."

The bed—actually a twin mattress laid on the floor and piled with a tangle of grubby-looking sheets and pillows—was along the end wall by the bathroom door. To our left was the door to a closet. The chief opened that and glanced inside. From what I could see, Chris's wardrobe was pretty minimal. And so were all his other possessions, if you took away the computer gear.

"Check the bathroom," the chief said over his shoulder. Horace trotted across the room and peered through the bathroom door. He turned, shook his head, and returned to where I was standing.

The chief was leaning over, studying the half dozen shoes on the closet floor, though without touching them. Two pairs of athletic shoes and one of Doc Martens. All black, all large—I could see that at least one pair was size thirteen, like the shoe Squeaky had found. No singletons, though.

Curious, I walked over and peered into the bathroom. Definitely more claustrophobic than cozy. The toilet was under the slanted part of the roof on one side—I wondered how many times Chris had absentmindedly stood up and bumped his head on the ceiling. On the other side, the shower was also under the slant, so anyone my height or taller would have to crouch to use it.

And no place in the tiny bathroom for Chris to be hiding.

I stepped out again. It occurred to me that if Kevin saw the contents of this room, he might be able to get an idea of what kind of computer work Chris did. So I pulled out my phone and, as I walked slowly back to the door, I snapped several dozen pictures of Chris's computer setup.

"I could have sworn I heard someone up here," the chief said.

"The house is about eighty years old," I said. "Or is it ninety? Old enough to have a lot of creaks and noises."

"True," the chief said. "He must have gone out the back door when we weren't looking."

"Maybe you should check to see if his van is still there," I suggested.

"Pretty sure it is," Horace said. "I booted it."

"Booted it?" The chief looked startled. "We don't have any grounds to do that."

"Actually, we do," Horace said. "Five unpaid parking tickets."

"Really," the chief said. "How interesting. Well, we'll catch up with him sooner or later."

Just then I heard a faint noise. A noise that seemed to be coming from behind the front wall. And it occurred to me that when Gloria had done the renovation to turn the attic into a bedroom, she'd have wanted to make use of every square inch of space in her tiny house. The shortened walls on either side of us defined the shape of the room—but there was almost certainly space behind them—a long, low, triangular-shaped space under the eaves that could easily be transformed into storage. I bent down and peered under the computer tables that lined the front of the room. Yes! Hidden under the tables were two half-height doors, one at each end of the short wall. One was held closed with a simple wooden latch. The latch on the other was open. I glanced at the opposite wall and saw two more small doors. Both of them were latched, though. If Chris was hiding—and I was starting to suspect he was—it would be behind that unlatched door.

I focused back on it.

"Let's go downstairs and strategize," I said. But as I said it, I put my finger to my lips and pointed, in an exaggerated fashion, at the door I was watching.

The chief frowned and opened his mouth to speak. Then he realized what I was doing and bent over to look under the tables. He glanced back and forth between the two doors and nodded.

"Yes," he said. "It's a little stuffy up here. Let's discuss our next move downstairs."

I mimed stomping vigorously. He nodded.

"But shouldn't we—" Horace asked.

"Downstairs," the chief said. Loudly. And he led the way out of the attic, gesturing to Horace, who looked puzzled but followed him. "I have some ideas about what we should do next. You brought your forensic gear with you, right?"

The two of them were descending the stairs. The chief was making rather a lot of noise. Horace just followed him, looking puzzled. I stopped just outside on the landing, in a spot where I could peer inside the room without being readily seen from the unlatched storage door.

"We should check the house for fingerprints," the chief was saying. "It's entirely possible that the killer looked for Mrs. Smetkamp inside the house before locating her out in the shed."

Horace said something in reply, but he wasn't really trying to be loud, so I didn't catch his words.

I heard a faint creaking noise and saw a flicker of movement in the attic room. I flattened myself against the wall outside.

A figure appeared in the doorway—a pale young man dressed all in black—black T-shirt, black jeans, and black Doc Martens. His hair was dark brown—not quite black—and looked disheveled, as if the last time he'd washed it he'd gone to bed before it was quite dry. And greasy enough to suggest the washing had been rather a long time ago. His face was shadowed with stubble, but he didn't quite have the panache to carry it off—I fought the impulse to shake him and order him to either grow a beard or shave properly. He was about my height—five ten or so—but not a particularly impressive figure. His body was rather paunchy, while his limbs were thin. No muscle tone. I waited to see what he was going to do—close and lock the door again? Sneak out? For now, he seemed to be trying to hear what Horace and the chief were saying downstairs.

Time to do something.

"Why, Mr. Smith," I said, loudly enough for the chief and Horace to hear. "We almost missed you."

He started, stared at me for a few seconds, then reached for the knob as if to close the door. Unfortunately for him, I'd stuck my foot in the doorway. The door bounced off it. He looked around as if trying to decide whether to retreat into the room or push past me. But Horace and the chief were already running up from the ground floor.

Chris retreated back into his room, looking around wildly, and I more than half expected him to try to escape through one of the dormer windows.

The chief strode into the room.

"Mr. Smith," he said. "I don't think we've met before. I'm Chief Henry Burke. I'm investigating several incidents that have occurred here on Bland Street the last couple of nights. I'd like to interview you to see if you can shed any light on them."

"I had nothing to do with it," Chris said.

"Nothing to do with what?" the chief asked.

"With whatever it is you think happened."

I wasn't buying it, and I could tell the chief wasn't, either. Chris was sweating and gnawing on his knuckles and didn't seem able to meet the chief's eyes.

"I'm not accusing you of being involved in either incident," the chief said. Was it just me, or did his tone add "not yet" to that statement? "But I'm interviewing all of the residents of this block, in the hope of finding some information that will be useful to my investigation. Would you be willing to come down to the station to talk with me? It's quieter there," he added, since just then the fire engine's siren went off. Presumably the firefighters were testing it. Or maybe giving some of the younger spectators a thrill.

"I don't know anything useful," Chris said. "I don't get out much and I hardly know any of the neighbors."

"Then it won't take long," the chief said, in a tone that suggested he would be delighted if his interview with Chris proved short. "But I would appreciate your making the time to talk to me."

That last bit suggested that if Chris didn't make the time, the chief would find a way of doing it for him. Reluctantly, Chris followed us out and locked his room door. Then he shot a venomous glance at me. At the hand in which I was still holding the master key.

"Gloria lent me her keys so we could check on you and Jennifer," I said, tucking the key in my pocket. "She was worried. I'll let her know you're okay."

He didn't answer—only turned and sullenly followed Horace and the chief downstairs.

I brought up the rear. I was tempted to stay behind. Wait until the chief, Horace, and Chris had gone down to the station and use the master key again to search Chris's room. But he seemed to be watching me suspiciously, and it occurred to me that if he was as reclusive and paranoid as he seemed, he might have laid traps that would let him know if people had been snooping. Threads or hairs strategically placed across doors or drawers. Faint siftings of flour around the objects on the desk.

"Meg, can you lock up the house after us?" the chief called, when I was halfway down the stairs.

"Can do," I replied.

Downstairs, I did a quick final walk-through. Okay, I was doing a little snooping. If anyone questioned me, I'd say that I was checking to make sure we weren't leaving anything out of order. Or at least no more out of order than it had been when we arrived. Clearly motherhood had altered me—I had to repress the urge to tidy Jennifer's little hellhole. Even a quick pickup—trash in a trash bag, dirty clothes in the hamper, dirty dishes to the sink—would have done wonders. But I wasn't Jennifer's mother, thank goodness. It had been years since either Josh or Jamie had left their rooms in anything like this condition. Michael and I must be doing something right.

And it wasn't likely that Horace or the chief had disarranged anything. They'd looked pretty carefully inside any open drawer or cabinet, but they'd been careful only to look, touching nothing except the doors of closets, which were large enough to conceal a body.

An example I should probably follow. So I stepped out of the front door and locked it behind me.

Chapter 24

I stood on Gloria's front porch and surveyed the neighborhood. The fire truck was gone. Some of Randall's workmen were loading most of the borrowed tables and chairs into a pickup. Two women were standing on the sidewalk in front of Mrs. Peabody's house, having an animated discussion. I recognized them as Garden Club members, although I drew a blank when I tried to remember their names.

I was about to head in a different direction—not that I had anything against either of them, I just didn't want to get sucked into a gossip session about the murder or the turkeys. But I saw a vehicle come to a stop at the end of the street. Cal Burke hopped out of the driver's seat and moved one of the construction barriers out of the way. One of the lurking firefighters jogged over to replace the barrier after Cal had entered the block.

Okay, he must be going to someplace on the block. Now could be my chance to tackle him.

As his car approached, I spotted Mother sitting in his passenger seat. Cal drove sedately past me and brought the car to a stop by the garden ladies. He even made an almost successful attempt to jog around the front of the car in time to open Mother's door. But Mother hopped out briskly and sailed over to where the two Garden Club ladies were.

I strolled in their direction. It was on the way to my car anyway. Cal was leaning against the Jeep, waiting. I suspected his grandmother had drafted him to haul Mother around for the day—although she was perfectly capable of driving, she loved being driven. I'd pay my respects to the Garden Club ladies and then ask Mother if it would be okay for Cal to help me for a few minutes. Then I could try to confirm my suspicion that he'd participated in the turkey prank and talk him into confessing to his grandfather.

I found the ladies engaged in a lively discussion of a plan for restoring Mrs. Peabody's yard to its pre-turkey condition. Pre-turkey and pre–*Marvelous Mansions*.

"After all, she is a club member, you know," the taller one was saying.

"Of long standing," Mother added, acknowledging the point with a graceful nod.

"Unfortunately, she doesn't get to many meetings," the shorter one said.

"Not her fault, of course," the taller one said. "She doesn't drive and she's shy about asking for rides."

"We need to be better at inviting her," Shorter said.

"But she always says she doesn't want to be a bother," Taller replied.

"Then we need to arrange rides for her," Mother said. "And convince her that she's needed at the meetings."

"What if we recruited her to the refreshment committee?" Shorter suggested.

"Perfect," Mother said. "You know, even if she wasn't a member, I'd have proposed that we take up restoring her garden as a civic project. It's too much for anyone, having to clean up after a disaster like this."

She made a sweeping gesture that took in the whole of Mrs. Peabody's yard. Disaster was the right word for it. The birds had clawed apart the neat brick walkway, presumably to get at insects underneath. They'd dug up the small, neatly mowed patches of grass, no doubt for the same reason. And all her neat, tidy, old-fashioned flower beds were a shambles. What the turkeys hadn't eaten they'd shredded. No wonder she'd been so willing to stay at our house. I wasn't anywhere near the gardener she was, but the sight of her yard depressed me.

"You just want to get the place back in shape before they have the judging for the Beautiful Block contest," Shorter said to Taller. "She lives on the corner," she added to me, pointing to the house that had hosted our headquarters during the roundup.

"I'll mention it to Randall," I said. "Maybe he can push back the judging a bit." And maybe I should ask the chief if he'd considered the residents of rival Beautiful Block contenders as suspects in the turkey prank. "Of course, you won't be able to get started until the chief gives his okay. He'll want Horace to work it as part of the crime scene."

"Well, that's not really a problem," Taller said. "It could take a while to gather all the plants we'll need."

"She has—well, had—some wonderful heritage plants that will be hard to replace," the shorter one said.

"We will do whatever we can to replace them if they cannot be rescued," Mother proclaimed, in her Joan of Arc voice.

"And we're going to have to wait until all the turkey . . . er . . . droppings have broken down a bit," Taller said, glancing up at Mother as if to see whether "droppings" was sufficiently euphemistic. "A good thing hers was a well-established garden. Not too many new plants to be harmed by the stuff."

"Harmed?" I echoed. "Turkey droppings aren't good fertilizer, then?"

"Oh, they're excellent fertilizer," Shorter said. "Very high in nitrogen. But too rich for tender young plants—it would burn them."

"If she had any tender young plants, the turkeys gobbled them up," Taller added.

"So does that mean in the long run, the turkey droppings will be a silver lining?" I asked. "What about the Smetkamps' yard? Do you have a plan for that?"

Mother, who was tolerating but not participating in the discussion of fertilizer, turned back and frowned. Both of the other women stiffened slightly and looked uncomfortable. Evidently the Smetkamps were not club members.

"I was talking to Myra Lord," I went on. "I gather she has been trying for years to talk Mrs. Smetkamp into getting rid of some of the more invasive of her alien species. It looks to me as if their whole yard will have to be redone anyway. Maybe if you came up with an attractive plan for redoing it with native species, you could help eliminate what I gather is a neighborhood environmental menace."

They all exchanged a look and then they relaxed and smiled.

"Myra is a gem," Mother announced. "I am sure she can come up with a plan."

I'd be willing to bet Myra already had a plan, whether or not she'd ever tried to sell Mrs. Smetkamp on it.

"And it won't be all that bad," Taller said. "I mean, we wouldn't be dealing with *her* anymore."

"And he's quite nice, actually," Shorter said. "Reg, that is. Never complains, no matter how many thankless jobs she piles on him."

"And look at how much he helps Emma," Taller added. "He's been a very good neighbor to her. But won't the television people be redoing the yard along with the house?"

"Not if we can help it," I said.

That made them both smile, and Mother nodded her approval.

"Are we kicking them out of town?" Shorter asked.

"We may not need to," I said. "I suspect the *Marvelous Mansions* people may be rethinking their involvement in the makeover. They may prefer not to be associated with a house in which a murder has taken place."

"I thought she was killed in the shed," Taller pointed out.

"You're correct," I said. "Make that a house in whose yard a murder has taken place. I bet right now they're looking for any loophole that will let them drop the project."

"Without cleaning up after themselves?" Mother pointed to the half-ruined house. "We're not going to let them do that to our neighborhood and just walk away, are we?"

"Of course not," I said. "But do we really trust them to fix things up? Much better to figure out how much it will cost for us to fix it up—and by us, I mean the Shiffley Construction Company—and hold their feet to the fire until they cough up the money."

"That's good," Taller said.

Shorter nodded vigorously.

"I'm sure Festus would be delighted to help with that," Mother said. "One of our lawyer cousins," she added to the ladies.

"I plan on suggesting him to Mr. Smetkamp," I said, and Mother beamed her approval.

"And, of course," Taller said. "I bet the chief will want them to stay in town until he's made sure none of them had anything to do with the murder."

"Or have any useful information," I added, in the interest of defusing negative gossip about the rank-and-file television crew.

Mother took out her cell phone, gave us all a nod and a smile, and walked a few feet away, either to answer a call or make one. I kept my eye on her. If she showed signs of leaving—and taking Cal with her—I'd interrupt.

"Poor Reg," Shorter said, with a shake of her head. "To lose his wife, and then have to deal with all this at the same time. And I never got the idea he was all that keen on the makeover."

"Maybe he'll just sell the ruins back to Creeping Charlie," Taller said. "And let him deal with it."

This sent them both into giggles.

"Creeping Charlie?" I asked. "Isn't that a weed?"

"Yes," Taller said. "*Glechoma hederacea*. A very aggressive alien invasive species, and quite difficult to get rid of because of its extensive root system. But it's also our nickname for Charles Jasper."

"Always creeping around," Shorter added. "Spying on what's going on in the neighborhood and telling people if their grass is too long or they haven't taken their trash cans back from the curb."

"People generally?" I asked. "Not just the Smetkamps?"

"Oh, yes," Taller said. "He harasses everyone. You'd think we had a homeowner's association and had elected him to enforce the rules. I thought he'd never stop harassing the Patels after they turned their front yard into a pollinator garden. And he used to nag Darlene Browning about reseeding her lawn and keeping her kids off the grass so it could grow in."

"Until she gave him a piece of her mind," Shorter added. "My, that was a day to remember."

They both giggled.

"You know, the chief should talk to him," Taller said. "If anyone was going to spot anything suspicious going on around here, it would be Creeping Charlie."

"Knowing him, he's probably already down at the station, telling the chief who he thinks did it and what he should be doing about it," Shorter said.

"And if anyone can handle him, the chief can," I said. "But I'll make sure he knows."

The Garden Club ladies chuckled at that and went back to their restoration plans.

Mother was tucking her cell phone back in her purse and heading my way.

"Meg, dear," she said. "Do you happen to know where the chief is? Minerva hasn't seen him for hours."

"Probably down at the station," I said. "I just helped him locate and apprehend someone."

"A suspect?" Mother asked. "Or a witness?"

"No idea," I said. "A person of interest, at any rate. So what do you need to talk to the chief about?"

"Nothing," she said. "But I think Cal Burke is finally ready to tell his grandfather that he was one of the people responsible for bringing the turkeys to Bland Street. It would be nice if we could find the chief before the boy loses his nerve."

"I love it when you take care of impossible chores before I even have the time to write them into my notebook," I said. "How did you figure out Cal was involved?"

"I didn't," Mother said. "The boys did. And they called me to say that they knew you could talk Cal into telling his grandfather, but they also knew you were so busy with the murder and the turkeys that they didn't want to dump anything else on you, and did I think I could give it a try?"

"Did you tell them, everything I know about persuasion and diplomacy I learned from you?" I asked.

"Of course not, dear," she said. "I just told them I'd take care of it. And also how proud I was of them for trying to help their friend." She smiled and headed back toward Cal's Jeep. He leaped to attention and managed to open her door this time.

I was watching them drive off when Horace appeared, carrying something—a brown paper evidence bag.

"Meg," he exclaimed. "Just the person I need. Can you help me with something?"

"Sure," I said. "What's up?"

"We're going to try tracking the owner of the shoe," Horace said.

"Cool," I said. "Is Dagmar bringing Piper?" Dagmar, Darlene's twin sister, had a black lab whose tracking abilities were much in demand.

"Unfortunately, Dagmar and Piper are off on the Appalachian Trail, trying to find some missing hikers," Horace replied. "But that's okay—we've got Winnie and Whatever."

"And Watson," I added.

"No, I told them to leave him out at your house," Horace said. "Winnie and Whatever are getting pretty good at general tracking. Watson only wants to find dead people, and you already did that. Oh good—here they are."

Aida's cruiser was coming to a stop in front of Mrs. Peabody's house.

"Did you bring them both?" Horace called.

Instead of answering, Aida hopped out of her car, came around to the passenger side of her cruiser, and opened the rear door a few inches. I spotted a pair of Pomeranians excitedly ricocheting around in the back seat. Aida reached in, snagged one, and handed it to me, along with a dog lead.

"Put the leash on Winnie and hang on to her," she said. "I'll get Whatever ready."

Winnie belonged to Rose Noire and Whatever was Aida's own dog. The two girls barked when they heard their names and wriggled or bounced even more wildly, but Aida finally succeeded in clipping the leash to Whatever's collar while I took care of Winnie. The chief, who had arrived during the battle, was observing with a slight frown on his face. I felt sorry for Mother, who might have been able to collar the chief if I hadn't sent her dashing down to the station. Should I call and tell her to return? Or text?

"If we're going to do this, let's get started," Aida said.

"If you're sure it's a good idea," the chief replied.

"It's not as if they're going to use up the scent." Horace held out his arms and I turned Winnie over to him. "And a few more people walking over the trail won't make it any harder for Dagmar and Piper if we have to bring them in."

"I'll leave you to it, then." The chief headed back to his cruiser. I spotted Cal's Jeep parked right behind it. Cal and Mother were standing nearby on the sidewalk. I deleted the text I'd been typing to Mother.

"How long will this take?" Aida asked, jerking my attention back to the tracking project.

"If you need to be someplace else, Meg can help me," Horace said, with great dignity.

"I'll stay for now," Aida said. "But let's get the show on the road."

We led the dogs through the Smetkamps' yard and carried them over the ladders to Myra Lord's backyard. She waved at us from where she was sitting on her deck, busily typing on her laptop. Horace put Winnie on the ground and handed over her leash to Aida. We all waited, dogs and humans, looking at Horace.

He put on a pair of gloves, then reached into the evidence bag and pulled out the remnants of the black athletic shoe. He held it down at ground level so Winnie and Whatever could sniff it—which they did with great concentration and enthusiasm. We all stood patiently watching as the dogs sniffed.

Actually, Horace looked patient. Aida looked as if she wanted to order the Poms to hurry up. There was a reason Horace was the one who did most of the dog training.

Horace finally pulled the ruined shoe away from the mesmerized dogs, slipped it back into the evidence bag, and said "Go find!"

The dogs spent a minute or so sniffing the air. Then, while Winnie continued to sample the air, as if appreciating its vintage, Whatever started slowly walking in a circle. No, make that a widening spiral. Eventually she stopped dead, sniffed the ground in front of her with great intensity, and uttered a single bark. As if roused from meditation, Winnie trotted over to her sister and sniffed the same bit of ground. Then the two of them took off, pulling so strongly that they almost toppled Aida over.

"I think they've found the trail!" Horace exclaimed.

"Come over here and take one of them, before they drag me off my feet," Aida said.

Horace did so, and I followed along, keeping an eye open to see what I could do to be helpful.

The two dogs were sniffing their way toward the side of Myra's yard, dragging Aida and Horace behind them. For such small dogs, they were strong and fast, and they weren't making life easy for us—especially Horace, who had brought along a bag containing some of his forensic equipment. I strode up to his side and offered to carry the bag for him, which he gratefully accepted. When the dogs reached the fence, they stopped and looked up at us, with peevish expressions on their furry faces, as if to say, "How dare you put a fence in right in the middle of this glorious scent trail?"

Horace and Aida tried to drag them along the fence toward the gate, about six feet away, but the girls wouldn't leave the spot where the scent crossed the fence.

"Let me help," I said. I went through the gate and positioned myself right across the fence from where the Poms had stopped. Horace handed me Winnie's lead, and then lifted her over the fence and into my arms. I put her down and she sniffed the ground and began pulling on the leash, heading away from the fence. I had to brace myself to hold on to her while Horace raced to the gate and joined us. I then repeated the process with Whatever and Aida. Whatever spent a little time sniffing at the place where they'd crossed the fence, as if to reassure herself that we silly humans hadn't pulled some kind of funny trick. Then she trotted over to Winnie. They touched noses and took off.

We were now in the yard with the thriving vegetable garden. I was pleased to see that the turkey wranglers had managed to avoid damaging more than just a few lima bean bushes. I hoped we could make the Poms' passage equally uneventful.

The dogs led us to the far side of the yard and then through the hedge into Mrs. Peabody's yard, on the side farthest from the Smet-kamps' house. They trotted briskly along just inside the property line until they reached the street. They turned to follow the street to the corner, then turned left onto the cross street. They eventually left the road to drag us through more backyards—by the time this whole adventure was over I'd probably have trespassed through every yard in the neighborhood. Then, to our growing excitement, they began tracking their way through a neat though rather minimally landscaped backyard and up to the back door of its house.

"Isn't this Gloria's house?" I asked. I hadn't seen any of the houses on this side of the street from the rear, but this was one of the Craftsman-style exteriors, which were greatly outnumbered by the generic stucco exteriors. There were only three Craftsman houses on this block, and I was pretty sure Gloria's was the only one on this side of the street.

"Yup," Aida said.

The yard was neat and tidy, but definitely minimalist. The small stretches of grass had been recently mowed, but there wasn't much landscaping. The patio's stone pavers were neatly swept, but empty apart from a weather-beaten picnic table and two plastic lawn chairs. The only bit of decoration was a rather obviously artificial ivy vine that ran up the side of the house and ended near one of the dormer windows with a few assorted artificial flowers wired to its tendrils. Probably something Gloria had done as a gag the last time someone had tried to yard-shame her. Maybe I'd talk the Garden Club into installing some simple, low-maintenance landscaping here, too.

Winnie sat down by the back door, looked back at Horace and uttered the short, sharp bark the Poms used to give orders to their clueless humans.

"Good girl," Horace said, as he fumbled in his pocket for the dog treats. He handed Winnie one. "Here," he added, tossing a baggie full of treats to me. "Give Whatever her treat."

I set Horace's forensic bag down and turned to reward Whatever, but she had left the back door and was walking slowly, sniffing the air.

"I'm notifying the chief." Horace had stopped fiddling with his forensic bag and was typing on his phone. "So he can start getting whatever permissions or warrants we need to continue following the scent. Wait—where's she going?"

Chapter 25

Whatever had dragged Aida over to where Gloria's trash can and recycling bin stood. She sat down next to the trash can and barked. I snapped a few pictures of her.

"Good idea, getting the paperwork underway," Aida said. "But maybe we should check this out first. Trash is fair game, remember, once it lands in the outside can. Meg, can you hang on to Whatever?" She handed me the lead.

"Good girl," I said to Whatever, as I handed over the treat. "Very good girl." She gobbled it eagerly, tail wagging. Evidently the treat was considered the right and proper conclusion to her scent work—once she finished inhaling it, she allowed me to lead her away from the trash can so she wouldn't be in the way as Horace and Aida examined it.

Horace handed me Winnie's lead.

"You, too," I said to Winnie. "You're both very, very good girls."

If they had been humans, the solemnity of my tone would have conveyed the message that this was way more than the kind of casual "good girl" they got for stopping something they shouldn't have been doing in the first place. I realized I needed to speak the Poms' language.

"The very goodest of good girls," I said, as I distributed another round of full-sized treats. Maybe some dogs didn't notice if you broke the treats into smaller pieces. I was convinced that the Poms noticed. And judged.

And to the dogs' delight, Horace had brought their favorite treats—a brand of chicken jerky with such a peculiarly strong fishy smell that I always wanted to wash my hands after touching the stuff. The dogs would come running whenever I shouted, "smelly treat!"

Meanwhile, Horace pulled a clean plastic sheet out of his forensic kit and spread it on the ground. He and Aida both donned gloves and began investigating the contents of the trash can, pulling each item out and depositing it neatly on the tarp.

Of course, since Horace was involved—and since this was obviously what he would define as a secondary crime scene—their investigation went at a snail's pace, as they stopped to take pictures of everything before they touched it. I tied the dogs' leashes to Gloria's picnic table and volunteered to handle the photographic part of the program, which speeded things up a little. Gloria got top marks for tidy trash handling—nearly everything they pulled out of the trash can was a neatly cinched garbage bag—large ones for the kitchen waste, smaller ones for trash cans from other rooms. So far Horace was content to examine the still-closed bags. Of course, he might end up having to go through all their contents eventually—but he could probably do that back at the station, with a sink handy for scrubbing up if he encountered anything nasty.

"Oooh," Aida said. "That last bag looks promising."

Horace's expression suggested that he agreed, but he still followed the same methodical procedure of having me photograph the bag in situ and then again once he'd placed it on the tarp.

While I was snapping the last few photos Horace wanted, the chief arrived, no doubt in response to Horace's text. He watched patiently. I wasn't sure if Horace had even noticed his arrival.

Horace knelt down by the tarp and took a deep breath—the sort of slow, steady breath Rose Noire was always advising us to take when we were overexcited and needed to calm down and focus. Then he reached for the bag.

Not a garbage bag—a plastic bag from the Caerphilly Drug Store, with its top tied in a loose knot. Horace untied the knot, reached into the bag, and pulled out a shoe.

"It's a match!" Aida exclaimed.

"Looks similar," Horace said.

"Black leather Nike, size thirteen." Aida was leaning over Horace's shoulder to get a closer look.

"Yes," Horace said. "But more importantly, both this shoe and the one Squeaky chewed to bits show the same telltale wear pattern. Whoever has been wearing them oversupinates."

"Which means he puts too much weight on the outside of his feet, right?" I asked.

Horace nodded—rather absently, since he was still regarding the shoe with an expression of delight.

"Is that going to be useful?" the chief said. "Don't most people wear out their shoes a little unevenly? The foot doctor has me wearing orthotics to correct my pronation."

"Only about a third of people have a balanced walk," Horace said. "And most of the rest pronate. It's twenty times more common than supination. Less than five percent of the population supinates."

"I see." The chief favored the lone shoe with a glance of approval—not quite the look of ecstasy you could still see on Horace's face, but still. "A potentially useful bit of circumstantial evidence, then. Does anyone remember if Mr. Smith supinates?"

Horace and Aida exchanged a glance and shook their heads slightly.

"No idea," Horace said.

"I think he does." I was flipping through the pictures I'd taken inside Gloria's house. "Aha. Here it is." I held up the phone to display the picture I'd taken in Gloria's hall closet. The pair of size thirteen men's shoes was front and center—with one shoe lying on its side to reveal that its sole was heavily worn on the outside edge.

"The very same pattern," Horace exclaimed. He beamed down at the newly found shoe as if longing to pet it. No wonder he got along so well with the Pomeranians. He was probably the only non-canine resident of Caerphilly capable of getting excited over such a smelly and unprepossessing object.

"Of course, we don't know for sure that those are Mr. Smith's shoes," the chief said.

"But you can inspect whatever he's wearing when you talk to him," I said. "Or wait—it wasn't all that long ago that you took him down to the station. Have you finished talking to him?"

"I've haven't even started," the chief said. "By the time I got him downtown, he'd changed his mind about being interviewed. Wanted to leave, and I decided I had enough evidence to charge him with the turkey prank. And he exercised his right to consult counsel before speaking with me."

Was that the reason for the chief's slight air of distraction and annoyance? Or had Cal managed to make his confession?

"So we still have him?" Horace asked.

"He's down at the station in one of my interview rooms, awaiting the arrival of his attorney."

"That's great," Horace said. "We can inspect his shoes. And if we get some of his DNA, we can probably prove that he was the wearer of the shoes Squeaky found."

"One step at a time," the chief said. "First we need to make sure we have grounds for taking his DNA. I'll get the town attorney working on that. Meg, can you send me that photo you took of his shoes? In fact, all the photos you took in Gloria's house."

"Consider it done," I said as I opened up my phone's photo app. "Although, there are a lot of them. Actually it would be easier to do that from a computer. There are a lot of them. I can head back to the house and send them from my laptop."

"Perfect," he said.

Horace and Aida returned to emptying the trash can.

"By the way," I added. "Have you interviewed Charles Jasper?"

"No," the chief said. "I assume you're asking because you think I should—any particular reason?"

"Only that he seems to be the closest thing Bland Street has to a neighborhood watch." I repeated what the Garden Club ladies had said. "If anything suspicious happened at the Smetkamps' house, or anywhere nearby, I bet there's a good chance he saw it."

"Yes, he could be useful." The chief scribbled a few words in his pocket notebook. "I haven't seen him here today, which is a little surprising."

"Maybe he took one look at what the turkeys did to his former yard and went home to recover from the shock," I suggested. "That's what Mother would be doing if her yard had been destroyed— lying in a dark room with a cold compress on her forehead. In fact, she might even react that way if she saw the damage the turkeys have done, in spite of how she feels about Mrs. Smetkamp—maybe I should go and check on her."

The chief chuckled at that, but the mention of Mother's name didn't inspire him to say that he'd just seen her. Then I heard a ding and he reached down to pull out his phone. He glanced at it, smiled, and then glanced over at where Horace and Aida were stuffing the various large and small bags they'd removed from Gloria's trash can into extra-large brown paper evidence bags.

"Unless you need me," he said. "I'm going to head back to the station. I've still got a few of the television people to interview, and with luck Mr. Smith's attorney will have arrived by now."

"We'll be fine," Aida said.

The chief strode off.

"We're finished with the dogs," Horace said. "Meg, could you take them back to your house?"

"I'll pick up Whatever when my shift is over," Aida said.

"Whenever," I said. "If you end up pulling a really long shift, she can stay over. Or you can give me a call and I'll bring her into town."

"Thanks," Aida said. "I'll let you know. It probably will be pretty late."

"If I'm not up, Kevin will be," I said.

"Watson's there, too," Horace said. Not surprising. Both Horace and Aida usually left Watson and Whatever at our house when they were at work, so the pups could hang out with Rose Noire's Winnie and Kevin's Widget. And Tinkerbell and Spike, of course; I'd gotten to the point where the house almost seemed too quiet if we had fewer than half a dozen dogs underfoot.

"Same offer goes for Watson, of course," I said. "Just let me know if you want to pick him up or have me deliver him."

I untied the Pomeranians' leashes from the picnic table and headed for my car.

When I arrived back at the house I took the Pomeranians to the kitchen and turned them over to Rose Noire. She welcomed them home with some of her homemade all-natural pumpkin treats. Watson and Widget, hearing the telltale chink of the treat jar lid, came running and were rewarded for their good hearing.

"How are our guests doing?" I asked.

"They're all in the library," she said. "I just took them some tea and cookies."

"Good," I said. "I'll just stick my head in to say hello."

"If you're going to do that, ask them if they'll be here for dinner," she said. "I forgot to do that. Spaghetti, with both meat and vegetarian sauce, tossed salad, and fresh bread."

"I'll ask."

I grabbed a cookie for myself, returned to the front hall, and then ambled down the long hallway to our library. The library was one of the features of our house that gave visiting architecture professors and students nightmares. It had been added to one end of the house around a century ago by a previous owner who had serious social aspirations and wanted a ballroom. When we bought the house, there had been holes in its roof that let in the rain, holes in the floor that allowed the invading rain to flood the basement, and several resident barn owls grown fat on the abundance of rodents living in its walls. Maybe it was a reaction to seeing the Smetkamps' half-demolished house, but when I walked into our library today, memories of the various stages of its long transformation flooded my mind. Today, it was a beautiful, serene, peaceful place. Floor-to-ceiling bookcases covered most of the walls, including those of the second-story balcony that ran three quarters of the way around the room. The windows and skylights let in so much natural light that we didn't usually need to turn on the lamps until evening. The shelves were half-filled with books—half-filled being a good thing, since it meant we had a lot more space to hold new books before we had to make difficult decisions about which books to keep and which to donate.

When I entered, I noticed that Rose Noire had been doing her best to comfort our refugee guests. New age music was playing through the hidden speakers so softly it was almost subliminal. And a little essential oil diffuser at one end of the room was pumping out a small cloud of mist scented with what I deduced was a calming blend of lavender, orange, and rose.

Gloria was seated at one of the sturdy Mission-style tables, surrounded by books and papers. She glanced up when I entered, gave me a distracted smile, and went back to whatever she was reading.

Mrs. Peabody and Mr. Smetkamp were seated at another table, playing chess with a large set that a woodcarver friend had crafted out of dark and light oak. She seemed about to move her queen—one of my favorite pieces in the set, since the friend had managed to give its face a distinct resemblance to Mother. He was fingering one of the carved unicorns that served as knights. They looked up, smiled at me, and focused back on their game.

Mr. Smetkamp looked calm. Not exactly happy, but remarkably calm for someone who had just lost his wife. Or did he not know yet? Surely the chief would have broken the news by now. Just in case he hadn't, I'd avoid the subject for now.

"Let me know if you think you'll be staying for dinner," I said. "Spaghetti, salad, and fresh-baked bread."

They exchanged a glance.

"If it's not imposing," she said.

"I hate to be a bother," he said. "But since I don't have a kitchen . . ."

"It's no bother," I said. "Rose Noire is cooking anyway, so it's just a matter of telling her how much pasta to throw in the pot."

"Count me in," Gloria said. "And I owe you one. Not just for dinner, for everything. Next time my gran brings me a country ham, I'll tell her to bring a spare for you."

"You're on," I said. "And by the way, the chief is currently interviewing your boarder. Chris, that is."

"Ooh," she said. "What's he done?"

"No idea," I said. "So far, nothing more than behaving suspiciously, although that might just be his natural personality. And given how much time he spends peering out of his windows with binoculars, maybe the chief is hoping he may have seen something useful." I figured the chief would rather I didn't mention the whole thing with the shoes for now.

She nodded.

"I've come to a decision," she said. "If the chief doesn't end up locking him up for something, I'm going to give him notice. Life's too short."

With that she went back to her books. I turned to Mr. Smet-kamp.

"I'm not sure if you've heard," I said. "It looks as if your make-over is kind of up in the air right now. Jared Blomqvist skipped town in the middle of last night."

"Skipped town?" His calm smile vanished. "Why?"

"We don't know yet," I said. "But the chief will be having him brought back."

"How can he leave now?" he asked. "It's the worst possible time—they've torn out the whole inside of the house and haven't even started putting in whatever's supposed to replace it all. And I can't deal with him. Imogen was doing that. There's no way I can do it. I'm no good at that kind of thing."

Evidently the chief had broken the news to him about his wife's murder.

"It will be okay, Reg," Mrs. Peabody said.

"I never wanted the makeover in the first place." His voice was a little ragged, as if the subject of the house opened the gates to let in his shock over his wife's death. "It was all Imogen's idea. I'm not sure what the point would be, going ahead with it when she's not here to enjoy it. Because I certainly won't. I just want them all to go away."

"You need for them to fix the house up first," Mrs. Peabody said.

"And what if they won't?" He shook his head.

"They just need a little firm handling," she said. "I'm sure they can be made to understand that you have no interest in going through with the makeover at a time like this. That you just want your house back in livable condition."

Perhaps she didn't realize how much work it would take to get the house back in livable condition. And firm handling didn't seem like something Mr. Smetkamp was going to be very good at. I had no doubt Mrs. Peabody could manage it, but would she have any influence with the *Marvelous Mansions* people?

"Given everything you've gone through, I'm not sure you should be the one dealing with them right now." I grabbed a pen and a piece of scrap paper from Gloria's table and wrote down Festus Hollingsworth's name and office phone number. "If I were you, I'd get a lawyer to negotiate with them. A tough, no-nonsense one—and if you don't already have one, call my cousin Festus. He's a bulldog of a negotiator. Tell him I sent you and he'll give you the friend-and-family discount."

"Thank you." He stared at the slip of paper for a bit. "Perhaps I should call him now."

"Good idea," I said.

"I'll do that from the sun porch," he said, rising. "Where I won't disturb anyone else."

Gloria hardly looked up.

Mrs. Peabody gave him an encouraging, reassuring smile.

I left them to it.

Chapter 26

As I strolled down the long hall from the library, I texted Rose Noire to say that all three of our houseguests would be staying for dinner.

I arrived in the front hall and felt suddenly rudderless. It wasn't that I had nothing to do—my notebook-that-tells-me-when-to-breathe was full of tasks and projects. But none of them were urgent. And none of them would help us find out who killed Mrs. Smetkamp, identify the person who'd inflicted the turkeys on Bland Street, or fix the mess the television people had made of the Smetkamps' house.

Then it occurred to me that I hadn't yet sent Horace and the chief all the photos of Chris Smith's lair and the contents of Gloria's trash can—which was the reason I'd come home in the first place. Last time I'd seen it, my laptop was in my office, which was back in the barn. I was heading for the back door when the doorbell rang. So I detoured to the front door.

It was Chief Burke.

"Hope I'm not interrupting anything," he said. "But since Mr. Smith is still conferring with his attorney, I thought I'd come and talk with Mr. Smetkamp. He was a little too much in shock this morning when I broke the news to him."

"He seems to be doing reasonably well now," I said. "He's back in the library. With Mrs. Peabody and Gloria, but you can take him out on the sun porch or bring him here to the dining room for a little privacy."

"Thank you," he said. "I know the way."

He headed down the long hallway to the library. I was resuming my course to my office when my phone dinged. I looked down at it. A text from Kevin.

"Who are these people staying here at the house?" he asked.

"Residents of Bland Street who wanted to escape the turkeys," I texted back.

I found myself wondering why he was asking. Normally, Kevin was pretty oblivious to the comings and goings of houseguests. It could be hard to lure him out of his basement lair for family gatherings. Although he did usually notice attractive young women—was Gloria his type?

I could always ask. Kevin did occasionally deign to divulge what he was thinking about.

"Why do you ask?" I texted back.

"You think the chief would be interested in knowing if any of them sneaked out of the house in the middle of the night last night?"

My fingers were already dialing Kevin's number before my eyes had quite finished reading that.

"I assume that means the answer is yes," he said, in place of hello.

"Absolutely." I was striding down the hallway as I spoke. "I'm going to find the chief," I said. "He just came out here to interview Mr. Smetkamp, and I want to catch him before he starts. And of course he'd want to know—why didn't you mention this before?"

"Didn't know about it before," he said. "Mainly because I've been so busy doing other kinds of work on the case. Tracing the emails that recruited those high school kids to help with the turkey prank. Checking all the security cameras anywhere near Bland Street that have online feed. Checking out the social media for Mrs. Smetkamp and all her neighbors, in case she was having any big conflicts with anyone. You know the drill. Since we're pretty far from both crime scenes out here, I didn't get around to checking the feed from our own home security system until just now."

I still had mixed feelings about the security system Kevin had installed. It still felt a little creepy and big brother-ish, having cameras covering the entire yard. But the system had already foiled a car theft and identified the porch pirate who'd been stealing packages from our doorstep. If it helped solve a murder . . .

"So you saw one of our house guests sneaking out?" I asked.

"Two of them. The two senior citizens. Practically tiptoed out the front door at—hang on, let me check. One fourteen A.M. Arrived back at two forty-seven."

"Plenty of time to get to town and back," I said.

"Yup. And looks as if they might have a motive for the murder. You'll probably figure it out when you see them."

"Hang on a sec." I opened the door and burst into the library. Everyone turned, startled by my abrupt arrival.

"Chief, before you start your interview, Kevin has something he wants you to see."

"Yes?"

I gestured for him to follow me out. He did, looking a little annoyed. I made sure we were halfway down the hall—and out of earshot of the library. "Kevin, here's the chief," I said before shoving my cell phone into his hands.

"Yes, Kevin?" the chief said into my phone.

I watched his face as he listened to Kevin.

"Can you send me that video? . . . Yes, so send it to her as well. Excellent."

The chief held my phone out in front of him, in a position

that gave him a good view of whatever video Kevin was sending. I shifted a little so I could see, too.

It was a video from the camera Kevin had installed on the roof of our front porch. I could see our front walk, a stretch of the road that ran past the house, and the small gravel parking area. The parking area held the Twinmobile, Michael's old but well-preserved convertible, and a moderate-sized sedan—possibly a Buick. I noticed a time stamp in the lower right corner—1:14 A.M. The feed from the night-vision camera was black-and-white, but impressively sharp and clear. After a few seconds, a figure appeared. Mr. Smetkamp, stepping down from the porch onto the walkway. He turned and held out his arm. A hand appeared on his arm, then Mrs. Peabody stepped into the picture. She glanced up and smiled at him.

"Good lord," the chief muttered.

I could see his point. That was not the smile of a nice little old lady expressing gratitude for the courtesy of a neighbor. It had heat, that smile.

Arm-in-arm they tiptoed down the front walk, then along the sidewalk until they reached the Buick. They seemed to be fighting to suppress giggles. They stopped by the Buick's passenger door. Mr. Smetkamp held out his car remote and clicked it. How did he manage, with that simple gesture, to conjure up Sir Walter Raleigh laying down his cloak over a puddle so Queen Elizabeth could keep her feet dry? He then opened the door for Mrs. Peabody and held out his arm to steady her. Very courtly and completely proper. When she was safely settled in the passenger seat, she turned her head, as if to thank him—then reached up and pulled his head down for a long, steamy kiss.

"Oh, my," the chief murmured.

After that, Mr. Smetkamp hurried around to the driver's side, got in, and drove off.

The picture went black for a second. Then it returned, although the time stamp had jumped to 2:46. Only the Twinmobile and the convertible were in the parking area, but toward the edge of the screen you could see the flicker of movement that had set off the camera's motion detector. Then the Buick returned and slid into the empty space. We watched as he hopped out, trotted around to the passenger side, and helped Mrs. Peabody out. They walked slowly along the side of the road, then up our front walk, until the porch roof eventually hid their contented, smiling faces from the camera.

"Good work, Kevin," the chief said, before hanging up and handing back my phone. "Probably a good thing I'm going to be talking at greater length to your visitors."

"No kidding," I muttered.

"Mr. Smith still looks good for the turkey prank," the chief said. "But his attorney has already informed me that his client claims to have an alibi for the time of the murder."

"An alibi," I echoed. "Is it believable?"

"Since he hasn't yet divulged it, I have no idea." The chief scowled. "Always possible that he's trying to scare up someone willing to cover for him. Still, even if his alibi turns out to be nonsense, we need to check out those two."

"Because if you don't, his defense attorney could use that fact to create reasonable doubt."

"I have a feeling that his defense attorney will be using those two to create reasonable doubt no matter what I do," the chief said. "I'm assuming if you'd heard anything about this from any of the neighbors, you'd have mentioned it."

"Before we found Mrs. Smetkamp's body, I'd have been discretion itself," I said. "But after that—yeah, I'd have mentioned it. I'd have blurted it out the second you walked into the shed. And so would anyone else in the neighborhood who knew about it. They must have done an amazing job of keeping it secret."

"Indeed," he said. "Well, I'll see what the grieving husband has to say. Don't mention this to anyone else for now."

"Of course not," I said. "And I'll make sure Kevin does the same."

He turned as if to head back to the library. Then he paused and turned back to me.

"Sorry if I've seemed a bit testy," he said. "I only just learned that my grandson Calvin was one of the teenagers responsible for inflicting the turkeys on Bland Street."

"Understandable." I hoped the use of Cal's full name wasn't a bad sign.

"So I'm going to let Judge Shiffley decide what punishment he and the others get," the chief went on. "Although I'm recommending more than a wrist slap."

"He's a good kid," I said. "I'm sure whoever talked them all into it made it sound pretty harmless."

"Yes," he said. "And at least he got up the gumption to tell me himself."

I nodded.

He headed back down the hall and disappeared into the library. Oh, to be a fly on the wall. But at least I could do something useful. I'd drop in to see Kevin, make sure he knew to keep quiet about the telltale video, and then get him to extract the photos from my phone and send them to Horace and the chief.

The Pomeranians came to attention when I entered the kitchen, then relaxed again when they realized I was just passing through rather than dispensing treats. But when I opened the door to the basement, Widget, Kevin's pup, detached himself from the pack and scampered down ahead of me.

I paused at the bottom of the stairs to adjust to the lower light level that Kevin found relaxing. The door to his section of the basement was open, and I could see flickering light inside.

"I have data," I called out. I thought those words would get his attention more quickly than a mere knock.

"Come in."

Chapter 27

Kevin's lair did bear a superficial resemblance to Chris's. A long, wide counter covered one entire wall. On it were more than a dozen monitors, attached to more than a dozen various computers and surrounded by at least a hundred peripherals, gadgets, and assorted bits of hardware. Lights blinked or glowed steadily throughout the room on various bits of equipment. But the space was somehow homier. There were posters on the walls, stacks of books mixed in with the hardware, dog beds on the floor and the counter. Widget and Spike, our eight-and-a-half-pound demon in canine disguise, were sitting side by side on the counter, staring intently at a monitor on which a *Road Runner* cartoon was silently playing.

"Do you actually pick Spike up and put him on the counter?" I asked. People had been known to need ER visits after meddling with the Small Evil One.

"Of course not," he said. "I built a ramp so he can get up himself." He pointed to the far end of the counter. Yes, there was a shallow ramp, Z-shaped, with wide spots at the two turns and a raised guardrail to make it less likely that an impatient dog would fall off while running up it. "Widget likes it, too. What's the data, and what do you want me to do with it?"

"A few hundred photos on my phone." I turned it on and handed it to him. "I want to send a lot of them to Horace and the chief and you, and I figured maybe you might have an easier way of doing it."

"Of the crime scene?" He sounded more interested.

"And of the turkey shenanigans, yesterday and this morning, which just might contain some clue to who committed one or both of the crimes," I said. "And of Chris Smith's room and its contents."

"Aha," he said. "You think that might offer some clue to his identity?"

"No idea," I said. "His space is pretty . . . impersonal." I glanced over at the part of the counter where twelve-inch Xena and Obi-wan Kenobi action figures were doing battle with a pack of similarly sized Ringwraiths and flying monkeys, while Spock and Aragorn, mounted on model motorcycles, rode to their rescue.

"Impersonal. Deliberately so?" Kevin asked.

"No idea," I said. "He's only been there about six months. Maybe he hasn't had time to unpack all his stuff and give it that lived-in look." I settled down in the less disreputable of Kevin's two ancient, overstuffed armchairs—another amenity I suspected Chris's decor would never include.

"Or maybe he's deliberately keeping it impersonal to keep his landlady from finding out anything he doesn't want her to know," Kevin countered. "And deliberately minimalist, so he can stay mobile."

"Doesn't look that minimalist to me," I said. "He's got almost as much computer equipment as you do."

"About the same amount visible, maybe," he said. "Remember I've got those RAID arrays in the storage room. Plus all the stuff down at the office. And—"

"Okay, I was exaggerating," I said. "I'm sure you have way more hardware than Chris. I'm a civilian, remember? A ton of hardware, half a ton—it all looks the same to me."

"Yeah, I can see how his setup would be kind of intimidating." Kevin was peering at one of the monitors, which now showed one of my shots of Chris's room. "But he doesn't have a whole lot of stuff other than the hardware. I bet if he wanted to leave town he could fit the entire contents of that room into a small truck."

"He has a van," I said.

"You see? And yeah, a van would work." Kevin was now studying a slightly different view of Chris's attic. "He's traveling light. Poised for a getaway. Give him an hour to shove everything in his van and he could be a hundred miles from here before we even know he's gone."

I nodded. I could easily imagine Chris waiting until Gloria and Jennifer were gone to make his exit—he'd have had time to figure out their class schedules. He could pull his van into the garage, load it up without anyone seeing him, and vanish.

"Maybe a good thing his van is currently booted due to unpaid parking tickets," I said.

"There are ways to remove those things, you know," he said. "Sometimes you can just deflate the tires and drive right out of it. Or so I've heard," he added, seeing my frown. "And he could always rent another van. Or steal one, if he's really desperate."

"Tell the chief if you find anything potentially incriminating," I said. "Maybe when he lets Chris go he can have him watched."

"Lets him go?" Kevin came to attention at that. "He's in custody? Did he kill the old lady?"

"The chief arrested him for the turkey prank." I explained about the shoe Squeaky had taken from a trespasser, and how the Pomeranians had tracked down its mate in Gloria's trash. "But since whatever misdeeds he committed by dumping the turkeys on Bland Street only amount to misdemeanors, he'll probably be out before too long."

"Then there's no time to lose," Kevin said. "The point is he's not there at the house now. Do you still have the key? You could let me in, and I could see what I can do. Get into his systems, document—"

"Too risky," I said. "When the chief does let him go, I bet Chris will be feeling pretty darned paranoid when he gets home and looking for any telltale signs that someone's been snooping. And that's if he doesn't catch you there, because are you really going to ask Chief Burke to give you a heads-up when he plans to turn Chris loose so you can schedule burgling his office? For that matter, as the official police computer forensic person, isn't it a bad idea for you to be doing something like this? What if the defense finds out? 'Mr. McReady, isn't it true that you took advantage of a borrowed key to gain access to the defendant's computer system without either his permission or a warrant? Your honor, I move that all of Kevin McReady's evidence and testimony be suppressed! My client's Constitutional rights—'"

"Okay, okay." Kevin scowled. "You've made your point. You're right—I can't go in there."

I almost sighed with relief.

"So let me brief you on what you should do when you go in. Get out your notebook."

For the next ten minutes or so, Kevin tried to explain the kinds of things I should be looking for when I sneaked into Chris's office. I was trying to take notes, but I was a little pessimistic about the whole idea. Not to mention daunted by some of the technical terms Kevin was using. It didn't help that he'd set up the largest of his monitors with a slideshow of the pictures I'd taken of Chris's setup, adding visual clutter to my already overwhelmed brain.

"This isn't going to work," I said finally, interrupting one of his explanations. "You keep saying I should look for something unusual, something suspicious, something out of the ordinary—none of this is ordinary for me. How can I flag something abnormal if I have no idea what normal is?"

"Good point." He looked discouraged. "I suppose I could call you. Talk you through it."

"And what if he goes to trial and his defense attorney realizes I'm a mere mortal and would need tons of help extracting clues from Chris's computers?" I asked. "They'd probably figure out who helped me. Heck, they could ask me under oath if anyone helped me. You're going to have to wait until the chief can get a search warrant. And if you can think of anything that will help him do that, don't be shy."

"You're probably right." Kevin didn't sound happy about it. "So I'll just finish extracting all these photos. Should I send them to the police and Horace?"

"Please. And to my computer. And then delete them, so they'll stop slowing down my phone."

Kevin got to work. I whiled away the wait by staring at the slideshow on one of his enormous monitors. Suddenly I noticed something—a detail that had been unreadable on my phone's tiny screen suddenly popped out.

"Done," Kevin said. "You can take your phone now."

"Thanks," I said. "What's PWrangler?"

"PWrangler?" Kevin repeated. "Could be short for PassWrangler."

"Okay," I said. "What's PassWrangler?"

"One of the common password protection programs," he said. "Why?"

"Because Chris has a Post-it note on one of his monitors," I said. "It says PWrangler followed by 'Chris1336' and then a long string of characters. Could it be—"

"A password!" Kevin exclaimed. "His username and password. Where did you see it? Did you take a picture of it?"

"Yes," I said, pointing to the screen. "That's why I'm asking—I just saw it go by. Can you go back a few slides?"

Kevin stopped the slideshow and navigated back through the photos until he reached the one I'd seen. He cropped it to show a close-up of the Post-it note, and we deciphered the slightly fuzzy password.

Kevin then looked up PassWrangler's website and spent a few minutes exploring it.

"This thing stores your data online." He sounded slightly disapproving. "Much more secure to store it only locally."

"But maybe easier to store it online if you might be logging in from a variety of places," I pointed out. "He has over a dozen computers, remember."

"True," he said.

"So give him a lecture on proper computer security later," I said. "And meanwhile see what we can learn from his lackadaisical approach."

He chuckled and went back to his laser focus on his computer's screen.

I sat back and watched as his fingers flew over the keyboard. From what I could tell, he seemed to be setting up his own account with PassWrangler and then . . . testing its capabilities?

"Interesting," he said finally. "They don't seem to use any kind of two-factor authentication."

"Is that a good thing?" I asked.

"It's a good thing for what I'm trying to do," he said. "Not good thing for Chris." Seeing my slightly puzzled expression, he went on. "Two-factor authentication would mean that if anyone—even Chris himself—tried to log in from a computer that's different from the one Chris normally uses, the program wouldn't let them unless they entered a security code. And they'd either text that code to his cell phone or email it to his email account, neither of which I'd have access to. So if I tried to log in, even knowing the password, not only would I still be on the outside, looking in, he'd also know someone had his password, so he could change it, and there would go our chance. But PassWrangler doesn't use two-factor authentication. I can't find any way that it could reveal that someone else had been logging in. Not very smart."

"But very convenient for our purposes."

"True. Of course, maybe a little too convenient. It's always possible that this is a decoy." He was frowning at the PassWrangler log-in screen, his fingers poised over the keyboard. "I set up something like this once. I was trying to get into someone's email—nothing illegal, just a prank. Long story."

"Of course," I said.

"Anyway, I sent him an email with a link that went to what looked like his usual log-in screen but was actually a very good copy. When he tried to log in, it captured his password, sent it to me, and then logged him in to the real thing. And it's possible to set up a log-in so it not only gives you fake data but also installs malware or spyware in your machine. That's what I'd do if I were really paranoid."

"*If* you were really paranoid?" I said. "Trust me, you are. Pass-Wrangler's a legitimate password manager, right? And you navigated to it yourself—you didn't use any links that would take you to a fake site. And you're on your own machine that Chris has never had access to. So unless Chris has hacked PassWrangler or is in cahoots with them—"

"You're right. I'm overthinking it." He took a deep breath, then carefully typed in the sixteen-character password we'd copied from the photograph. He reached out and scratched Widget behind the ears—something I'd seen him do before. Something he seemed to do for luck. Then he hit return.

The next few seconds seemed like a century.

"I'm in," he said.

I started breathing again. Kevin was hunched over his keyboard, his face only inches from the screen, saying nothing.

"So is this going to be useful?" I asked, when a minute or so had gone by.

"Useful? It's golden. The keys to the castle."

"So you can get into all his stuff."

"Some of his stuff. Maybe. Eventually. Right now it would be pretty stupid to try to get into anything unless I'm positive it wouldn't leave any clue that he could pick up on. But just seeing what he's got access to will tell us a lot. It'll probably take me a little while to figure out everything he's up to. But here's an example—something we should tell the chief about. Old Chris's got the log-in information for the Gmail account that was used to recruit those high school kids to help move the turkeys."

"Can you log in and see what else he's up to?" I asked.

"Bad idea," he said. "Not wanting to leave clues, remember? Google definitely does use two-factor authentication. So on top of me probably not being able to get in, he'd know someone was trying to."

"Good thing you're the one doing this part, not me," I said.

He smiled, nodded, and focused back on the screen. I watched for a few minutes. He seemed to be mostly staring at whatever he'd found in PassWrangler. Occasionally he'd scroll up or down, or toggle over to type something in another window.

Widget padded over to Kevin, hopped down into his lap, and curled up for a nap. He probably knew from long experience the signs that Kevin would remain nicely immobile for quite some time, making his lap a prime spot for prolonged and undisturbed napping. Spike didn't seem to mind being deserted. He remained glued to his cartoons, growling occasionally when the screen showed a closeup of Wile E. Coyote.

I pried myself out of the dilapidated chair, retrieved my phone from the counter, and began tiptoeing out of the room. Then I realized that Kevin wouldn't even have noticed if I'd marched out singing "La Marseillaise" with a military band accompanying me. I climbed the stairs without making any special effort at stealth, though I did go slowly, because I was busy thinking.

Chapter 28

Normally, as soon as I'd reached the kitchen, I'd have opened my notebook to today's to-do list and crossed off "send pictures to the chief." Actually, I wasn't sure I'd taken the time to add that item, which meant I'd probably have written it in just for the satisfaction of being able to cross it off. But instead, I stood in the kitchen, pondering the implications of Kevin's discovery—actually, I could probably call it Kevin's and my discovery, since I'd not only taken the very useful photo of the Post-it note but also spotted its usefulness. If Chris had the log-in information for the Gmail used to recruit Darlene's sons and their friends for the turkey prank, he was probably the ringleader of the prank. Probably? Almost certainly.

Did that make him more of a suspect for the murder, or less? I had no idea what his motive would be—but then his motive for the turkey prank wasn't exactly obvious, either. It might be that he merely thought dumping the turkeys in someone's yard would be hilarious and had only picked the Smetkamps' yard because it was directly across the street from his lair, making it easy for him to enjoy seeing the results of his handiwork. If that was the case, Mrs. Smetkamp getting murdered the very next night was a monumental bit of bad luck, not only for him but also for the chief, who'd have to do a full investigation of him along with all the others who seemed to have a motive.

But what if he'd deliberately chosen the prank location to get back at Mrs. Smetkamp? If that was the case, it could be crucial to find out what his motive was—because what if the same motive had led to the murder? It was hard to think of anything she could have done—or that Chris might imagine she'd done—that could reasonably inspire first a stupid if elaborate prank and then a vicious murder. But then I found it hard to think of anything that could reasonably inspire murder under any circumstances. Murder was profoundly unreasonable. It was one thing, after yet another maddening interaction with Mrs. Smetkamp, to mutter "I could kill that horrible woman!" I'd done that a time or two myself. But it was quite another thing to actually do it.

Unless you were crazy. Obviously, I didn't know Chris well enough to opine on whether he was sane or bonkers. I doubted anyone in town did—not even Gloria. If he was a psychopath or a sociopath—one of these days I'd let Dad explain the difference to me—then all bets were off. He could be killing for something that seemed trivial to a normal person. Or something imaginary. For example, Gloria had mentioned that Mrs. Smetkamp had been asking her nosy questions about Chris. What if she'd also interrogated Chris directly and somehow hit a nerve?

But what could she possibly have said or done that would do that?

And what if the prank wasn't just a prank? What if whoever had done it—we didn't yet know for sure it was Chris—had deliberately planned to use it as part of a murder plan? A plan to create chaos and distraction that would help cover his tracks when he slipped across the street to carry out his homicidal intentions.

If I'd learned about Chris's connection to the prank an hour ago, I'd probably have made a beeline for our library to see what I could learn about him from three people who knew as much about him as anyone in Caerphilly—Gloria, his landlady, and Mrs. Peabody and Mr. Smetkamp, two of his nearest neighbors. No chance now of talking to the last two—even if the chief released them after interviewing them, he probably wouldn't appreciate my butting in. I could always see what else Gloria knew. Not just about interactions between Chris and Mrs. Smetkamp, but also about Mr. Smetkamp and Mrs. Peabody. Had they managed to pull the wool over the eyes of all the neighbors or was their affair an open secret on Bland Street?

Bland Street. I could go back there and strike up conversations with some of the neighbors. Darlene seemed to have a good idea what was going on in the neighborhood. Myra Lord might have noticed more than just what invasive plants Mrs. Smetkamp was growing. And if Charles Jasper really was constantly haunting the neighborhood, he might have noticed something. Yes, a visit to Bland Street might be useful.

The neighbors had also had ringside seats for what *Marvelous Mansions* was up to, so they might have some idea if the friction I'd observed between Jared and Mrs. Smetkamp was just noise in the universe or if it had been heated enough that it could have inspired murder.

And the television people. It occurred to me that I hadn't heard from Randall. Had he found someplace for them to stay? If he hadn't, I might need to help out. Preferably not by offering to put them up here. Taking in a few neighbors was one thing; hosting an entire television crew who might be stranded here for days . . . no. If it came to that, maybe I could talk Ekaterina into giving them a day's grace. And even if Randall had found them a place, I should drop by and make sure they're settled in. See if they needed anything. Or knew anything that would help us figure out what Jared was up to.

I was still standing in the kitchen, debating whether to head for Bland Street to gather information or tackle some of the items already in my notebook, when Rose Noire dashed in.

"The chief took Emma and Reg downtown for questioning," she exclaimed.

"I figured he would," I said.

"But why?" She sounded indignant. They'd spent a night under our roof—they were our guests. She was in full mama bear protective mode.

By way of an answer I pulled out my phone and showed her the video Kevin had pulled from our security cameras. I had to smother my laughter as her indignation gradually changed to astonishment.

"Oh, my goodness," she said. "They're . . . involved! Does that mean they're suspects?"

"Well, technically, he always was," I said. "The spouse is automatically the first person they look at when someone's murdered. The chief just didn't spend much time looking at him because we knew he was staying out here and assumed that gave him an alibi. Now, of course . . ."

"I can't imagine either of them killing anyone." She looked stricken. "They're such nice people. They have very nice, gentle auras."

"I have a hard time imagining it myself," I said. "But Mrs. Smetkamp wasn't the least bit nice. I can very easily imagine him wanting a divorce. What if she wasn't cooperating?"

"She couldn't actually stop him from getting a divorce, could she?" Rose Noire asked.

"I don't think so," I said. "But I bet she could create all kinds of obstacles if she wanted to. She could object to the terms and delay things, run up his lawyer bills. And I'm pretty sure you have to be separated for a while before you can get a divorce, and they're still living together. Were, I mean."

"They could have been occupying separate bedrooms."

"And that would be hard to prove. A he-said, she-said situation."

"Perhaps his relationship with Mrs. Peabody is relatively new," she said. "And he hadn't yet had the chance to break the news to his wife that he wanted a divorce."

"Or perhaps he hadn't yet gotten the nerve to bring up the subject," I said. "He's pretty . . . mild-mannered."

"And she's an ogre." As soon as the words were out of her mouth, Rose Noire gasped and covered her mouth with both hands. "I can't believe I just said that. What a very . . . negative thing to say."

"Accurate, though," I said.

"You can't go around calling people names," she said. "It's so . . . harsh."

"Especially not dead people that everyone thinks you should be feeling sorry for," I said. "How about this: she was a very forceful personality, and he's not. That's not harsh, is it."

"No." She sighed. "And it is accurate. Those poor people. They're going to have to go through all the interrogation and scrutiny that comes with being murder suspects. And even if—even *when* the chief arrests the real killer and proves their innocence, they will always have the memory of this hanging over their relationship."

"And after they survive it together, their relationship will be that much stronger," I said.

"Let's hope so." She still looked troubled. "I'm going to go and make some desserts."

Some people ate when they were stressed or distressed. Rose Noire cooked. Or gardened.

"Putting in my bid for crème brûlée," I said. "Meanwhile, I'm going to head into town. See if I can find out anything else that will help the chief with this."

"Yes," she said. "You need to do all you can to help dispel the unjust suspicion against them." She nodded and drifted into the pantry.

Interesting. I had a hard time imagining either Mr. Smetkamp or Mrs. Peabody hurting anyone, not even the massively difficult Mrs. Smetkamp. And Rose Noire approved of their auras. I didn't exactly believe in auras, but I had a good deal of confidence in Rose Noire as a judge of character.

I hoped we were right.

I dropped by the library, planning to talk to Gloria before I left. Unfortunately, she wasn't there. All her books and papers were there, suggesting that she'd be back sooner or later.

I decided to give it a few minutes, in case she'd gone to the bathroom or something. And while I was waiting, I pulled out my phone and called Randall.

"What's up?" he asked.

"Did you find a place for the television people?" I asked.

"I did indeed." He sounded pleased with himself. "You know my cousin Jeanine."

"The real estate agent?"

"That's her. She's got a house that's been on the market awhile, mainly because the price the owner wants for it is completely unreasonable, even by Caerphilly's standards. She's going to let the television people stay there until the chief says they can leave town, which he promises won't be more than a few days."

"And the owner's okay with it?"

"Jeanine offered to reduce her fee if he went for it."

"That's generous of her."

"Actually, it probably won't cost her anything. She figures he's about to dump her and move on to another agent. She's the third one he's had trying to sell the thing. She figures the lower fee will keep him happy for a few weeks—plus she planted the notion that maybe one of the television people will fall in love with the place and want to buy it."

"I don't think any of them could possibly afford it," I said. "They all seem too young and broke to be buying houses. I mean, they're worried about paying their bill at the Inn."

"Yeah, but the owner doesn't know that. He's got the naïve idea that anyone with any connection to movies or TV must be rich. Anyway, they'll probably have gone home by the time he decides to fire Jeanine and move on."

"Nice," I said. "I should probably go over and see how they're settling in."

"And see if they know anything that would help solve the murder?"

Was I that transparent?

"That, too," I said. "I'm really hoping it turns out to be Jared, instead of the latest suspects the chief just took downtown to be interviewed." I explained about the video.

"Holy cow! I didn't see that coming."

"I don't think anyone did," I replied.

"I'm having a hard time imagining either of them stabbing Imogen Smetkamp," Randall said.

"Rose Noire says they both have nice, gentle auras," I said. "Let's hope she's right. So where did you put all the television people?"

"Five eighteen Thaddeus Court," he said.

"Isn't that in Westlake?" No wonder Jeanine was having trouble selling the house. Westlake was full of McMansions with manicured lawns whose residents were mutinous that the town kept rejecting their attempts to transform their neighborhood into a gated community. There was only a limited market for houses that enormous—especially since the owners usually expected to sell them at even more enormous prices.

"Eight bedrooms, media room in the basement with theater seating, Olympic-sized pool, hot tub—"

"Okay, I no longer feel the least bit sorry for them," I said. "But how come the construction workers get tents and the TV people get Westlake?"

"The construction workers are out there, too, now," he said. "They seem to be getting along just fine with the TV people, now that Jared's not among them."

"Good," I said. "Maybe I'll still go out and make sure they're all settling in okay."

I let Rose Noire know where I was going and waited long enough for her to pack a picnic basket full of cookies and scones for the television people. And then I took off for town.

I was heading for Westlake. I really was. But while I was picking my way through the outskirts of town, to avoid the tourist traffic, I noticed an out-of-town police cruiser. From Stafford County. I knew the chief had borrowed some deputies from neighboring counties to help with the turkey roundup, but I didn't recall him mentioning Stafford as one of them.

And it occurred to me that if you took I-95 up to Washington, D.C., you drove right through the middle of Stafford County. Which meant it was one of the counties Jared might have to travel through on his way to Dulles.

So when the cruiser made a right turn onto the street where Caerphilly's police station was located, I made the same turn. I didn't follow it all the way into the station parking lot, but I did pull to the curb and watch. The cruiser parked near the front door and two uniformed deputies got out. They retrieved a prisoner from the back seat—Yes! It was Jared!—and escorted him into the station.

I was torn. I knew I should be celebrating the fact that they'd apprehended him. Uttering my silent thanks to the Stafford County Sheriff's Department for bringing him back to face whatever charges the chief was going to be filing against him. And waiting patiently to find out what he'd actually done, whether he'd seen anything useful, how the turkeys had ended up on Bland Street, who had committed the murder . . .

Patience was never my strong suit. I was a lot better at doing than waiting.

I spent ten or fifteen minutes parked there, trying to think of a reason to go into the police station. If only I'd extracted the photos from my phone myself. I could have put them on a flash drive and delivered that to the chief. But then I wouldn't have spotted the Post-it note with Chris's passwords.

The only excuse I managed to come up with for going into the station—and it was definitely an excuse, not a reason—was that I could take in the basket of baked goods and pretend Rose Noire had packed them as a thank you to the police, for all the overtime they'd been putting in during the mini crime wave on Bland Street. Rose Noire wouldn't mind—in fact, she'd be delighted to have her cookies and scones shared even more widely and would gladly pack another basket for the television people. But the chief would almost certainly see through it.

I was still pondering this idea when Randall's truck pulled up next to me.

"You going into the station?" he asked.

"Only if I can think of a plausible excuse so it won't be totally obvious I just came to kibitz and pick up gossip," I said, opting for honesty.

Randall burst out laughing so hard that he let up on the brake for a second and his truck lurched a foot forward.

"Come along inside with me, then," he said. "I actually do need to talk to the chief about a couple of things. For starters, I found something he might find useful. Figured I'd drop by and tell him about it."

"Not sure that gives me an excuse to tag along."

"No, but you'll find it interesting. And you are a part of the other thing I want to consult him about—finding out what we can do to put Bland Street back together and what we need to leave alone till he finishes investigating all the crimes. Since you'll probably be helping out with whatever we can do—"

"You're on," I said.

I started my car again, followed his truck into the parking lot, and strode beside him to the station door—bringing the basket of baked goods with me.

Chapter 29

Inside the station we found Sammy, one of the deputies, talking with two unfamiliar uniformed deputies. I could see Randall eyeing them curiously.

"From Stafford County," I explained in an undertone. "They just delivered Jared Blomqvist."

"Excellent," he said. "Maybe I should go over and express our official gratitude for their assistance."

I nodded to George, the civilian staffer who was running the front desk and set the basket on the counter.

"From Rose Noire," I said.

He gave me a thumbs-up and grabbed a chocolate chip cookie. I leaned against the counter to watch Randall at work.

The chief appeared in the door that led back to the rest of the station. He handed a stack of papers to George.

"You looking for me?" he asked, turning to me.

"Randall is," I said. "I came along with him. He has some questions about what, if anything, we can do to help get Bland Street back to normal."

The chief nodded. Noticing the basket, he grabbed a cookie.

Randall had reached into his pocket and was giving both of the Stafford deputies the familiar bright-red pig-shaped cards that would get them each a free pulled pork sandwich at the Shack, which was run by another batch of Shiffley cousins. He was very free with those gift cards, and the Shack didn't mind, now that they'd figured out that in addition to the small fee Randall paid them for the cards, the free eats definitely led to repeat customers. In fact, their business had picked up so much that long-standing customers were getting a little testy about how hard it was to get in these days. As a result, the Shack's owners were about to open a second location, not too far from the first so they could share the same kitchen. But the whereabouts of the new restaurant, the Secret Shack, would be revealed only to the locals. I'd already been sworn to secrecy.

"Come on back," the chief said. "Randall can join us when he finishes charming our guests."

He said that both to me and to George, who nodded. I followed him back to his office.

It was a little less tidy than usual, which showed how very busy he'd been. I settled into one of his guest chairs while he sat down in his desk chair with a tired sigh.

His reading glasses were pushed up onto his forehead. He took them off entirely, set them on the desk, and rubbed his eyes. He looked exhausted. Not surprising, given how early he'd been up and how hard he'd been working.

I felt a sudden intense desire to fix everything. Solve both of his cases—no, he'd rather do that himself. Bring him the vital clues that would let him solve them. Yeah, that was more like it.

Although just maybe the most helpful thing I could do was to not get in his way.

"I guess you've got a full house over there in the jail," I said.

"Not quite a full house," he said. "Aida's finishing up some routine paperwork with Mr. Smetkamp and Mrs. Peabody, and we'll be sending them home pretty soon."

"On their own recognizance?"

"That only really applies if I'd arrested them for something," he said. "Technically they're still just persons of interest. Apart from not having an alibi, we don't have anything against them."

"They'd have a motive," I pointed out.

"So do a lot of people where our highly unpopular victim is concerned."

"True," I said. "Are they going to need a ride back to my house?"

"Possibly," he said. "Although probably only to collect their belongings. I gather they're planning to stay at her house tonight."

"Should be easy to keep an eye on them there," I said. "Since last I heard you still had someone guarding the crime scene."

"And it's not as if either of them is a serious flight risk."

I nodded. I was trying to find a polite way to suggest that perhaps he was taking them a little too lightly. Just because they were senior citizens, longtime Caerphilly residents, and pleasant people did not automatically clear them of murder.

"Just to be on the safe side, I got Kevin to set up his cameras to cover all possible exits from her house," he added. "And in addition to the guard at the Smetkamps' house, my deputies will be driving through the neighborhood rather often. In case you were thinking I was not taking them seriously enough as suspects."

"I should know better than to doubt you," I said. "I really hope they didn't do it. I like them."

"So do I," he said. "But until I can either definitively clear them or get solid proof that one of the others is the killer, we'll be keeping an eye on them."

"And the other two will be staying in jail, I hope. Chris and Jared."

"They'll be having bail hearings first thing in the morning," he said. "Mr. Blomqvist will be staying put, at least in the short term. He has multiple warrants in Illinois for grand larceny and wire fraud, but the Rockford Police Department is being very co-operative about letting us keep him until we determine if he's the killer. Murder does take priority over financial crimes, regardless of how far-reaching they are. And Kevin just texted me to hang on to Mr. Smith no matter what, because the FBI might want to talk to him."

"The FBI?" I echoed. "Why?"

"Kevin hasn't yet divulged that yet," he said, sounding slightly irritated. "And I didn't have the time to interrogate him. He hasn't said anything to you about it, has he?"

"No," I said. "I'd offer to see what I can get out of him if I thought he'd actually tell me something."

"Most of the time I appreciate Kevin's thoroughness," he said. "Right now I'm just hoping he realizes that I don't need a fully developed, bulletproof case against Mr. Smith. I just need enough to make sure we can hold on to him as long as we need him."

"What about the shoes?" I asked.

"Your grandfather's lab is working on the DNA," he said. "And Cal gave me some useful information just now. He said—without prompting from me, mind—that toward the end of the roundup, he heard the ringleader let out a really salty exclamation."

"Using some of those words you can't say on TV?" I asked.

"Using most of them, I should think," the chief said. "Turns out the guy was walking around in his stocking feet at that point and stepped on a board with a nail in it."

"Oooh," I said. "That means the ringleader would have a tell-tale wound in his foot. Can't you inspect Chris for that? Or would the judge have to force him to show his foot?"

"Assuming he ever finishes conferring with his lawyer, we can ask to see his foot, and if he refuses we can try to get a judge to force him. And obviously if anyone wants to prove he wasn't the ringleader, all he has to do is show me his soles. All the high school kids were happy to do that. I've seen a lot of naked feet today."

"Don't you sometimes get frustrated with all the hoops you have to jump through to get your job done?"

"Sometimes," he said. "But then I remind myself that those hoops represent our constitutional rights, and trying to skip them leads to unjust convictions. And it's okay. With luck we should be able to figure out which of our suspects is the killer before we have to either release them or extradite them for whatever other crimes they've committed."

"Luck?"

"Luck, and a lot more sleuthing, and maybe a little help from the cell phone tower records I've requested," the chief said. "All four of our suspects are on record as having been someplace nowhere near Bland Street when Mrs. Smetkamp was murdered. Even Chris said as much before he lawyered up. So if anyone's phone pinged the closest tower to Bland Street during the critical time period, I'll be having a heart-to-heart with the owner."

"A lot of other cell phones will be pinging that tower," I said. "It's a populated area."

"Yes," he said. "Not as many as there would be in daytime, but still, just being in the area won't be any kind of proof that someone's the killer. Especially for residents. But if someone has already given us a statement that they were somewhere else at the time of the murder and their phone shows up on Bland Street instead—that would take a little bit of explaining."

He smiled. Randall appeared in the doorway, bearing a plate of Rose Noire's cookies.

"Sorry, Chief," he said as he set the plate on the chief's desk and eased into the second guest chair. "Wanted to make sure the Stafford cops knew how much we appreciated them."

"No problem," the chief said. "Meg tells me you want to talk about Bland Street. Do you—"

"Chief?" Aida appeared in the doorway.

"Excuse me for a minute." The chief went over to the door. He and Aida exchanged a few words in an undertone. He nodded, she turned and left, and he returned to his chair. He was frowning.

"Bad news?" Randall asked.

"Unfortunately, I may end up having to release Mr. Smith before too long," the chief said. "To my complete astonishment, it appears that he may actually have a valid alibi for the time of the murder."

"An alibi for the whole time between midnight and four in the morning?" Randall asked. "Should be interesting."

"Apparently, he went over to Clay County and had a few drinks at the Clay Pigeon." Did the chief realize that he'd wrinkled up his nose slightly at the name of our sister county's notoriously sleazy drinking establishment?

"That'd only cover him through the state-mandated closing time," Randall pointed out. "Which was still two A.M. last time I checked. And while I have no difficulty believing that the Pigeon plays fast and loose with the state drinking laws, I doubt if anyone in Clay County is going to testify under oath that the place was open past the legal closing time. No way they'd want to get the owner into hot water."

"Since nearly everyone who was there is probably related to him," I said.

"And more importantly, he's the sheriff's uncle," Randall said.

"All true," the chief said. "But whatever they do normally, when there's an outsider present, they tend to follow the rules, on the off chance he might be an undercover investigator for the Alcoholic Beverage Control Authority."

"So what was he doing there?" Randall asked. "Especially from two to four A.M.?"

"Drinking by himself in a corner," the chief said. "Until closing time, when he reached for his wallet to settle his tab and found it was missing."

"Nice to know they gave him the full Clay County experience," I said.

"So he went down the block to the sheriff's office to report the crime," the chief went on. "Someone from the Pigeon followed him and tried to get him arrested for failing to pay his bar tab. And they were down there, trading accusations and filing reports and pressing charges until someone showed up at the sheriff's office with a wallet he claimed to have found in the Pigeon's parking lot."

"Chris's wallet?" Randall asked.

"Yes." The chief grimaced slightly. "Had his driver's license but was minus both of his credit cards and most of his cash. Only just enough left to settle the bar bill."

"Bit of a coincidence, that," Randall said.

"Indeed," the chief said, deadpan. "Luckily for him, the booking process had enough witnesses, along with a sufficiently robust number of time-and-date-stamped electronic records, that he was able to demonstrate that he didn't leave Clay County until after dawn."

"Not the killer then," Randall said.

"No chance they're protecting him for some reason?" I asked.

"Probably not," the chief said. "Vern's over there right now, documenting the alibi."

"Good," Randall said. "Somehow he manages to get along okay with the Clay County folks."

"He gets along with them very well indeed," the chief said. "He called the station just now to let us know that so far they're all sticking to their story. In spite of the fact that I don't think they liked Mr. Smith that much. Initially, they dropped some broad hints that if we didn't want him to have an alibi, Vern should just let them know what time they wanted him unaccounted for."

"And they wonder why that tourism campaign of theirs failed," Randall said.

"You have to admit that 'Come Play in Clay!' wasn't exactly a world-class advertising slogan," I pointed out.

"Vern managed to convey the idea that no, we'd actually be fine if Mr. Smith's alibi *was* solid."

"So if the alibi is genuine, Chris's not the killer," I said.

"That's a big if," the chief replied.

"Can't you still hold on to him for the turkey prank?" Randall asked. "He still looks good for that, doesn't he?"

"He does indeed," the chief said. "In fact, he's already under arrest for that. I only invited him down here to interview him about both crimes, but when he got here he balked, and since the evidence that he'd organized the prank was good and getting better all the time, I charged him. And let him call his lawyer."

He glanced at his watch, from which I deduced that he was getting impatient.

"Can't he refuse to talk?" Randall asked.

"At this point, I'm betting that's just what he's going to do," the chief said. "And while I have no doubt that Judge Shiffley would be quite happy to deny bail to a homicide suspect with no real ties to the community, she'll probably set bail for the turkey prank, since so far we've only identified misdemeanors to charge him with on that. And I'm betting if we let him out we'll never see him again."

"Would grand larceny be enough to hold him?" Randall asked.

"Depends on the judge's mood," the chief said. "It wouldn't hurt. What is he supposed to have stolen?"

"Probably several thousand dollars' worth of someone else's electricity," Randall said.

Chapter 30

"That sounds promising," the chief said. "But how do you know this?"

"I was looking at some of Meg's pictures of them finding his other shoe in the trash can," Randall explained. "I noticed something weird in the background. So I went over to check it out. Found a heavy-duty electrical cable running up the side of Gloria's house and into the attic."

"An electrical cable?" I echoed. "Was it sort of camouflaged by a very fake plastic ivy vine?"

"That's it," Randall said. "Disappears into the ground by the foundation, and I haven't yet figured out whether he's stealing from one of the neighbors or directly from Dominion Energy. Got my head electrician over there to see if he can figure it out without our digging up Gloria's whole backyard. Either way, he's stealing power."

"But surely not enough to amount to grand larceny," the chief said. "It would have to be at least a thousand dollars for that."

"Gloria told me her electrical bill was up nearly eight hundred dollars the first month Chris was living there," I said. "And she complained, and later he told her he'd found the problem and fixed it, and her bill went back to normal."

"That's what she told me," Randall said. "Looks like that cable is the way he fixed it—she hadn't even noticed it was there. And if something he's doing sucks power at that rate, he'd hit the grand larceny mark after maybe a month and a half—two months, easy. He's been there for six, so it's probably well over that by now."

"That's promising," the chief said. "But what could he possibly be doing that uses so much power?"

"That used to be one of the clues you'd look for that some-one was running a marijuana farm inside their house or barn," Randall pointed out. "Between the grow lights and the need to optimize the temperature and humidity, those operations were real power hogs."

"They still are," the chief said. "But they're legal now—at least if you get a grower's license."

"And the licenses are pricy," Randall said. "Something like ten thousand dollars. The reason I know is that a cousin of mine is thinking about getting into the business, and the family's discussing if we're going to help him out with all the up-front expenses. But I bet a lot of people just skip the formality of a license."

"True," the chief said. "But we've been inside Mr. Smith's quarters, remember. No sign of cannabis cultivation—unless Ms. Willingham has a basement we didn't see."

"No," Randall said. "None of the houses in that neighborhood have basements. And the bogus power cable definitely runs up to the attic. Must be something else."

"I'll see if Kevin has any ideas about what Mr. Smith could be up to that would use that much power." The chief was scribbling in his notebook. "Meanwhile, how soon can you find out who he's stealing power from?"

"Like I said, my head electrician's over there now. And I'm

working on getting Gloria's permission in case figuring it out requires digging."

"Good." The chief was typing rapidly on his phone. "But don't start digging until I can get Horace over there to document what you're doing—it's a crime scene, remember. I'm texting him now."

"Roger." Randall saluted and stood up. "I'll head over there."

"Before you go," I said. "Did you give the television people gift cards for the Shack?"

"No," he said. "Drat. I should have."

"Let me have a handful," I said. "And I'll be sure and tell them it's from you."

Randall handed me a sheaf of the red pig cards, then ambled out.

"What do you suppose Chris was doing over in Clay County?" I asked, as I tucked the cards into my tote. "Call me paranoid, but what if he's up to something?"

"That thought had occurred to me," the chief said. "I'm going to send Vern back this evening to see if he can charm any more information out of them."

"It would be interesting to know if he was meeting with anyone," I said.

"Witnesses at the Pigeon said he was all by himself," the chief said. "And maybe—just maybe—they were telling the truth." He tilted his head. "Are you thinking of anyone in particular?"

"No," I said. "But I'm trying to think of reasons for Chris to drive all the way over to Clay County. He wouldn't have to do it just to get a drink—there's a couple of places in town that would still be serving till two."

"Only the Caerphilly Inn and that new place over by the bus station," he said.

"The Nameless Bar," I said.

"Yes," he said. "You'd think they'd have gotten around to nam-
ing it by now."

"They did," I said. "That's what they named it. The Nameless
Bar. I think it's meant to be edgy and ironic."

"Ah," he said.

I didn't have to point out that for its intended clientele—
Caerphilly College students—calling the place the Nameless
Bar probably enhanced the impression that it was a disreputable and slightly dangerous dive bar, a holdover from a rougher,
pre-gentrified incarnation of the town. Actually, it was only a few
years old, and had been decorated, surprisingly, by Mother. Her
workmen had spent countless hours implementing its deliberately seedy downscale decor—creating hundreds of water rings
on the bar and the tables, beating all the furniture until it looked
so rickety and shabby that no self-respecting thrift shop would
take it, and hurling bricks and bowling balls at the walls and floor
until they looked as if the place had seen hundreds of bar fights.
Never had I seen a better example of Mother's motto that, as a
decorator, she tried to express the customer's taste, not her own.
It was actually quite entertaining to watch the students going into
the place, some furtively, as if embarrassed to be seen in such
unprepossessing premises, others swaggering boldly into a place
that even Chief Burke had pronounced as—in the immortal
words of Douglas Adams—"mostly harmless." And the college of-
ficials secretly approved of it, once they'd figured out that with it
nearby, the more rebellious students who wanted to go slumming
no longer had any reason to brave the more authentic dangers of
the Clay Pigeon.

"I can't see him carousing at the Inn," I said. "But if he merely
wanted a drink in a dark, dank atmosphere, the Nameless Bar
would be a lot more convenient. So far, meeting someone's the
only reason I could come up with for going to the Pigeon. I mean,
it wouldn't be for the beer or the food."

"Or the company."

"Or the ambiance."

"In short," he said, with a smile, "there is no reason for a sane person who doesn't live in Clay County to voluntarily visit the Clay Pigeon. I found out that every time Vern has to go over there as part of an investigation, he comes home, takes a long hot shower, and then goes over to Judge Shiffley's farm to spend a few hours watching old movies and hanging out with all her hounds. Gets him back in a good mood."

"He needs a dog of his own," I said.

"He doesn't think that'd be fair to a dog, with the crazy hours he keeps."

"I know," I said. "But he could do what Horace and Aida do and leave the dog with another dog owner while he's at work. Heck, he could leave his pup with us if he picks one that gets along with Tinkerbell and the Pomeranians."

"And Spike," the chief added.

"No one gets along with Spike," I said. "But he hasn't killed anyone yet."

"You've sold me," the chief said. "Why don't you work on Vern? The man needs a dog."

I thought of pointing out that maybe Vern was the best judge of whether he was ready for a dog. After all, I had Michael, the boys, and Rose Noire to help out with the care and feeding of our dogs. Vern lived alone. And while he was welcome to drop a dog off at our house, was he going to want to do that, day in, day out?

But the chief was frowning at me, so I pulled out my notebook and entered a new task: talk to Vern about getting a dog.

"I'm not going to bulldoze him," I said. "But I'll make the suggestion. Getting back to Chris—it's always possible that he felt the sudden need to get out of the attic but is so antisocial that he didn't want to run even the slightest risk of encountering anyone he knew."

"Meeting someone there seems more likely," the chief said. "Someone he didn't want to risk being seen with."

"In that case, the joke's on him," I said. "Having his top-secret meeting in a place where he and whoever he was meeting would be the only strangers and would stick out like a pair of sore thumbs."

"Unless whoever he was meeting was a Clay County resident," the chief said. "In which case the locals will probably protect their own and claim Mr. Smith drank alone all evening." He was writing in his notebook again. "We'll see what Vern can find out. Now that's odd."

He had glanced down at his phone and was now staring at it, frowning.

I repressed the urge to ask "what?" Either he'd tell me or—

"Kevin just texted to say he's on his way to town to see me," he said, looking up from his phone. "He says the information you gave him did the trick. What information?"

"Those pictures I took of Chris's attic," I said. "I asked him to send them to you."

"He did." The chief glanced over his shoulder at the laptop perched on the credenza behind him. "So far I haven't seen anything earth-shattering in them."

"One of the pictures showed a Post-it note stuck to one of Chris's monitors," I explained. "When we enlarged the picture we were able to decipher a password."

"To anything interesting?"

"To Chris's online password manager," I said. "So, in theory, Kevin has the passwords to everything interesting. But at least when I left, he hadn't started using any of them yet, because he doesn't want to set off anything that would let Chris know we have his passwords. Still, the password manager will make it easy for Kevin to do his investigation, once you get a warrant to search Chris's attic and computers—"

"*If* I get a warrant." He glanced at the *Star Wars* clock on the wall of his office—a Father's Day gift from his grandson Adam. "I called Judge Shiffley just now, and she was over at the beauty salon, getting her hair done. She promised to let me know when she was back at her office to hear my request for a warrant. It would be nice if—"

The vintage intercom on his desk squawked to life.

"Chief, Kevin McReady's here to see you."

"Send him in."

Chapter 31

"That was quick." The chief turned back to me. "Here's hoping whatever he's got makes the warrant a no-brainer."

"Does the fact that Chris lawyered up help at all?" I asked.

"It's not supposed to," the chief said. "It doesn't mean he's guilty. Only that he's not a complete fool."

Kevin strode in with an air of suppressed excitement that I found encouraging. The chief's expression suggested that he felt the same way. Kevin threw himself into the other guest chair.

"You've still got him, right?" His expression was anxious. "You didn't let him go? Because the FBI's definitely going to want to talk to him."

"If you mean Mr. Smith," the chief said. "I still have him. He's currently meeting with his attorney."

"Still?" Kevin seemed surprised. "What could be taking so long?"

"Maybe he's got a lot of crimes to confess," I suggested.

"Actually, he probably does," Kevin said. "But would he really want to spill the whole thing to a small-town public defender? He probably needs a hotshot big-city attorney."

"Attorney-client privilege applies just as much to a small-town public defender as a hotshot big-city defense attorney," the chief said. "And as a matter of fact, he didn't go with one of our public defenders. He's got a very seasoned—and expensive—criminal defense attorney from Richmond. Just what do you think he's done?"

"Well, among other things, he's running a password-hacking farm."

Kevin said this dramatically, and with a note of triumph. I deduced that this meant Chris was the cyber equivalent of Jack the Ripper. Or at least Bernie Madoff.

Our subdued reaction probably disappointed him.

"That sounds bad," the chief said, after a pause. "Just what is it? And why is the FBI interested?"

"You probably want the layperson's version," Kevin said.

"Always," I replied.

"You know, right, that no password is uncrackable," Kevin began. "I mean, even if you go for the maximum length, which is usually fourteen or even sixteen characters, and choose a completely random string of characters, someone could eventually figure it out by trying one option after another."

"But that would take a long time, right?" the chief said.

"Depends on how long your password is," Kevin said. "There are about a hundred characters to choose from, counting lower and upper case, numbers, and all the punctuation marks and stuff. So if you only had a one-character password, someone could crack it with a maximum of a hundred tries—or an average of fifty tries. When you go to two characters, the maximum number goes up to ten thousand tries. With sixteen characters, do you know how many possible combinations there are?"

The chief and I both shook our heads.

"It'd be in the octillions," Kevin said. "More than thirty digits. Maybe even the nonillions."

"And those are still crackable?" the chief asked.

"Only with some serious computer power," Kevin said. "Which is what Chris's got. One of the pictures Meg took showed something that I took at first for a rack of servers. But—I'm going to skip all the technical stuff that would put you to sleep here— it's actually a rack of machines set up for password hacking. He's crammed an immense amount of high-powered hardware into each of them and he's running some kind of password-guessing software on them twenty-four seven."

"What does he do with the passwords when he gets them?" I asked.

"Sells them. To bad people. Probably on the dark web."

"This does sound like someone the FBI might be interested in," the chief said.

"Especially since he just might fit the profile of someone they've been trying to catch for a long time," Kevin said, nodding. "For this and a bunch of other things, including some that are pretty nasty. If it's illegal and you can do it online, he's probably done it."

I had the feeling Kevin was getting just a bit stressed by the effort of explaining this to us in layperson's terms. He wasn't leaning back in his chair but sitting on its edge, watching the chief, and occasionally glancing at me. It occurred to me that he would be much happier once he got to talk to whoever at the FBI would be interested in Chris. People who spoke his language.

An idea occurred to me.

"Would these hacking servers use a lot of electricity?" I asked.

"Tons of it," Kevin said. "If he's doing it in Gloria's attic, her power meter would be spinning like a pinwheel in a hurricane. I'm really surprised she hasn't noticed the increase."

"She did," I said. "And complained, and he took care of the problem by running a power line from someplace else up to his room."

"He probably tapped directly into the Dominion Power lines," Kevin said.

"Probably," the chief said. "Horace and Randall are over there documenting that."

"Is there any way you can get his fingerprints?" Kevin asked. "If he's who I think he is, the FBI got his fingerprints when they tried to raid his place six months ago, and if they could compare them to—"

"We already have his fingerprints," the chief said. "We took them when we booked him for the turkey prank. And if George hasn't already uploaded them to IAFIS, he will soon. Is—"

"Can you also send them here?" Kevin grabbed a Post-it note from the pad on the chief's desk and scribbled something on it—an email address that ended in fbi.gov. He handed it to the chief. "This is my contact in the FBI's cybercrimes unit. She'll be over the moon if this turns out to be her guy."

"I'll go get George on it." The chief stood and left the office. His face was impassive, but he was moving faster than usual, from which I deduced that he was at least a little enthusiastic about Kevin's information.

Kevin was still sitting on the edge of his seat and jittering one leg in what looked like impatience.

"Relax," I said. "Chris's still here, talking to his lawyer. He's not going anywhere before the chief can notify the FBI."

"Yeah, I figure," he said. "But I need to get back so I can start doing the forensics on those two phones."

"What two phones?"

"Our geriatric lovebirds," he said. "I told the chief I could probably use their phones to prove they were where they said they were when the murder was taking place."

"And just where did they say they were?"

"They drove down to where the road dead-ends at Caerphilly Creek and parked behind the Spare Attic." He snickered softly. "Just where all the high school kids go. I think if I was going to lie, I'd make up something less embarrassing."

The chief returned.

"Mr. Smith's fingerprints have been uploaded to IAFIS," he said. "And emailed to your FBI contact. And would I be correct in assuming that Smith will probably turn out to be an alias?"

"One of many, I suspect," Kevin said. "I'm not sure I actually know his real name. I'm going to head back home. Work on those phones."

"Sounds good," the chief said. "Thanks."

"And I'm going to head over to make sure the television people have everything they need in their temporary quarters," I said.

On my way over to Westlake, I felt a momentary pang of guilt for having given away the basket of baked goods. In fact, halfway there I pulled over long enough to text Rose Noire what I'd done and warn her not to ask the television people how they liked the cookies. She immediately replied that she would pack another basket for me to take to them tomorrow, and Michael was picking up the boys at the zoo, and if I was hungry I should hurry home because she was serving dinner at six and the boys were already reported to be ravenous and Gloria had brought home leftovers from the New Life Baptist potluck lunch.

I almost turned around and headed home immediately. But I was curious to see what kind of palatial quarters Randall's cousin had found for the television people. So I stuck to the plan. I could use dinner as an excuse to leave whenever I wanted.

And it really was one of the nicer houses in Westlake. Unreasonably big, like most of the houses in the neighborhood, but a lot less over-the-top than most. I found the television people all gathered around the pool, eating pizzas from Luigi's, our favorite local Italian restaurant, and sipping red and white wines from the recently established Caerphilly Winery. They seemed a lot happier than they had the last time I'd seen them. And happy to see me.

"Have a slice!" Maddy said, waving at the patio table on which the pizza boxes were stacked. "Best pizza I've had in a long time,"

"Ever," one of the others corrected.

"I would if I wasn't on my way home to dinner," I said. "I just came by to make sure you all had everything you needed."

"We're fine," one of them said.

"Do you know if they've caught Jared?" Maddy asked.

"Yes," I said. "I just saw him escorted into the police station."

A few of the television people emitted small cheers or greeted the news with fist pumps.

"Do they think he's the killer?" Maddy asked.

"No idea yet," I said. "But whether or not he is, he won't be coming back to work on the project anytime soon. They'll be extraditing him to Rockford."

"Knew he was up to something there," a crew member muttered.

"Serves him right," another added.

"I hope he gets what's coming to him for that," Maddy said. "But I'm not sure he's a killer. Have they looked into that guy across the street?"

"You mean, the vampire dude?" another crew member asked.

"Vampire dude?" I echoed.

"The really pale one who doesn't usually come out in the daylight," Maddy explained. "But either he's up all night or he sleeps with his lights on. I've never been there when they weren't on. The second night we were here I had to go back at two in the morning because I realized I'd left my phone at the site, and when I got there all his lights were on."

The vampire dude was Chris Smith, obviously. I thought of explaining that yes, Chris was already down at the police station, not only under arrest for the turkey prank but also under serious suspicion in the murder case and whatever crimes the FBI wanted him for. But I wasn't entirely sure of the ethics or etiquette involved—was it altogether appropriate to reveal that someone was being arrested or interrogated before the police made it public knowledge? What if it turned out that Chris was innocent after all?

"I'm sure the chief has looked into him," I said. "If for no other reason than that he's right across the street from the crime scene."

"Yeah," Maddy said. "And was probably awake whenever it happened."

"That, too," I said. "Was there any other reason to look at him in particular?"

"They had a big blow up a couple of days ago," she said. "Him and Mrs. Smetkamp."

"Exactly what happened?" I tried to keep my tone matter-of-fact, rather than revealing how very interesting this news was.

"It was like the second day we were here," she said. "We were all having a production meeting inside Mrs. Peabody's garage. You know, the lady next door, the nice one who's letting us make use of her space on account of the Smetkamps' yard being so small."

"I know her," I said. "And yes, she's very nice."

"The garage door was open," she said. "And I was sitting next to it and happened to see the vampire guy drive off. He has a really old brown van, like he bought it secondhand from UPS or something. And Mrs. Smetkamp saw it, too, and a minute later she said she was tired and had a headache and needed to lie down and we should call her if we needed her. And we were all relieved, because it was like impossible to get much done with her around. And when she left, she closed the garage door after her. So we'd have some privacy, she said."

I nodded my encouragement.

"And I was thinking that was kind of a weird thing to say, so I stood up and looked out of the windows in the garage door. And she didn't go back to her own house. She went across the street. To the house where the tall, chic African American lady lives."

"That's Gloria," I said. "Chris—vampire guy—rents her attic."

"Yeah, we didn't figure there was any way those two were a couple," Maddy said. "Anyway, she walks up to the front door, tries the knob, and goes right in."

"That's odd," I said.

"I thought so, too," she said. "So I kept watching. About twenty minutes later, the brown van returns and the guy—Chris—gets out and goes into the house. And I kept watching, and a minute or two later they both burst out again. She's running, and Chris is chasing after her, yelling at her about how she's trespassing and snooping and he's going to call the cops on her. I'm not sure what she was saying—she wasn't as loud. But she ran inside her house and slammed the door, and he pounded on it for a while, and then he threw some things at the windows of her house— rocks and pinecones and stuff. And then he kind of stomped back across the street, went inside, and slammed the front door behind him—he'd left it hanging open. She didn't come out again for hours, and I thought of asking her what happened, but she wasn't exactly easy to talk to, you know?"

"Tell me about it," I said. "Did you let Chief Burke know about this?"

"No." She looked anxious. "I wasn't sure it was relevant. Do you think I should have?"

"I tell you what," I said. "I'll let him know about it, and if he wants more information, he'll get in touch."

"Am I going to be in trouble for not telling him already?"

"You were probably still in shock when you spoke to him earlier today." I figured she'd talk more freely to the chief if I gave her an easy out. "He'll understand that. And it is only the first day of his investigation. Don't worry."

"I did tell him about some of the other people she had shouting matches with," Maddy said. "I just forgot about this one."

"Many other people?" I asked.

"Pretty much everybody who came within ten feet of her," she said. "Darlene, the lady next door, and Mayor Shiffley, and the mailman, and that tall scrawny guy who nags everyone about their yards—I guess he's from the homeowner's association."

"They don't actually have a homeowners association," I said. "He's just a freelance busybody."

"Seriously?" Maddy laughed. "Then maybe she had a right to chew him out. But it's pretty hard to think of anyone who didn't go at least one round with her."

"Including me, a time or two," I said.

We both laughed.

"Well, yeah," she said. "But you already knew that."

I made a mental note to remind myself of this moment the next time I felt resentful of Kevin's security cameras.

"Thanks," I said. "This will make it even easier to smooth your path with the chief. I'll just tell him you're worried that you forgot to mention all the people she clashed with."

"Solid!"

I reminded them, one last time, to let me or Randall know if they had any problems or needed anything. Then I cemented my popularity with them by passing out Randall's gift cards and headed back to my car—pulling out my phone on the way. I called the chief from the car and relayed everything Maddy had told me.

Chapter 32

When I'd finished, the chief was quiet for a minute or so.

"Very interesting," he said finally.

"And I'm betting Chris never called to report her for trespassing."

"No, he didn't," the chief said. "Of course, if what Kevin suspects is true, Mr. Smith would probably be actively trying to avoid the police."

"Because if he reported her, you'd talk to her, and he was afraid she'd have seen something incriminating. Something that would blow his cover. I have no idea what."

"If Mr. Smith's misdeeds were technological in nature, I doubt if Mrs. Smetkamp's snooping would enable her to figure them out," he said. "I don't get the sense that she was particularly cyber-savvy."

"But he might not realize that," I said. "He could be like Kevin—more than a little clueless about what ordinary mortals like you and me understand about his beloved tech. What if Chris panicked because he thought she saw something that would have been like a flashing neon sign to Kevin but was just gobbledygook to her. And bumped her off to keep his secret, whatever it is."

"Entirely possible." He sighed. "I should go. George tells me he has a call for me from the FBI."

We signed off. I almost wished he hadn't mentioned the call from the FBI. Now I'd be wondering what was happening with Chris until the next time I saw the chief again, which probably wouldn't be until sometime tomorrow. And I'd just have to keep my curiosity in check.

Unless, of course, I could find out something from Horace or Aida when either they picked up their Poms or I returned them.

With that thought to cheer me up, I headed home.

Supper was relaxing. Restorative, in one of Rose Noire's favorite words. Gloria was still staying with us, the better to be near her research materials, and the goodies she brought home from the New Life Baptist potluck lunch transformed an already satisfactory meal into a feast. On top of the spaghetti, salad, and French bread, we had fried chicken, corn bread, potato salad, green bean casserole, sweet potatoes, black-eyed peas, and macaroni and cheese. And a good thing Gloria'd brought all that, since Josh and Jamie had invited Adam and Eli to come home with them to dinner, and an afternoon of helping Grandfather at the zoo had given them all impressive appetites.

Jamie found a moment to pull me aside.

"Have you seen Grandma recently?" He looked anxious.

"If you're wondering whether she talked Cal into confessing to his grandfather, the answer is yes," I said. "He'll be serving whatever punishment Judge Shiffley comes up with for the turkey pranksters, but his grandfather is pleased that he spoke up."

"That's good," he said. "And Chief Burke doesn't have to know we all had to talk Cal into it, right?"

"You'd be amazed at how well Grandma and I can keep a secret," I said.

He grinned and went back to the table, although I saw him give a quick nod to Josh and another to Adam before returning to his food.

Having the boys around gave us both an incentive not to dwell on the murders during dinner and plenty of other topics to discuss. After dinner, Michael and I spent a lively evening with the boys, playing Settlers of Catan and other favorite board games until Darlene came by to pick up Eli and Adam. And Willie Mays, the Pomeranian the chief's family had adopted.

I was checking to make sure there was food and water down for the resident dogs and the visiting ones who'd probably be staying overnight when my phone rang. I pulled it out and glanced at the caller ID. Aida.

"What's up?" I asked.

"Not much," she said. "I'm stuck here on Bland Street, standing guard while Horace does his forensic thing inside the Smetkamps' house."

"Is that safe?" I asked.

"The asbestos tests came back negative," she said. "And Randall had his crew put in a lot of pillars and braces and everything, so the whole thing won't fall down while Horace is in there. But still, probably a good idea to have someone standing by, just in case. You know how he gets when he's working a crime scene—an armored tank division could sneak up on him. Does that offer to bring Whatever into town still hold?"

"Absolutely," I said. "And have you eaten?"

"Not yet. Not since lunchtime, which was a long time ago."

"I can pack you a dinner basket," I said. "You want Rose Noire's spaghetti or leftover Baptist fried chicken?

"Yes," she said. "Either. Both. And Horace is probably also starving."

"I'll pack him a basket, too," I said. "A basket and a Pom. See you soon."

Out in the kitchen, Rose Noire and Gloria had finished the post-dinner cleanup. I suppressed the guilt I felt at having left them to it. Besides, they were happy, seated across the kitchen table from each other, sipping cups of hot jasmine tea and discussing herbal medicine. Evidently they were planning an expedition to the southwest corner of the state to introduce Rose Noire to Gloria's grandmother, a well-known herbalist.

They interrupted their tea-drinking long enough to grab the two picnic baskets out of my hands and fill them to the brim. Rose Noire even helped me get leashes on the exuberant Watson and Whatever and secure them in the back seat of my car.

I took off for town with a passenger seat full of food and the two Poms alternately bouncing around in the back seat and straining to inhale every molecule of scent emitted by the picnic baskets.

Bland Street was blissfully quiet. When I arrived at the Smetkamps' house, I found Aida sitting outside in her cruiser, filling out paperwork. Ironic that the thing that would have discouraged me from pursuing a career in law enforcement—the high probability of having people shoot at you and having to shoot back at them in return—didn't seem to bother Aida, or Horace, or any of the deputies I knew. It was all the paperwork they had to fill out that they seemed to consider the job's biggest drawback. Then again, maybe they were onto something.

I parked behind her and began the challenging task of untangling Watson's and Whatever's leashes so I could extricate them from the car. Aida spotted me and hopped over to help.

"She behave herself?"

Whatever launched herself into the air in Aida's direction. Luckily this was standard for the Poms, and thus predictable. Aida caught her and cuddled her while I finished the untangling.

"As far as I know," I said. "Rose Noire was on dog duty most of the day. I didn't hear any complaints. You heading out now?"

"I'm supposed to be watching Horace's back while he finishes up the crime scene," she said. "Of course, it should be pretty safe at the moment. Sounds as if the chief's got the killer."

"Or killers." I handed her one of the picnic baskets.

"Or killers," she agreed. "Horace and I have a bet on—I'm backing Chris and he's got Jared. You want to join in? You can have Romeo and Juliet."

"No deal," I said. "I don't think they did it, And Rose Noire approves of their auras."

"Don't say I didn't ask." She chuckled. "Anyway, even if Horace isn't in any danger, someone should make sure he doesn't stay here all night, going down forensic rabbit holes. He said he was almost finished half an hour ago."

"If that's a subtle hint that you'd like me to keep an eye on Horace so you can head home, feel free," I said. "I won't leave till he does."

"Hallelujah," she said.

Just then I freed the last bit of tangled leash, so Aida wished me goodnight, stowed Whatever in the back seat of her cruiser, and drove off.

I grabbed the second picnic basket and headed for the house. Watson stuck close to my side. He was probably coveting the fried chicken.

The front door was open, though the screen door was closed. Closed but not latched. I knocked on the doorframe.

"I brought you Watson," I called. "And some dinner."

"Come on in."

The house was as much of a disaster as the last time I'd seen it. Maybe more, since now various surfaces were coated with fingerprint powder, and the additional braces Randall's crew had added to prop up the roof added to the cramped, cluttered feeling. And it was only dimly lit by the light coming from the door to the kitchen.

Watson pulled toward the kitchen—evidently Horace's voice

was, at least momentarily, even more enticing than the fried chicken.

Horace was sitting on the floor with a clipboard braced against his knees. Paperwork. Beside him was a battery-operated camping light, and I remembered that Randall had had the power to the house turned off, for safety's sake.

Horace looked up with a tired smile.

But to my surprise, instead of running over to Horace, Watson lifted his head, sniffed, then went over and sat down very deliberately in the middle of the kitchen floor. He looked over at Horace and barked once.

Chapter 33

"He's alerting," Horace said. "You know—telling me he's found a body."

"But that's not where we found Mrs. Smetkamp."

"No." Horace shook his head vigorously. "We're nowhere near the shed."

"Could she have rested there for a while before being dragged outside?"

"Unlikely." Horace's voice suggested that only politeness kept him from saying "Are you kidding? No way!"

"She was definitely killed in the shed, then?"

"Absolutely," he said. "Both your dad and I think so. There's no sign of her being moved. No drag marks, and no blood here, or anywhere between here and the shed."

We stared at Watson for a moment or two. No bodies in the middle of the kitchen floor, either—only linoleum scraps and the plywood floor. Watson wagged his tail slightly and uttered another peremptory bark.

"Maybe there's a body in the basement," Horace said.

"There isn't a basement," I pointed out.

"Didn't think so," Horace said. "I'd have noticed."

"There's a crawl space," I said. "We could check that out."

Horace closed his eyes and nodded. He was somewhat claustrophobic. In fact, seriously claustrophobic.

"Yes," he said, after a moment. "I guess we should. Stay there," he added to Watson.

"Does he actually obey when you say that?" I asked. "Because if he does, he's unique among the Pomeranians."

"Only if he's alerting on something. So if he doesn't follow us, it's a lot less likely to be a false alarm. Actually, maybe we should bring him. Maybe he'll lead us away from the crawl space."

"We can always hope."

"You bring him," he said. "Come," he added to Watson. He picked up a large flashlight and led the way out of the house. I grabbed the end of Watson's leash and he followed, a little reluctantly, as if waiting for proof that we'd gotten his message.

Outside we circled around to the side of the house, where we found a small square wooden door that gave access to the crawl space.

Watson liked the door. He pulled so hard that if he'd been any larger he might have dislocated my shoulder. He dragged me over to the door, pawed at it, then sat down and looked back reproachfully at Horace and me.

"Maybe some animal got into the crawl space and died there," I suggested.

"No." Horace shook his head. "He doesn't alert on dead animals. Only dead people."

Watson pawed at the door again.

"Let's see what he's found, then," I said.

The access door was held in place only by two simple wooden latches, one on either side of the doorframe. Horace twisted them open and removed the door. Watson surged forward, but I pulled him back.

"Wait," Horace said. He turned on his flashlight and peered through the two-foot-square opening. I took hold of Watson's leash just short of the collar so he couldn't go far, and stepped closer so I could peer over Horace's shoulder.

It wasn't a big space. Of course, it wasn't a big house, but surely, since it wasn't subdivided into rooms, I'd have thought the crawl space ought to look more spacious. But it was only about two and a half feet tall at most, and in some areas pipes and ductwork ran along overhead, just below the flooring, making the space even shorter. The cobwebs didn't help, either—the corners were filled with them; they festooned the pipes and ductwork, and even hung down in some of the otherwise open areas like makeshift sheer curtains. And it didn't have a floor, of course; just a rough dirt surface. I could make out the outlines of another access door directly across from us, on the opposite side of the house.

"Are you sure Watson couldn't be alerting on a dead animal?" I asked. "Because this looks like just the sort of place an animal would crawl into to die."

"I hope not," Horace said. "That's an important part of a ca-daver dog's training—only alerting on dead humans." He leaned a few inches closer to the trapdoor. "I should check it out."

He sounded so anxious that I took pity on him. After all, I wasn't nearly as claustrophobic as he was. I could remember Horace curl-ing up in the fetal position after the time his job had required him to go through the tunnel from the town square into the courthouse basement. The whole town was proud of this relic of Caerphilly's participation in the Underground Railroad, but very few residents had ever voluntarily traveled through it.

"You've had a long day," I said. "Pulling a double shift. Why don't you let me check it out?"

"More like a triple shift," he said, with a small, tired sigh. "But it's my job. I can't ask you to go into someplace where there might be a dead body."

"I'll go slowly," I said. "And if I see anything that even looks like a dead body, I'll come back out immediately and we can call the chief. And Randall," I added. "He could rip out that section of the floor so you can just look down from the kitchen. The place is a wreck anyway."

"That's true," he said. "And we'd need to do that anyway, if there's really a body down there. But technically I should go in myself."

I glanced at him. The night had grown cool, but he was sweaty and anxious at the mere thought of going into the crawl space. And he was starting to breathe oddly. Even Watson, in spite of his focus on whatever he'd scented, noticed his human's distress and jumped up to lick Horace's face.

I rummaged in my tote and pulled out the little cobalt glass bottle Rose Noire had given me—was it only yesterday?

"Here." I unscrewed the top of the bottle and stuck it under Horace's nose. "Smell this and take deep breaths. You're panicking or hyperventilating or something."

Horace followed my instructions. In a minute or so, he was sounding better.

"Sorry," he said. "This place was already getting to me, even before I realized I'd have to go into the crawl space."

"And you don't have to go into the crawl space after all," I said. "Because I barged in before you could stop me and you had to stay behind to secure Watson. So watch my back."

I was starting to get down on my hands and knees when something occurred to me.

"Hang on a sec," I said.

"You see," Horace said. "You don't want to go in there, either."

"I just want to do something first."

I went around the front of the house to the other side. I undid the latch to the other access door and opened it. Then I returned to where Horace and Watson were waiting.

"Making sure you have a good escape route?" he asked.

"Making sure any animals that might be lurking under here have a good escape route," I said. "I do not want to deal with a cornered skunk or something like that."

"Good thinking," Horace said.

"Well, here goes," I said.

I pushed past him, gently, dropped to my knees, and crawled through the door. I stopped when I was all the way in and played the flashlight beam over my surroundings, until I was sure which part of the space ahead was under the kitchen.

"See anything?" Horace asked.

"Dirt and cobwebs. Watch my back."

I began crawling toward the kitchen. I glanced over my shoulder at one point to see Horace and Watson both peering in after me.

I reminded myself that while Watson was very good at finding dead bodies, he didn't always find recent ones. In fact, he was getting quite skilled at finding long-buried bodies—he and Horace were in great demand with archaeologists from the college who were trying to find Colonial cemeteries or pre-Colonial indigenous burial grounds. Maybe the house had been built over a grave so old the marker had disappeared.

With those reassuring thoughts, I crawled ahead, slowly, studying the ground ahead of me for anything I didn't want to crawl into. Like dead animals. Or live animals. Or animal droppings. And every foot or so, I stopped, raised my phone, and took a flurry of flash pictures of my surroundings.

I had just crawled past a protruding pipe that had been partially blocking my view of the part of the crawl space that was under the kitchen when I spotted something.

"Uh-oh," I said.

"What do you mean, uh-oh?" Horace asked.

I pulled my phone out to take a picture of what looked like finger bones lying on the surface of the dirt in the rough shape of a hand, as if their owner had been reaching up from a shallow grave for help and had then given up trying and let the hand drop onto the surface.

"You're going to owe Watson a T-R-E-A-T," I said.

"What do you see?"

"Bones." I wriggled a little closer to get a better angle on the skeletal hand. With luck, that would be enough to keep Horace from having to crawl in himself. "I'm taking pictures."

"Good," he said. "Then back out of there so we can call the chief."

"And Randall." I decided I'd taken enough pictures. I took the time to text a few of the best to Horace. "Check your phone," I called out.

Turning around in this part of the crawl space would be a little awkward, and I was curiously disinclined to turn my back on those outstretched fingers. Although they didn't feel threatening. Just sad and ominous. So I started backing away from the hand.

"Wow," Horace said behind me. "Watson was right. He did find a body."

"At least part of one." I could tell his normal forensic enthusiasm was a little muted, probably because of the dread he must be feeling at the prospect of entering the crawl space. "I was careful not to get too close to the bones. I only hope I didn't mess up any evidence. Like traces of someone coming in here to bury the body."

"I doubt if you did," he said. "From the look of it, those phalanges and metacarpals have been there for a while."

"Still, you're not going to want to work this scene through the crawl space." I had backed far enough from the hand that I was ready to turn around and head for the access door. "When you let the chief know, why not suggest that we notify Randall before it gets too late to wake him. Get him to bring back that crane he was using earlier, and the work lights. You could get them to just rip up the floor in the kitchen—in the whole house, for that matter—and work the crime scene properly."

I had reached the door. Horace stepped aside to give me space to crawl out.

"That's true." He sounded more cheerful—although it was hard to hear him because Watson had begun to bark furiously. "And a good thing—I get the creeps just being in that house, much less under it. Besides—Oh!"

I emerged from the trap door and looked around to see what Watson was barking at—and what had interrupted Horace.

"I'm afraid I can't allow you to call Chief Burke," a voice said.

Charles Jasper was standing over us, pointing a gun at Horace.

Chapter 34

"Why are you pointing that gun at us?" I said, pitching my voice as loud as I dared, in the hope that someone nearby would hear me. This was Bland Street, after all, where the yards were small—and given the warm spring weather, surely someone would have their windows open.

"Shut up. And put your hands up." Jasper stepped back a few paces, probably so he could more easily cover both of us with his gun. "Nobody's going to hear you. They're all either asleep or watching television."

"They'll hear you if you fire that thing," Horace said, nodding at the gun.

"They'll just think it's a cop show on TV," Jasper said. "Hands up."

"And there's no need to fire it, now that you know it's us, not intruders," I said, standing up and brushing dirt from my jeans. While doing so, I slipped my phone into my pocket, trying to press one of the redial buttons as I did. "Very public spirited of you, keeping an eye on the neighborhood like this, but you can stand down now."

"Nice try," Jasper said. "Put your hands up and go back into the house. Move."

Horace and I complied, going as slowly as possible. Jasper seemed happier once we were inside and out of sight. I was listening intently for any noises from my phone. With luck, I'd managed to redial the chief, and he'd catch some of what Jasper was saying. And if I'd miscalculated and redialed someone else, surely they'd call 911 when they heard what was going on. Of course, maybe I'd just punched the wrong buttons.

"Sit down," Jasper ordered.

"Does this have something to do with the bones in the crawl space?" Horace asked, as he carefully took a seat on a clear stretch of the plywood floor. "And who is it down there?"

"Don't ask stupid questions." Jasper was scanning his surroundings as if looking for something.

"You haven't kept up with the neighborhood gossip," I said to Horace. "I bet the bones belong to the late Mrs. Jasper. Who, according to him, ran off with the man she was having an affair with. Only I kind of doubt that ever happened. Is it just her in the crawl space, or did you also do away with her boyfriend?"

"Just her." Jasper was patting some of the upright supports. "I invented the boyfriend."

I noticed that Horace had let go of Watson's leash. He still kept his hand near the leash, so Jasper wouldn't notice. Unfortunately, Watson hadn't noticed, either. If Horace was expecting his dog to pull a Lassie and run for help, it wasn't working out very well so far.

Horace reached and nudged Watson with his toe. Watson looked back at him with a puzzled expression on his furry face.

I figured it was my job to keep Jasper distracted.

"No wonder you were so distraught when you had to sell your house," I said. "Didn't it occur to you to dig her up and take her with you before you left?"

"Don't think I didn't try," Jasper said. "When the bank fore-closed on the place, they didn't give me much time to get out. And they were watching me pretty closely—guess they figured out I wanted to take something away. Joke's on them, isn't it? I bet they'd all have been happier if I'd managed to take her away. After a while I figured it was probably safe enough. The smell had pretty much cleared out by the time I had to move, and I didn't see the Smetkamps having much reason to crawl under the house."

"Until *Marvelous Mansions* showed up."

"Yeah. And then I knew I had to stop her. Imogen Smetkamp. She was bound and determined to put in a basement."

"*Marvelous Mansions* wasn't going to do that," I pointed out. "Wasn't in their budget, and—"

"She was going to make them," Jasper said. "She had some-thing on that producer guy. The slick one. No idea what—she was just dropping hints. But I gather it was something he could get in serious trouble for if she told on him. She was going to use that to force him to give her a basement."

"Maybe she was going to try," I said. "But the town wouldn't have let her. There's an underground spring running through this part of town, and a town ordinance against building base-ments. Some kind of environmental regulation."

Watson finally figured out that Horace wasn't holding his leash. He stood up, shook himself, and began trotting away. Yes!

"What's the dog doing?" Jasper snapped.

"He probably just needs to go out," Horace said.

Jasper began backing away, trying to find a vantage point where he could keep an eye on us and Watson.

"Stop him," he ordered. "Or I'll shoot him."

"Here, boy," Horace called. "Come here."

"Smelly treat!" I called. "Come get a smelly treat!" Watson was normally as enthusiastic about the smelly treats as the rest of the

Poms. But tonight he was on a mission. He arrived in the kitchen area, sat down in the middle of the floor, and uttered his sharp, peremptory alert bark.

"Déjà vu all over again," I said.

"Make him stop that," Jasper ordered. "Why is he doing that?"

"He's a cadaver dog," Horace explained. "He's telling me he's found a body."

"He'll probably just sit there and bark occasionally," I said.

"Well, I'll be damned." Jasper seemed to find the situation hilarious. "You mean that's how you found her? On account of that fluffy little mutt?"

Horace frowned, and bit back whatever defense he wanted to make on Watson's behalf.

"Yes," I said. "And if you dig her up and take her away someplace else, it'll be your word against ours that she was ever here. Heck, you can even make us do the digging."

I saw Horace opening his mouth, probably to protest that this wouldn't work. I frowned and shook my head slightly.

"I don't think so," Jasper said. "Go into the kitchen with the mutt."

Horace hurried to comply. I moved more slowly. I had a sinking feeling I knew what Jasper was planning. The roof looked to be the most badly damaged over the back of the house—especially over the remains of the kitchen. And Jasper was hovering just outside the kitchen area, eyeing a precarious-looking upright that appeared to be the main support for the roof in that part of the house. If he managed to knock that out, a good portion of the roof might come tumbling down . . . right on top of anyone sitting in the kitchen.

"And what if trying to bring the house down on top of us doesn't actually kill us?" I asked.

"Then I'll come over and finish the job with a piece of lumber," he said. His cool, matter-of-fact tone suggested that yes, he was absolutely prepared to do this. "And then I'll set it on fire. I can probably make it look like an electrical fire."

Horace opened his mouth—no doubt to point out that the electricity had been turned off—and then shut it again. No need to help Jasper figure out how to murder us.

"You won't get away with this," he said instead.

No, Jasper wouldn't. He'd screw it up somehow, and the chief would catch him. But fat lot of good that would do Horace and me if we were already dead.

"Do you really want to burn down the house you love?" I asked.

"The house I love?" Jasper repeated. "That's gone, thanks to those horrible television people. I might as well cremate the remains."

Watson barked again—the demanding bark of a cadaver dog whose humans are ignoring his find.

"At ease," Horace said.

Jasper had found a four-foot-long piece of two-by-four and was hefting it. I suspected he was planning to use it to knock the vertical support down.

"And what are you going to do when the roof starts falling," I asked. "Run like hell for the exit?" I looked at Horace as I said that last part, and he nodded.

"At least let me put my poor dog outside," Horace said.

"You're not going anywhere," Jasper said.

"I can order him outside." Horace reached down and unhooked the leash from Watson's collar. "Outside! Go!"

"Keep your hands in the air!" Jasper shouted.

Horace complied. Watson, realizing he was free, began sniffing the picnic basket.

Jasper took an experimental whack at the base of the upright. One-handed, he couldn't get that much power into it. Still, it moved an inch or so, and the roof lurched down a bit and shed bits of debris. A big chunk of something landed on the picnic basket, startling Watson, who yelped and ran outside.

Horace breathed a sigh of relief, then focused back on Jasper.

"You'll bring down the whole roof," Horace exclaimed.

"Only the part over your heads," Jasper said, with a chuckle. "And that's kind of the point. I figure the part I'm under will stay put long enough for me to get out." He drew the two-by-four back again and swung. This time he tried to put more power into it, and his gun veered away from us.

"Move!" Horace and I shouted this to each other simultaneously. We both leaped toward the back door. I was faster but Horace was right on my heels, and we both managed to scramble through the door just as we heard the thud of the two-by-four hitting the upright again.

"Stop! Get back here!" Jasper shouted. Two shots rang out, but neither hit me. Horace also seemed to be dazed but uninjured.

"Watson!" he called. "Here boy!"

Just then the kitchen section of the roof trembled and collapsed. Its fall seemed to have a domino effect, with other sections collapsing, one after another, until the entire house was a flattened heap of debris.

"Where's Watson?" Horace shouted. "If he went back inside to find me—"

"He's fine." I spotted Watson, huddled up against the fence between the Smetkamps' yard and Myra Lord's. I strode over, scooped him up, and handed him to Horace.

"You take care of Watson," I said. "I'm calling nine-one-one."

"Already called it," came a voice from across the fence. I glanced over to see Myra Lord peering through the shrubbery. "Squeaky was going crazy inside, which usually just means he heard a possum or a fox outside, but after he found that shoe that turned out to be evidence I figured maybe I'd see what he was up to. Saw that jerk marching you inside at gunpoint and called nine-one-one. Listen—I can hear the sirens already."

"Now that you're sure he's safe, let me hold Watson," I said to Horace, holding out my arms. "You get out your gun and guard the rubble, in case Jasper's still a menace. I'll stay close so Watson can see you."

Horace nodded and handed over his Pom. Watson, still a little spooked, licked my face a couple of times, then curled up in my arms.

"While you're at it," I said to Myra. "Can you call nine-one-one again and tell them to send the fire department? We're going to need them to rescue Jasper." Or recover his body, though I decided that was too depressing to mention.

"You've got it," she said.

"Call Randall, too," Horace said. "We're going to need his crane."

"Roger," I said. "I'll do that."

"And maybe you should take Watson back home with you when the chief's finished debriefing you," he said. "I could have a long night ahead of me here."

Curiously, he didn't sound tired. He sounded energized. He glanced back at me, and we exchanged a smile. Yes, he had a long night ahead of him. But he was alive and well to see it. We all three were.

"I'll take good care of Watson," I said. "And spoil him rotten with T-R-E-A-T-S. After all, he solved two murders tonight."

Chapter 35

"Bland Street's starting to look a little closer to normal," Randall said.

"Most of it, anyway," I replied.

The ruins of the house were still there, of course, and looking worse than ever. Tuesday night, Randall and his crane had lifted up enough of the debris to locate Charles Jasper's unconscious body and haul him off to the hospital. He was still there, under guard, recovering from assorted broken bones, with Dad hovering over him to watch for signs of concussion.

"I approve," the chief had said. "We want to make sure he lives to stand trial. For both murders."

Once they'd extracted Jasper, the workers left the rest of the house in place until daylight when, with the chief supervising and Horace documenting every move they made, Randall's workers had slowly and carefully lifted up beams, boards, and every other kind of debris from the rubble. They focused on the corner where the kitchen had been, of course, and although they started promptly at 7:00 A.M., as permitted by the town noise ordinances, it was mid-afternoon before they'd cleared away enough of the rubble that Horace—with the assistance of Dad, in his role as medical examiner, and two consulting archaeologists from the college—could begin excavating the place where Mr. Jasper had buried his wife's body. They were still at it when I went home for dinner, and this morning I'd heard that they'd finally finished up under portable floodlights just short of midnight.

But the rest of the wreckage would have to stay put, in case it was needed as evidence in the case against the *Marvelous Mansions* production company. Although at least they were able to load the rubble they'd removed into a moving pod, rather than piling it up in the yard.

So the neighborhood wouldn't completely return to normal until the *Marvelous Mansions* production company and Mr. Smetkamp finished battling over who was going to foot the bill for repairing his house—or, more likely, tearing it down and building a replacement. Correction: until the *Marvelous Mansions* production company and Mr. Smetkamp's very able attorney finished battling. I'd convinced my cousin Festus Hollingsworth that he needed to take the case—for Caerphilly's sake as well as Mr. Smetkamp's.

Festus, in his usual impeccable three-piece white suit, was even now prowling about the ruins, using his cell phone to take pictures of the wreckage from various angles. He spotted Randall and me and strolled over to say hello.

"How's it looking?" Randall asked.

"The house? A disaster. But Mr. Smetkamp's case is looking better and better." Festus smiled with anticipation.

"So can we look forward to a dramatic court battle?" Randall asked.

"Unlikely." Festus shook his head. "I've already spoken to their counsel. He's not giving away anything, of course, but I can read between the lines. They're doing everything they can to put all the blame on Blomqvist and distance themselves from him. But they'll settle. Unless they're complete fools."

"They just might be complete fools," Randall said. "Given what they did to that house."

"Oh, they're pretty clueless about construction," Festus agreed. "I know more about it than they do, which is rather unfortunate for a company that's trying to film a home makeover show."

"Haven't they learned anything from previous makeovers?" Randall asked.

"Not really," Festus said. "Since this was only the second makeover they've tackled. Apparently they thought they saw a market opportunity and were rushing to get some episodes done to take advantage of it. Didn't take the time to check out Jared Blomqvist's résumé and figure out it was all fiction. He talks a good game, but his only previous television experience was filming a few commercials for a used car dealership in Fresno. I figure they'll fold once they see our witness list."

"And just who is on your witness list?" Randall asked. "Apart from Meg and me, that is."

"We've got those construction workers from out of town," Festus began.

"I thought they never set foot in the house," I pointed out.

"Oh, not the skilled ones Randall has working for him now," Festus said. "I mean the unskilled guys they hired to do the demolition. Mr. Blomqvist treated them like dirt and shorted their pay. They're fired up to testify."

"How'd you ever find them?"

"The other television people helped," Festus said. "All the crew members—Jared treated them like dirt, too. Pro tip: if you want to get away with something unethical, if not downright illegal, make sure you're reasonably civil to the minions you get to carry out your dirty work. One of them hired a bunch of day laborers for the demolition crew."

"So he could easily find them again, I assume," Randall said.

"Well, not easily," Festus said. "Most towns and cities have at least one place where men looking for day labor show up hoping to connect with someone who will hire them. Blomqvist sent one of his people down to Richmond to find a place like that. The guy remembered the address he went to, and all the television people looked in their phones and cameras and found me the best pictures of the guys he hired. I sent him and my investigator down to ask around, and they managed to find a couple of the guys. They weren't too keen to talk, until he explained that we were going after the guy who cheated them. Now they're fired up to testify."

"Nice work," Randall said.

"Y'all get to claim some of the credit," Festus said. "Putting the crew up in that mansion in Westlake and sending in food from the Shack and Luigi's and who knows where else. Got them all on Team Caerphilly."

"You make it sound as if we were trying to bribe them," I said. "We were just treating them decently."

"Which isn't something they were used to, working under Blomqvist. He's out, by the way. As I said, the production company fired him and they're doing their best to distance themselves from him. Apparently, at the only other makeover he did, he stiffed all the local vendors and contractors and pocketed the money."

"I heard the Rockford cops are due today," Randall said. "Extraditing him back to face charges."

"So I hear." Festus frowned and pointed across the street at Gloria's house. "Is that an FBI vehicle over there?"

"It is indeed," Randall said. "They're seizing all of Mr. Smith's computer equipment."

"And Mr. Smith himself?"

"They've already got him," Randall said. "Or will as soon as all the paperwork is finished so the chief can hand him over."

"What's he done?" Festus had come to attention—no doubt his professional instincts were aroused by the possibility that Chris might have committed some interesting federal crime.

"Nothing you'd want to defend him for, trust me," I said. "According to Kevin, Chris's main activity is running something called a password-hacking farm, but he's also got profitable sidelines in ransomware and the more unsavory sorts of pornography and—well, just about every kind of cybercrime you've ever heard of."

"You're right," Festus said. "Not my kind of client. Friend of mine defended one of those cybercriminals. Got him off with only ten years for several dozen wire fraud charges that could have earned him up to twenty years each. And then when the client got the bill, he not only refused to pay it, he hacked into my friend's home and office computers, planted ransomware and nasty pictures on them. It was a nightmare."

"I can imagine," I said. "What did your friend do?"

"Luckily, in his first panic he called me," Festus said. "And I introduced him to Kevin. He's okay now, and if Kevin ever needs a lawyer, my friend will probably knock me down running to take the case. So I'm not saying I'll never defend anyone with highly developed hacking skills—but they'd need to have Kevin's seal of approval before I'd take them on."

"You don't want Chris as a client, then," I said. "Kevin says he's a nasty piece of work."

"I'll stick to Reg Smetkamp," Festus said. "A very nice man. I never met his late wife—"

"Consider yourself lucky," Randall muttered.

"But I think he deserves some happiness," Festus continued.

"And it looks as if he's going for it." Randall pointed down the block to where Shiffley Moving Company trucks were maneuvering to place two large moving pods in front of Mrs. Peabody's house.

"He's moving in with Emma Peabody?" Festus said. "Good."

"Good for them," I said. "But how are they ever going to fit all his stuff in? Her house is already a little . . . whatever's the opposite of minimalist."

"I'd say cozily cluttered," Festus said.

"Cozy's in the eye of the beholder," I said. "And her place is neat as a pin, but cluttered for sure. How are they ever going to fit in two pods full of stuff?"

"They aren't," Randall said. "One of those two pods is empty. My guys are going to drag the stuff out of the full pod, one item at a time, so Emma and Reg can give a thumbs-up or thumbs-down. The rejects go into the other pod. When they're finished, we take whatever they don't want out to your parents' barn, and your mother's going to organize a big estate sale."

The two pods were now placed end to end, with their doors facing each other and about ten feet apart. Mrs. Peabody and Mr. Smetkamp had come outside and were standing on the sidewalk, arm in arm.

As we watched, the movers carried a large object wrapped in quilted moving blankets out of the full pod, set it on the pavement, and unwrapped it. A large, overly ornate china cabinet. Obviously antique, but the sort of antique that would inspire Mother to sniff deprecatingly and remark that someone should have chosen their ancestors more carefully. Mr. Smetkamp and Mrs. Peabody stared earnestly at it for a minute or so. Then they turned to look at each other and simultaneously shook their heads. They both burst into laughter—she had a delightful lilting laugh—and he waved toward the empty pod. The movers rewrapped the ugly china cabinet, carried it onto the empty pod, and went back for another piece of furniture.

"That's going to take some time," I said.

"They can take as long as they need," Randall said. "I'm not charging Reg anything extra for my guys' time. He's lost enough already."

I nodded.

The workers hadn't even finished removing the quilted blankets from the next object, a sofa in a nauseating shade of brownish maroon, before the happy couple were shaking their heads vigorously.

"Then again, if they're that decisive, maybe it won't take all that long," I said.

"Reg said he mainly wants his clothes, his books, and a few mementos," Randall said. "Apart from that, anything Emma wants can stay, and all the rest can go."

"So if they're moving in together, what happens with the house next door?" I asked. "Soon to be the vacant lot next door."

"I doubt if that will happen all that soon," Festus said. "Depends on how long my negotiations with *Marvelous Mansions* take."

"Not a problem there," Randall said. "When you no longer need the ruins as evidence, Reg wants to have the whole lot cleared so Emma can expand her garden. They're actually thinking of making it a sort of neighborhood park, full of native plants."

"Sounds like a lovely idea," I said. "I bet the Garden Club will pitch in."

Gloria strolled over to join us.

"Never thought I'd be happy to see the FBI raiding my house," she said. "But they're hauling away all of Chris's stuff. Good riddance."

"Of course, now you're minus a tenant," I said.

"Minus two tenants," Gloria said. "Jennifer's moving in with her boyfriend—says this neighborhood has become too crazy. But that's okay. I've already got replacements lined up, thanks to Randall."

"My niece Hannah is going to take Jennifer's room as soon as it's available," Randall said. "She's going to be a sophomore at the college in the fall, and you know how tough they make it to get a dorm room if you live in the county. Nice for her, having her aunt Darlene right across the street."

"And for the time being, I'm going to rent my attic to Randall's bricklayers," Gloria added.

"Your bricklayers?" I echoed, turning to Randall.

"Two of those guys from Pulaski are awesome bricklayers," Randall said. "And I've got a lot of projects coming up that I can use them for. With luck, they'll get to like Caerphilly and move up here—but in the meantime, they're going to rent Darlene's attic so they have a nice place to stay when they're here. Probably working long hours and going home most weekends, so it won't be as crowded as all that."

"And if it's crowded and noisy, I won't mind, now that you and Michael have said I can keep using your library for the time being," Gloria said. "I promise, I won't be a bother. But you can't believe how much faster it's going, having a quiet place with no students, no Jennifer, and no Chris."

"Glad we can help," I said.

"And when—Whoops! I need to run! I've only just barely got time to get to my class."

She sprinted across the street, dashed into her house, and half a minute later her garage door opened and she took off in the convertible.

"So unless Hannah is very different from most college students," I said, "she probably isn't all that keen on having an older relative that close by. But the mother in me approves."

"Yeah, Darlene and Gloria both can keep an eye on her," Randall said. "She's whip smart, but a little naïve."

"Not to mention her uncle Vern regularly patrolling the neighborhood," I said.

"That, too," Randall agreed. "Speak of the devil—here comes Vern. I think he has a surprise for us. Well, for you, anyway."

Vern parked his cruiser behind Randall's truck. He hopped out and strode over to us, moving a lot faster than his usual relaxed pace.

"Mission accomplished?" Randall asked.

"Yeah." Vern was beaming with happiness. He turned to me. "Meg, were you serious that if I got a puppy I could drop him off to hang around with all your dogs when I'm on duty?"

"Absolutely," I said. "You need a dog, and a dog needs company, and it's not as if one more dog would be a hardship around our house. The more the merrier."

Vern let out a breath as if he'd been worried.

"Then let me introduce you to someone." He hurried back to his cruiser, opened one of the back doors, and reached in to pick up something. Then he strode back to rejoin us.

"Haven't figured out what to call the little devil yet," he said. "But here he is."

He was holding a puppy cradled against his shoulder—a sleek little thing with a glossy reddish coat and big, floppy ears.

"One of Judge Shiffley's best Redbone coonhounds had a litter a couple of months ago," Vern continued. "She's been trying to talk me into taking one, but I kept saying, no, it wasn't fair to a dog, with the hours I keep. But if you're really okay with him staying out at your place with all the other dogs when I can't be with him, I think we can give the little fellow a good life."

The puppy yawned and opened his large, soulful, deep-brown eyes.

"He'll be very welcome." I reached out to scratch the puppy behind one ear, and he wagged his tail gently.

"Just one thing," Vern said. "Spike's not going to go after him, is he?"

"Not with Tinkerbell around," I said. "She's very protective of any creature smaller than she is."

"And there aren't many bigger," Randall added.

"The Pomeranians will probably help her," I said. "They've figured out how to gang up on Spike when he gets out of line. And anyway, coexisting with them has mellowed Spike a bit. Or maybe just worn him down. He'll probably just ignore the newcomer. Ostentatiously. The way he does with the Poms."

"That's good, then." Vern tilted his head to gaze down at the sleepy puppy with the sort of look you see on new fathers in the delivery room. "They're awesome dogs, Redbones. Tireless hunters but also great family dogs. Gentle, loyal, protective. And Judge Shiffley's one of the best Redbone breeders anywhere."

"Sounds as if he'll be a good influence on our dogs," I said.

"You going to train him for scent work?" Randall asked.

"Just for hunting," Vern said. "I'll leave the scent work to Horace."

"Meg! There you are!"

We all turned to see Grandfather striding toward us.

"Afternoon, Dr. Blake," Randall said. "How are the turkeys doing?"

"Fine," Grandfather said. "Just fine. Clarence has finished vasectomizing all the toms. Of course, some of the hens will still be laying fertilized eggs for a month or two, so we may eventually have to fix any young toms that hatch, but I think we've finally taken care of the town's feral turkey problem."

"And in a way that won't freak out the tourists if they find out," Randall said.

"But you haven't heard the best news," Grandfather said. "We've been testing Seth Early's sheep. Almost all of them are naturally low methane emitters. Almost as low as those New Zealand sheep, and the Kiwis have been working on that for a decade. And that was before we started putting the methane-reducing spices in their feed. Great news for the planet!"

"What's this low methane—" Randall began.

"That's great," I said, before Randall could ask a question that would set Grandfather off on a lengthy explanation of his sheep emissions project.

"I caught a ride here with your mother," Grandfather said. "But she's going to be busy for a while—any chance you could take me back out to the zoo?"

"I can do it," Vern said. "As long as you can hold this little guy while I drive." He held up the nameless puppy.

"Glad to." Grandfather focused on the puppy. "Look at those paws," he said. "Going to be a big boy, isn't he? What breed?"

He and Vern strolled off, with Vern giving him chapter and verse on the virtues of Redbone coonhounds.

"Maybe I should go figure out why Mother's here," I suggested.

"No big mystery," Randall said. "She's supervising the cleanup of Mrs. Peabody's yard. The chief cut a deal with the teens who helped with the turkey prank—and their parents. They pleaded guilty to some kind of misdemeanor charge, and Judge Shiffley sentenced them to spend some vast number of hours undoing what the turkeys did. Your mother and I have joint responsibility for making sure they put in those hours."

The teens were already hard at work. Two of them were filling a wheelbarrow with the bricks that had once made up the front walk and piling them up along the side of the driveway. Another two were shoveling turkey droppings and dead plants into black plastic garbage bags. And the final two—one of them being Cal Burke—were setting up a small canopy over the folding chair in which Mother would be supervising.

"We're going to put up a fence in front of the ruins," Randall said. "To get everything ready for the Beautiful Block judging. A solid eight-foot privacy fence. Your mother's got a couple of artists lined up to paint murals on it."

"Great," I said. "And—wait. Isn't that Tyler Lord? He wasn't involved in the prank."

"No," Randall said. "But he wants to help. Since it means he gets to show off his new outfit."

Sure enough, Tyler was sporting a bright blue Shiffley Construction T-shirt, and a junior-sized blue Shiffley Construction hard hat with TYLER stenciled across the back.

Just then a pickup truck and an SUV pulled up in front a little way down the block. Seven or eight people hopped out, grabbed tools from the bed of the pickup, and hurried over to Mother as if reporting for assignments.

"Aren't those the television people?" I asked.

"Yup," Randall said. "I guess they want to help make up for what Jared got wrong."

"I bet they're feeling relieved, now that he's on his way back to Rockford," I said.

"Yup." Randall nodded. "They're all heading back to L.A. in a day or two. Asked what they could do to return our hospitality, and I suggested a few hours over here would be much appreciated."

"If you ask me, they already helped enormously by sharing some of their photos and video with Festus," I said. "I hear they've got Jared on tape telling the day laborers not to worry about the load-bearing walls, just whack everything in sight."

"That, too," Randall agreed. "And—What's that guy doing?"

I turned to see an Amazon truck stopped in the middle of the nearest intersection. Its driver was leaning out of his window as if trying to scout out what was happening here on Bland Street before proceeding any farther.

"I wonder if it's Benny," I said.

"Benny?"

"The driver who was unfortunate enough to be delivering something when the turkeys were here."

A car honked, and then another. Evidently the Amazon truck was blocking the way for several tourists traveling on the cross street. The truck lurched slowly into motion and crawled along Bland Street until it reached Mrs. Peabody's house. Between the moving pods and the volunteers' vehicles there wasn't a parking space along the curb, so the truck double-parked by one of the moving pods. The driver—Benny, I was almost positive—seemed to look around carefully before opening his door and stepping out with a brown cardboard package in hand, leaving the engine still running.

Mrs. Peabody spotted the truck, exclaimed something, and ran to meet him. He flinched away from her and kept her at arm's length as he handed her the package. Then he watched, transfixed, as she ripped open the box and unfurled a six-by-four-foot orange banner that featured a larger-than-life cartoon turkey under the words GIVE THANKS!

"Thank you!" she said. "I can't wait to put this up."

Benny had turned pale and was running back to his truck. He was still fastening his seat belt when he set the truck in motion and floored his accelerator. We heard the siren start up a few seconds after he left the 1200 block.

"I hope they let him off with a warning," Randall said. "He did have a pretty tough time here the other day."

Then we went over to join the crew of volunteers. Several of them had already propped stepladders against the side of Mrs. Peabody's house and, under Mother's supervision, were figuring out how to hang the banner over her front door.

"Perfect!" Mother exclaimed. "Just you wait—by the time we're finished, this neighborhood's going to be a shoo-in for the Beautiful Block contest."

We all cheered, and then went back to making her words come true. With this many people pitching in, Bland Street would be back to normal in no time.

Just then Aida drove up in her cruiser. She didn't have her lights and sirens on, but she was driving noticeably faster than the speed limit. She pulled up beside Randall and me.

"Chief needs your help," she said. "Got a complaint from some tourists, and it looks as if our bird roundup isn't quite complete."

"We missed some of the turkeys?" Randall said. "How is that possible?"

"Not turkeys," Aida said. "Maybe the tourist is hallucinating. But it sounds as if this time we may have feral peacocks."

Acknowledgments

Thanks once again to everyone at Minotaur Books, including (but not limited to) Claire Cheek, Hector DeJean, Stephen Erickson, Nicola Ferguson, Meryl Gross, Paul Hochman, Kayla Janas, Andrew Martin, Sarah Melnyk, and especially my editor, Pete Wolverton. And thanks also to the art department for another beautiful cover.

More thanks to my agent, Ellen Geiger, and to Matt McGowan and the staff at the Frances Goldin Literary Agency for taking care of the business side of things so I can concentrate on writing.

Special thanks this time to Erin Mitchell, who shared with me the real-life adventure that inspired the *Marvelous Mansions* makeover.

Many thanks to the friends who brainstorm and critique with me, give me good ideas, or help keep me sane while I'm writing: Stuart, Aidan, and Liam Andrews; Deborah Blake; Chris Cowan; Ellen Crosby; Kathy Deligianis; Margery Flax; Suzanne Frisbee; John Gilstrap; Barb Goffman; Joni Langevoort; David Niemi; Alan Orloff; Dan Stashower; Art Taylor; Robin Templeton; and Dina Willner. And thanks to all the TeaBuds for two decades of friendship.

Above all, thanks to the readers who make all of this possible.

About the Author

Donna Andrews has won the Anthony, the Barry, and three Agatha Awards, an RT Book Reviews Award for best first novel, and four Lefty and two Toby Bromberg Awards for funniest mystery. She is a member of the Mystery Writers of America, Sisters in Crime, and Novelists, Inc. Andrews lives in Reston, Virginia. *Between a Flock and a Hard Place* is the thirty-fifth book in the Meg Langslow series.

Visit her website at www.donnaandrews.com.